THE ICEMAN
INHERITANCE

MICHAEL BRADLEY
THE ICEMAN INHERITANCE

Prehistoric Sources of Western Man's Racism, Sexism and Aggression

With a New
Introduction by
John Henrik Clarke

KAYODE PUBLICATIONS LTD.
15 West 24th Street
New York, N.Y. 10010

First published 1978 by
Dorset Publishing, Inc.
Kayode Publications Ltd. 1st Printing June 1991

Cover illustration by Joe Gillians

Bradley, Michael, 1944-
The Iceman Inheritance

1. Caucasian race.   2. Physical anthropology.
3. Human evolution.   I. Title.

GN537.B73   572.8'034   C78-001497-9

ISBN 1-879831-007   10 9 8 7 6 5 4 3 2 1

For Jason Bradley, Susan Sevage, Deanna Bean
and Michael Twose

What is the hardest thing of all?
That which seems the easiest
For your eyes to see,
That which lies before your eyes.

— Goethe

CONTENTS

Author's Acknowledgements
and Foreword

First, I would like to acknowledge immediately my own limitations of scholarship in preparing the argument put forward in this book. Although I am very confident about the general defensibility of the thesis, I am also acutely aware that the defense provided could have been much better (although only at the cost of many more pages).

Secondly, I would like to emphasize the fact that *The Iceman Inheritance* has always been intended as a 'popular' book. Therefore, notes and the bibliography represent the bare minimum required to lead the general reader to the major sources.

Thirdly, I would like to acknowledge the generosity of the Chilton Book Company for permitting me to quote from the text of Ivan Sanderson's *Abominable Snowmen: Legend Comes to Life* and to reproduce the Neanderthal footprint and the footprint of the *Guli Yavan* contained in the appendix of Sanderson's book. I am indebted also to Alfred A. Knopf, Inc. for permission to reproduce illustrations from Professor Carleton Coon's *The Origin of Races*.

Many people have contributed to the presentation of ideas contained in *The Iceman Inheritance* during the past fourteen years of this book's preparation. Some have contributed through conversation, discussion, argument and encouragement. Some have supplied specialized material, or have expedited my access to it. Others have entered into sometimes lengthy correspondence in order to answer my queries. Still others read the manuscript for errors and criticism.

I am indebted to the late Dr. Georgio de Santillana of M.I.T.; to Dr. Bruce Mazlish of the Princeton Institute for Advanced Study; to Dr. Thomas D. Langan of the University of Toronto; to Dr. R.C. Tennyson of the University of Toronto's Institute for Aerospace Studies; to Dr. Bruce Raemsch of Onteonta College; to Dr. J.T. Fraser, Secretary and Founder of the International Society for the Study of Time; to Dr. Jagdish Hattingadi of York University; to Dr. John Yolton, Dean of Rutgers University; to Dr. G.J. Whitrow of the Imperial College of Science and Technology; to Dr. Sidney Bolkosky of the University of Chicago.

Special thanks are due to Imre de Csepreg Nemeth, Director of the Social Work Program at Toronto's Seneca College, who wrote one of the Introductions to this book, and to Dr. Judith Posner, Co-ordinator of Women's Studies, Atkinson College, York University, who wrote the other. I would also like to take the opportunity to thank Professor Carleton Coon, author of *The Origin of Races*, for his encouragement and patience during several conversations. Although it proved impossible not to criticize Professor Coon's racial *emphasis* in some respects, it remains obvious that the argument presented in this book relies heavily upon Professor Coon's comparative analysis of Neanderthal-Caucasoid skeletal material. I think it also needs to be said that Professor Coon has been the object of unremitting, and generally unfair, criticism from 'liberal anthropologists' who have 'excommunicated' him from the contemporary anthropological belief structure, but who have failed to answer Coon's careful research with comparable rigour. I feel that research of the next few years will tend to vindicate the views of both Coon and Franz Weidenreich.

Popular writers entered into correspondence in order to extend encouragement and, in some cases, to supply information. In this category are: Elaine Morgan, author of *The Descent of Woman*; Adrian Desmond, author of *The Hot-Blooded Dinosaurs*; and especially Duncan Lunan, Scottish astronomer and author of *Man and the Stars*, whose information about extra-terrestrial contact and astrophysics was of great assistance.

I would also like to thank faculty members, and students, of Seneca College, Malaspina College, Syracuse University and the Princeton Institute for Advanced Study who participated in lectures and seminars on the theory presented in *The Iceman Inheritance*.

Although I am indebted to all those mentioned above, none are responsible for the nature of the argument presented in this book and, in spite of their assistance, it must be acknowledged that most of those mentioned disagree, at least in part, with the major thesis of *The Iceman Inheritance*.

Some colleagues in both journalism and market research helped considerably by agreeing to tackle the manuscript and to judge its popular readability. I would like to thank Tracy Walker of Powell River, British Columbia; Alan Seymour and De Anna Bean, both of Adcom Research Limited, Toronto; Malcolm 'Mac' Vagg of K.M. Vagg Research Associates, Toronto; Edward Palmer, Toronto.

Particularly, I appreciate the efforts of David Kilgour, editor, who was instrumental in getting an unwieldly manuscript ready for publication. At the same time, thanks plus a certain degree of awe are due to Larry Goldstein, President and founder of Dorset Publishing Inc., who not only possessed the determination to establish a publishing house in Canada's uncertain economic climate (a climate notoriously fatal to publishers), but who also somehow possessed the courage to commit cheerfully to *The Iceman Inheritance* as his first book under the Dorset imprint.

Finally, I thank my friend and wife, Wendy Bradley, for her constant encouragement and support over more than a decade.

Michael Bradley
Toronto, Canada
July, 1978

In most respects this 1990 edition of The Iceman Inheritance is identical to the original Canadian publication which was released in November 1978. A new Introduction by John Henrick Clarke has been substituted for the two original Canadian introductions written by Imre de Asprey Nemeth and Dr. Judith Posner, the dedication has been altered slightly and some typos that found their way into the original book have been corrected. But in other respects the book remains the same because no changes were necessary. I still stand behind the argument presented in The Iceman Inheritance and no new evidence has emerged to refute it. On the contrary, some new evidence has emerged to support the thesis.

Drs. Eric Trinkhaus of Harvard's Peabody Museum and T. Dale Stewart of the Smithsonian Institution jointly undertook a forensic-style examination of all known Neanderthal skeletal material. They discovered a much higher incidence of violence inflicted injuries (bone lesions) among Neanderthals". Trinkhaus and Stewart thus demonstrated empirically what I argued theoretically in The Iceman Inheritance: that the Neanderthals were more aggressive than other ancestors of modern man.

In 1985 a previously unpublished and unpublicized paper was found among Sigmund Freud's manuscripts. This 12 page essay suggested that Western man's psychosexual aggressions and ambivalences were caused by glacial evolution during the last European Ice Age. The new Freudian manuscript was published under the title of A Phylogenetic Fantasy and caused something of an uproar in anthropological circles and much popular press coverage - of which the most accurate was, perhaps, the London Observer's August 6, 1986 article "Hangups Due to Ice and Id of a Byegone Era". The Iceman Inheritance argued in 1978 precisely what Sigmund Freud wrote in his 12 page paper which was not discovered until 1985 (but was probably written around 1919).

In short, the years since the original publication of this book have not seen any evidence that the theory should be discarded or revised, but, on the contrary, have seen new evidence that The Iceman Inheritance is more valid and more vital than I knew in 1978.

Michael Bradley
Toronto, Canada
November 1990

INTRODUCTION

In his book, The Iceman Inheritance, the Canadian writer, Michael Bradley has made the most glaring admission about the European's attempt to dominate the world through racism. There are a large number of books on this subject but the writers tend to hedge on the subject by inferring that in spite of the atrocities and the racism brought to this world by the Caucasian race, they have given the world some order, some technology and arts and letters of lasting benefit. What the authors of these books do not take into consideration is that in spite of the contributions that benefit the world Europeans in their attempt at world domination created a disastrous climate for the world's people.

Caucasians, in general, have an inferiority complex about their world position. If they were secure within their alleged superiority they would not have to shout it to the world so often and so loudly. When a people feel called upon to repeatedly announce their superiority to the world it is suspected that behind all their pretense they do not believe it as much as they want other people to believe they do. In contrast, if the same people believed in the inferiority of the rest of the world its people and its cultures they would not spend so much time trying to prove their point. Inferior things normally fall into an inferior position and usually stay there without any help from anybody. All the European laws, lies, manipulation or religion have not kept most of the non-European world in the inferior position the European world have assigned to it.

Throughout their history, which is short in comparison to the history of other peoples, especially the Africans and the Asians, they have been astute record keepers, when it suited their purpose they have also been astute record changers. As a result the Europeans have caused us to read the history of the world in their favor. This book has provoked some non-Europeans into taking a new view of world history in order to understand how European people related to non-Europeans throughout history. The first thing we learned is that there was no Europe in ancient times. The geographical area that would later be called Europe was not a functioning entity in world affairs when early civilizations were being developed in the Nile Valley and other river valleys in Africa and later in Western Asia (now mistakenly called the Middle East) and in mainland Asia in countries like India, China and later Japan.

When we look at the chronology of world history we discover that the first real show of European literary intelligence surfaced around

1250 B.C. (depending on your source), with the publication of two books of folklore, the Odyssey and the Iliad, credited to an author named Homer, who we have little information about. In the book, A History Of The Modern World, by R.R. Palmer and Joel Colton, they tell us that:

Europeans were by no means the pioneers of human civilization. Half of man's recorded history had passed before anyone in Europe could read or write. The priests of Egypt began to keep written records between 4000 and 3000 B.C., but more than two thousand years later the poems of Homer were still being circulated in the Greek city-states by word of mouth. Shortly after 3000 B.C., while the pharaohs were building the first pyramids, Europeans were creating nothing more distinguished than huge garbage heaps. Ironically, like the pyramids, they still endure and are known to archaeologists as "kitchen middens." At the time when the Babylonian King Hammurabi, about 2000 B.C., caused the laws of a complex society to be carved on stone, the most advanced Europeans were people like the Swiss Lake Dwellers, simple agriculturists who lived in shelters built over the water to protect themselves from beasts and men. In a word until after 2000 B.C. Europe was in the Neolithic or New Stone Age. This was in truth a great age in man's history, the age in which men learned to make and use sharp tools, weave cloth, build living quarters, domesticate animals, plant seeds, harvest crops and sense the returning cycles of the months and years. But the Near East - Egypt, the Euphrates and Tigris valley, the island of Crete and the shores of the Aegean Sea (which belonged more to Asia than to Europe) - had reached and passed the Neolithic two thousand years before Europe.

When Europeans finally got themselves together and created the semblance of what could be referred to as a state or a nation they soon made a glaring discovery - Europe could not furnish them with enough food to properly feed them or enough material to properly clothe them. They began to look with covetous eyes at the more developed parts of the world. Soon they would find a rationale for their initial military aggression under the young Macedonian Greek known in history as Alexander the Great. He would invade North Africa in the year 332 B.C. following the invasions from Western Asia by the Assyrians in 666 B.C. and the Iranians in 550 B.C.

These invaders and their ruthless administrations would cause the Africans of North Africa and the Nile Valley to cry out, in effect, Oh God - If you cannot send us a liberator - send us a conqueror who would show some mercy. Alexander did show some mercy - he also showed that he was a greater diplomat than he was a warrior. As a conqueror he did what conquerors do- he raided the granaries of Egypt to feed his soldiers and his armies continued the bastardization of Egypt that was started by the Western Asian invasion of 1675 B.C. whose forced co-habitation with the women changed the population and the cultural temperature of the declining Nile Valley civilization. Alexander's and the Greeks' conduct in Africa was more arrogant than racist. Some of the racism that we know today did have its genesis in the Greco-Roman period although this racism can in no way be compared with what non-Europeans have experienced at the hands of Europeans for the last 500 years.

With the military rise of Rome and the decline of Greek military power, after Alexander, the Romans were determined to control the trade of the Mediterranean and had no intentions of sharing this trade with the Carthaginians who had built one of the most advanced commercial cities of the world of that day. The Roman conquest of a large area of North Africa and the consolidation of that conquest with the death of Hannibal and the end of the Punic wars would install the Romans as the dominant power in the Mediterranean for the next 500 years.

Because of the stubborn refusal of white "scholars" to read books like, Stolen Legacy, by George G. M. James, published in 1954, African Origins of the Major "Western Religions", by Dr. Yosef A. A. Ben-Jochannan, published in 1970, The Destruction of Black Civilization: Great Issues of A Race From 4500 B.C. to 2000 A.D., by Chancellor Williams published in 1974, Ages of Gold & Silver, by John A. Jackson published in 1991. White scholarly pretenders who are often authorities on things they know little or nothing about are not aware of the early European intellectual dependency on North Africa and Western Asia. They are also not aware that most of the so-called Greek philosophers not only studied in Egypt but consulted Egyptian texts on a regular basis. According to Theophile Obenga in his work, The Pharaonic Origins of Greek Philosophy, published in 1990. The word "Philosophy" is not of Greek origin. This European practice of attributing the achievements of other people to themselves started during the Greco-Roman period and continue to this day.

The racism that plagues us today had its origins in the 2nd rise of Europe in the 15th and 16th centuries. During this period that the Europeans refer to as their Middle Ages or Dark Ages, Europe had lost their previous skills in seafaring and the concept of longitude and latitude had been also lost from their memory. They came out of this period in history, according to Professor Leonard Jeffries of City College of New York, land poor people poor, and resource poor. The

European established the slave trade and used it to begin its economical recovery. After the Crusades and the famines and plagues that had arrested the attention of Europe for over 300 years, Europe's self-concept was damaged. Since 711 A.D. the year of the African Arab conquest of Spain, Europe had been held at bay by what they referred to as the 'Hated Infidels', African and Arab armies in North Africa and in the Mediterranean area and by the continuous rise of Islam.

Europe began to break out of this bind in the 1400's with the port assault on the city of Creta, in Morocco, in 1415 and again in 1455 when in settling an argument between Portugal and Spain, the Pope authorized Portugal and Spain to reduce to servitude all infidel people - most of the declared infidels were African and Asians.

This was the official rationale for the Atlantic slave trade. During this period Europeans not only began to colonize most of the world they also colonized information about the world. They colonized the Bible. They colonized all complimentary images that non-European people held of themselves. The most effective of all of these colonized images was their colonization of the image of God. Through missionaries, adventurers, free-booters and slave traders they began to propagate the concept that God favored them over other people. They were saying, in essence, that all Europeans were the chosen people of God. Often in their teaching about God they ran into a contradiction. They taught of a God who was king and loved mankind - who was no respecter of kith or kin. By pretending that God favored them over other people they had made God into a bigot - they had made God ungodly. Most of the non-Europeans had misconceptions about the European's relationship to Christianity then, and have the some of the same misconceptions now. Europeans have a tendency of proclaiming ideas to the world that they do not believe themselves and would not dare to live by if they are going to hold power over most of the people of the world. The war on non- European culture that had been going on before the emergence of Europe now continued, mainly under European control. The Europeans were now telling their victims that the world waited in darkness for them to bring the light. Where in actuality, everywhere the European went outside of Europe he put out the light of his victims' culture, spirituality and cultured way of life. Not only did he not understand their culture, he had no intention of understanding their culture. Europeans declared war on the structure of every society they invaded or were welcomed into as visitors. Many societies that the European pretended to civilize would have been better off had the Europeans left them alone. In Africa, the Pacific

Islands, and in large areas of mainland Asia people had built safe and spiritually endowed societies before the first European wore a shoe or lived in a house that had a window. In large areas of Africa a cluster of civilizations were built without an organized jail system or a word in their language which meant 'jail' because there was no need in their society for one.

There is a need to look at European racism in the opening up of the so-called New World.. The best of the early recorded accounts come from Father Bartholome De las Casas who came to America on the third voyage of Christopher Columbus. When Christopher Columbus noticed the rapid disappearance of the native American, over the time of his three visits, he would go to De las Casas and request that he petition the Vatican for an increase in the Atlantic slave trade with the pretense that this increase would save the souls of the native Americans. De las Casas is considered the first historian of the New World. His account of mass murder and the disappearance of the natives of the New World - mistakenly called, 'Indians' is entitled, The Devastation of the Indies: A Brief Account, was published in 1974. Father De las Casas' account of the island of Hispaniola (Haiti) and the people he observed there is as follows:

> ...all the land so far discovered is a beehive of people; it is as though God had crowded into these islands the great majority of mankind.
>
> And of all the infinite universe of humanity these people are the most guileless, the most devoid of wickedness and duplicity, the most obedient and faithful to their native masters and to the Spanish Christians whom they serve. They are by nature the most humble, patient, and peaceable, holding no grudges, free from embroilments, neither excitable nor quarrelsome. These people are the most devoid of rancors, hatreds, or desire for vengeance of any people in the world. And because they are so weak and complaisant, they are less able to endure heavy labor and soon die of no matter what malady. The sons of nobles among us, brought up in the enjoyments of life's refinements, are no more delicate than are these Indians, even those among them who are of the lowest rank of laborers. They are also poor people, for they not only possess little but have no desire to possess worldly goods. For this reason they are not arrogant embittered, or greedy.

If Father De las Casas' account of the people on Hispaniola is true, and I believe it is, what excuse can the Spanish Christians offer for their wholesale torture and murder. De las Casas goes into a detailed description of the continuous annihilation of the Indians in the occupation and destruction of the civilizations of Mexico. Further in his book he describes the occupation of the Indies in this manner:

> *They were very clean in their persons, with alert, intelligent minds, docile and open to doctrine, very apt to receive our holy Catholic faith, to be endowed with virtuous customs, and to behave in a godly fashion....*
>
> *Yet into this sheepfold, into this land of week outcasts there came some Spaniards who immediately behaved like ravening wild beasts, wolves, tigers, or lions that had been starved for many days. And Spaniards have behaved in no other way during the past forty years, down to the present time, for they are still acting like ravening beasts, killing, terrorizing, afflicting, torturing and destroying the native peoples, doing all this with the strangest and most varied new methods of cruelty, never seen or heard of before, and to such a degree that this Island of Hispaniola, once so populous (Having a population that I estimated to be more than three million), has now a population of barely two hundred persons.*
>
> *The island of Cuba is nearly as long as the distance between Valladolid and Rome, it is now almost completely depopulated. San Juan and Jamaica are two of the largest, and most productive and attractive islands, both are now deserted and devastated. On the northern side of Cuba and Hispaniola lie the neighboring Lucayos comprising more than sixty islands including those called Gigantes, besides numerous other islands, some small some large. The least felitcitous of them were more fertile and beautiful than the gardens of the King of Seville. They have the healthiest lands in the world, where lived more than five hundred thousand souls; they are now deserted, inhabited by not a single living creature. All the people were slain or died after being taken into captivity and brought to the Island of Hispaniola to be sold as slaves.*

Racism, with its accompanying fear and frustration, was the cohesive force that held the plantation system together. It created a new way of life for the European in the Caribbean Islands and the Americans over and above any amount of creature comfort they could have enjoyed in Europe at the same time in history. The Europeans who were successful in Europe generally stayed in Europe. What was referred to as the New World was brought into being by a large number of people who were failures at home. It was once said that Europe dumped its human garbage can into the New World. In spite of some exaggeration, there is some truth in this statement. Many of these Europeans felt called upon to make non-Europeans feel inferior so that they could convince themselves that they were a superior people.

The physical resistance against European dominance and the need and greed that influenced their attitude and the personality started in a formal way early in the eighteenth century. In Africa there were anti-colonial revolts. The Africans were fighting to regain what slavery and colonialism had taken away. In the Caribbean Islands and in South America the Africans on a different geography and under different circumstances were fighting for basically the same thing. There are 250 recorded slave revolts in the United States, alone. The people of Asia had been reacting against the occupation and domination almost from the beginning of the European presence in their country. They had a different landmass to deal with and a different political situation, but they were fighting against the same thing.

Early in the twentieth century the world began to witness the military rise of modern Japan. In the Russo-Japanese War (1905) the Japanese were strong enough to match their military power against a major European nation, and win. Racism against Asians although with some variations, was radically different from racism against people of African descent and was spreading world wide with the stereotyping of Asians, mainly Chinese, in early movies. While the cry against the "Yellow Peril" was directed against the Japanese, after the Russo-Japanese war it was generally directed against all Asians. This matter is reflected in great detail in the book, The Revolt of Asia, by Upton Close, published in 1927. One of his comments worth repeating here is:

> *Having witnessed the wide-sweeping reverse swing of the pendulum against white dominance in Asia today, especially as shown in the revolt in China, it is now time to turn back from the present, surcharged with the motion' of impending and fundamental change to examine, first the broad contacts between the races which culminated in the 'White man's world,' and second, the successive steps which have recently brought his supremacy of the verge of collapse.*
>
> *...The one question upon which the human creature is perhaps even more ignorant than where he is going is where he came from... we are almost totally ignorant as yet of even the meaning of 'race.' Differentiations into racial stocks are approximate and uncertain. The one principle upon which all ethnologists seem to agree is, that any people, wherever found, must certainly have come from somewhere else.*

Upton Close states further in his book about the Origin and end of the "Yellow Peril":

> *This final great irruption of the 'barbarian push,' flaring westward through Russia into central Europe as well as driving southward upon China, was, dramatically enough, what abruptly awakened*

self-centered Europe to the existence of the other half of the world. The military machine perfected by Genghis Khan swept through feudal Russia and as far as Vienna. No resistance offered could check it. Not the chivalry of Europe, but the decision of the Mongol commander to go home and attend the funeral of the dead Khan (and share in the inheritance) saved Christendom from the same iron heel which left such terrible scars of oppression on the soul of the Slav.

This was the origin of the 'Yellow Peril' scare, a fright which now seems almost a congenital instinct in the west.

This era was followed by pseudo-scientific racism and the widespread propagation of the teutonic origin theory.

Early in this century, the elder scholar among African-Americans, Dr. W. E. B. DuBois said: "The problem of the twentieth century is the problem of the color line." Unfortunately, his prophecy was correct. In spite of all the talk and the sociology - good and bad - we have not made much progress in resolving this issue. We have talked about it extensively without really dealing with it. To deal with it we will have to ask ourselves some hard questions and we will have to be boldly honest with our answers. Some of the hard questions are: How did racism start in the first place and for whose benefit was it created? Who benefits from it now? Why do we lack the strength , or the courage, to destroy it?

In this Introduction I am dealing, mainly with the form of racism that affects people of African descent. In a speech delivered to the Pan-African Students Organization in the Americas, New York City, November 1964, Richard B. Moore observed:

In an attempt to justify the conquest and enslavement of African people, European rulers and their spokesmen found it expedient to regard and set forth Africans as beings of a low and brutish order who indeed were hardly human. Such creatures then were deemed to have done little or nothing which could be dignified as history.

The dehumanization of the African people had already been started. The false images were already in motion. The stereotype and mental images of 'savage Africa' and the 'Dark continent' were deeply impressed upon the minds of the Europeans. The distortions were repeated until some of the victims began to believe it themselves.

In his book, Race, Science and Humanity, published in 1963, Dr. Ashley Montagu refers to the belief in race as a "widespread contemporary myth in the Western World." He further states that, it is the modern form of the older belief in witchcraft." This point of view is extended in the following quote from the Introduction to his book:

> *I am convinced that when the intellectual history of our time comes to be written, the idea of 'race' both the popular and the taxonomic, will be viewed for what it is: a confused and dangerous idea which happened to fit the social requirements of a thoroughly exploitative period in the development of Western man. The idea of 'race' was developed as a direct response to the exploitation of other peoples, to provide both a pretext and a justification for the most unjustifiable conduct, the enslavement, murder, and degradation of millions of human beings.*

European interest in formalizing the concept of race dates back to the early part of the eighteenth century. Dr. Montagu maintains that the development of the idea of race, may be traced, with some justification, back to the scholastic naturalization of Aristotle's doctrine of Predictable Genus, Species, Difference, Property, and Accident. In the year 1457, the Council of Cardinals met in Holland and sanctioned, as a righteous and progressive idea, the enslavement of Africans for the purpose of their conversion to Christianity, and to be exploited in the labor market as chattel property. He further maintains that the concept of race had another development during the early days of the "Age of Enlightenment" when in 1735 Swedish botanist, Linnaeus took over the concept of Class, Species and Geunus from the theologians to serve them as systematic tools. These conclusions show how important it is for us to deal with both the genesis and the present application of racism.

This devilish scheme speedily became the standard policy of the church for three centuries. And thus the ghastly traffic in human misery was given the cloak of respectability and anointed with the oil of Pontifical righteousness in Jesus' name. And so the slave trade began, inaugurating an era that stands out as the most gruesome and macabre example of man's disregard of the humanity of all men.

There is no way to understand the African slave trade without understanding slavery as an institution. Slavery is almost as old as human societies. Every people has at some time or another been slaves. In fact, Europeans enslaved other Europeans for a much longer time than they enslaved Africans. This slavery did not give birth to racism, but it did lay the basis for feudalism. European racism had manifested itself in many dimensions outside of Europe, and what is called the Holocaust is just European racism turned inward toward itself, within Europe, making Europeans the scapegoat of other European people.

Slavery was a permanent feature in the ancient world, in Egypt,

Kush, Greece and Rome. The African slave trade is better known to us because it is the most recent and the best documented. The "Christians" of European descent have never felt at ease in an honest discussion of this subject because every examination of it will prove that slavery and the slave trade were the incubator for present day racism.

The Christian Church was the handmaiden for the development of racism. While it propagated the theory that all men were created equal in the sight of God; in practice, it found all sorts of arguments to prove that non-European people, especially Black men, were inferior and could not be considered as men in the general sense. A search for ways to justify European domination led biologists to the works of Linnaeus and Buffon. Thus, the classification of races began. In deciding the distinctions between higher and lower races, the Europeans, of course, became the hierarchy of races.

In many ways this was a continuation of the rationale set up to justify the slave trade. The African slave trade-like African history in general - is often written about and rarely understood. There was at first a concerted effort to obtain labor to open up the vast regions of the New World. It is often forgotten that, in what became the United States, white enslavement started before Black enslavement. In an article, White servitude in the United States, "Ebony Magazine". November 1960, the African-American writer, Lerone Bennett, Jr., gives the following information about this period:

> When someone removes the cataracts of whiteness from our eyes, and when we look with unclouded vision on the bloody shadows of the American past, we will recognize for the first time that the Afro-American, who was so often second in freedom, was also second in slavery.
> Indeed, it will be revealed that the Afro-American was third in slavery. For he inherited his chains, in a manner of speaking, from the pioneer bondsmen, who were red and white.

Forced labor was widely used in England. This system was transferred to the colonies and used to justify a form of slavery that was visited upon red and white men. Concise information on this system and how it developed is revealed in the book. Slavery and Abolition, 1831-1841, by Albert Bushnell Hart, first published in 1906.

> It was decreed that the apprentice must serve his seven years, and take floggings as his master saw fit; the hired servant must carry out

his contract for his term of service; convicts of the state, often including political offenders, were slaves of the state and sometimes sold to private owners overseas. The colonists claimed those rights over some of their white fellow countrymen. A large class of "redemptioners" had agreed that their service should be sold for a brief term of years to pay their passage money, and of 'indentured' or 'indented' servants bought by their masters under legal obligation to serve for a term of years and subject to the same penalties of branding, whipping and mutilation as African slaves. These forms of servitude were supposed to be limited in duration and transmitted no claim to the servant's children. In spite of this servitude, the presumption, in law, was that a white man was born free.

The English settlers at once had begun to enslave their Indian neighbors, soothing their consciences with the argument that it was right to make slaves of pagans. In large numbers, the Indians fled or died in captivity, leaving few of their descendants in bondage. The virgin soil of the new English settlements continued to need more labor. This led to a fierce search for white labor that subsequently led to search for Black labor.

American Abolitionists, both Black and White, began fighting against a form of racism that had begun to crystallize itself in the embryo of the colonies' educational systems, filtering down from the attitude prevailing in the colonies' churches. During the period of the founding fathers, the African-American heard promises about democracy and liberty and justice and did not know that these promises were not meant for them. They deluded themselves into thinking they were but the African soon learned that the African was not brought to this country to be treated democratically and the American promise was not made to him. That was the dilemma during the formative period of this country - it is the basis of its dilemma now. This country was born in racism and it has evolved in racism.

In the early years of the nineteenth century, the system of chattel slavery gave way to the colonial system. This was not the end of racism as it affected Africans and other non-white people throughout the world; it was only a radical change in how it would be manifested. The European would now change the system of capturing Africans and other non-white people and enslaving them thousands of miles from their homes. They would enslave them on the spot, within their own countries and use them as markets for the new goods coming out of the developing European industrial revolution and out of their countries and their labors to produce grist for new European mills. The industrial rise of the West has as its base a form of racism-racism helped to lay the base of the present economic system we now call capitalism.

In the main, theoretical racism is of nineteenth century origin in America and in Europe, and yet the nineteenth century was a century of the greatest resistance against racism. It was during that century when Africans the world over began to search for a definition of themselves. The highwater mark of the Africans reaction to European racism came in the middle of the nineteenth century in the presence of great Black intellectuals such as Martin R. Delany and Edward Wilmot Blyden. Toward the end of the nineteenth century, the great intellectual giant, W. E. B. Dubois took up the fight and ably carried it into the middle of the twentieth century. There is now an international struggle against racism on the part of people of African descent. The struggle has been taken to the world's campuses, where the theoretical basis of racism started. This has helped to create new battlelines and a lot of fear and frustration on the part of white scholarship. Their fear prevents them from recognizing that the removal of the racism that they created is the healthiest thing present-day Black scholarship can contribute to the world.

The important contribution that Michael Bradley has made to this subject is in the realm of an alarmist - calling attention to what has already happened and what needs to be done about it. Western racism is a disease that has affected the whole world. Its after effect might, in the final analysis, do more harm than good to its creators.

This book is not a masterpiece of scholarship or analysis. The content of the book, The Iceman Inheritance, is an important message for our times and all times if we have the hopes of creating a world free of - war - race hatred - and tension. His inquiry into this subject, his bold admissions and revelations will inevitably open other doors and put other subjects on our intellectual agenda for investigation.

In my opinion this is the meaning of his investigation and the essence of his contribution to the subject of race in a changing world.

John Henrik Clarke
Professor Emeritus
African World History
Hunter College
New York City
February, 1991

Part One

The
Contention

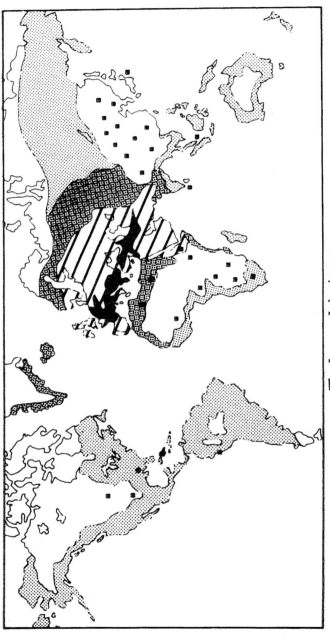

The Iceman Inheritance:
The Expansion of Neanderthal-Caucasoid 'Western' Influence

Neanderthal homeland
100,000 - 30,000 B.C.

Neanderthal-Caucasoid
expansion 30,000 - 1,500 B.C.

Euro-Arabic 'Western' expansion
1,500 B.C. - A.D. 1,400

European colonial expansion
A.D. 1,400 - 1850

'Western' colonial, technological
cultural expansion A.D. 1850 - present

Modern resistence to Western expansion and
colonialism based upon borrowed Western
cultural, political, technological developments.

1

Greek Gifts:
Western Technology

This book is racist.

For, among other things, I will attempt to show that racism itself is a predisposition of but one race of Mankind — the white race.

I believe that I can show that our converging contemporary crises, like racism itself, have their origins in the prehistory of the white race alone. We attribute various threats to our survival to 'Man's' folly... but this is a conscious and self-protecting euphemism.

Nuclear war, environmental pollution, resource rape... all are primary threats to our survival and all are the result of peculiarly Caucasoid behaviour, Caucasoid values, Caucasoid psychology.

There is no way to avoid the truth. The problem with the world is white men.

If this insight has generally escaped us it is only because we Caucasoids have dictated much history, written most of it, and judged it in terms of our own self-image. But we have never looked at ourselves in an objective biological mirror.

And that is what we shall now proceed to do.

Our racial psychology has brought the world to the brink of disaster. We therefore have some obligation to attempt to correct matters, and there isn't much time. The task is a hopeless vanity, the obligation is betrayed, if we are unwilling to try to know ourselves.

Even if we undertake racial psychoanalysis in good faith difficulties arise. There are so many defense mechanisms designed to obscure the profile of our Caucasoid racial personality. For instance, one of the most potent contemporary defense mechanisms is the existence of liberal anthropology. The tendency of modern anthropology is to deny the very concept of race. It is a position most vehemently articulated by Ashley Montagu among contemporary writers. I will argue that the denial of racial behavioural differences is, at best, a Greek gift that serves to cloak our true nature. The denial of race and racial proclivities is a mechanism to disguise the white race's proclivity for racism.

As a defense mechanism, the denial of racial differences is potent in our time because so many people eagerly embrace it, more as an article of faith than as a reasoned position. But although Montagu and allied writers have welded together a strongly supported tenet of modern liberalism, the strength of the anti-race posture is the strength of many: quantity, not quality. The denial of race and racial proclivities, like most faiths, is vulnerable to facts. Unfortunately for the credibility of modern liberalism and contemporary anthropology, truth is still enshrined by facts and not by consensus, no matter how well-intentioned. We will look at the facts.

Other defense mechanisms are more formidable because they boast at least a grain of truth. The grain is magnified in the lens of our racial vanity until the small speck appears to eclipse the whole. Our perspective is distorted, our values deranged. Our reflection is cosmeticized.

Here comes a grain of truth. Progress.

Progress is vindication of all the crises which threaten our survival. It is the materialist conception of hope itself. And if little good can be said of us and our civilization, we Caucasoids can be proud that *we* brought progress to *them*. After some hard thinking, medicine and literacy are generally cited as benefits enjoyed by *them*. The profits, of course, accrue to us.

Take literacy, which generally consists of our teaching 'them' one of our Western European languages under less than optimum conditions, guaranteeing a necessarily low level of competence.

How could it be otherwise when the level of public literacy is appallingly low even within our advanced Caucasoid strongholds? Abroad, our gift of literacy means the basic ability to succumb to simplified Caucasoid religion, simplified Caucasoid ethics, and simplified Caucasoid ads. Even within the Industrialized West public education accomplishes little more with the vast majority of students.

And medicine? It is undeniable that our exported progress has brought the wonders of Western medicine to afflicted and 'less advanced' non-Caucasoid people... a very small fraction of them. It is not to denigrate the superhuman effort and devotion of doctors, nurses and doctor-missionaries to suggest that, on balance, it wasn't worth it. By infinitesimally improving the infant mortality rate we have succeeded in contributing to overpopulation in the undeveloped and for the most part non-Caucasoid world. If more people live longer, more people also endure their span of years in poverty and in the shadow of famine.Our medicine has consigned more to life, but in too many instances to a life not worth living.

Besides, there is an apocalyptic geometry to progress, a dark Malthusian quality to the entire concept. Even within the advanced Caucasoid redoubts of the Industrial West it is not so much a question of progress *and* medicine, but a question of progress *versus* medicine. In 1974, the United Nations' World Health Organization released statistics that were a bitter pill for our progressive pretensions to swallow. Of all males reaching the age of 20, men in industrialized countries have a *lesser* chance of attaining the age of 65 than their brothers in undeveloped countries. The inescapable conclusion is that non-Caucasoids were always better off without our notion of progress and we ourselves are beginning to be better off without it. We have already exceeded critical mass in our experiments with progress. Progress and medicine vie for human life.

In addition to the well-known fact that progressive pollution of ourselves and our environment has increased the incidence of degenerative diseases like cancer and heart disease throughout the Western World, there is the lesser-known fact that our war technology may very well be promoting epidemic diseases of rare virulence.

More than one expert has voiced the opinion that the mysterious Legionnaire's Disease which struck delegates to an American Legion convention in Philadelpia in 1976 was caused by escaped toxins associated with chemical-biological warfare research. The swine flu scare of 1975-76 also has suspiciously military overtones. The four original casualties of swine flu were soldiers stationed at Fort Dix, New Jersey. Biological warfare agents are stored at Fort Dix and the swine influenza is a prime CBW research agent.

As early as 1969 U.S. Congressman Richard D. McCarthy published evidence linking epidemic diseases in men, domestic cattle, wildlife, and food crops to escaped CBW toxins. Most incidents up until 1969 had taken place in the vicinity of the Fort

Detrick (Maryland), Pine Bluff (Arkansas) and Dugway Proving Grounds (Utah) CBW research installations. Thanks to experiments at Fort Detrick, Rocky Mountain spotted fever now in New England, and Venezuelan equine encephalitis occurs among wildlife in the Southeastern states. Both are CBW experimental strains. In September of 1976, researchers learned that bubonic plague is present among Colorado wildlife in the vicinity of Rocky Mountain Arsenal, where that agent is stored.

Recent evidence raises the ominous possibility that CBW research may have already promoted a massive *Clostridia* epidemic among U.S. domestic cattle. Over the past three years some 1,500 cattle in 22 American states have been found mysteriously mutilated. 'Mutilated' is a misnomer. The dead cattle have been found with selected organs and tissues *surgically* removed, and the organs and tissues in question are usually those needed to determine *Clostridia* infection. Of all mutilated cattle later autopsied, some 40 per cent have been found to be infected with *Clostridia* bacteria. The mysterious mutilators, whoever they are, apparently use military helicopters and the conclusion is becoming inescapable that they must enjoy government protection since the mutilators are never revealed by official searches. It is as if some government agency were attempting to monitor the extent and virulence of a still-secret, but widespread, *Clostridia* epidemic. It only remains to be said that there are 93 species of the *Clostridia* bacteria genus. Several species are CBW research agents, particularly *C. Botulinum*.[1]

It seems that medicine as one proof of progress is rapidly losing lives in the struggle against other aspects of progress. Medicine cannot be considered a vindication of rampant progress. Rather, medicine is rapidly becoming an inadequate defense against it.

Our military activities, purposeful and accidental, are not the only threats our culture presents to the rest of the world. Even our peaceful activities are proving harmful. A report prepared by the U.S. Central Intelligence Agency in 1974, designated "Office of Political Research-401", attempts to assess the political and social implications of climatic change. The report notes that although there appear to be natural cycles of climatic change and the world appears to be entering a natural period of cooling, man-made industrial pollution in the atmosphere must now be regarded as a major contributing factor to the *severity* and *rapidity* of climate alteration. The CIA estimated that from twenty to thirty percent of all atmospheric dust is now man-made.

This unnatural addition to atmospheric dust has two effects. The first is the enhancement of the 'greenhouse effect' and contributes to warming of the earth's surface. But the second and much greater effect is a reduction in the amount of sunlight which reaches the earth's surface. The dust reflects more sunlight back into space. The net result of these two effects is a distinct cooling of the earth's surface and climatologists have already concluded that it is having an adverse, and possibly irreversible, influence upon global weather patterns. Wind patterns which we once regarded as 'normal' have, in the northern hemisphere, shifted southward by an average of about thirty miles since 1940. The average annual temperature in Iceland has dropped almost 2 degrees F. since 1945. The growing season in the British Isles has been reduced by a week.

The tropics have not gone unaffected by the southerly shift of wind patterns. Since 1950 the desiccating winds of northern Africa have shifted southward and the Sahara desert has expanded to encroach on the once-arable lands of the Sahelia. The resulting famine in sub-Saharan Africa has been a world tragedy for the past decade. The monsoons have failed twice since 1964, visiting famine upon the Indian subcontinent and Southeast Asia. Soviet crops failed in 1972.

The CIA report lists the adverse climatic changes of the early 1970's tersely:

> *The world's snow and ice cover had increased by at least 10 to 15 percent; in the eastern Canadian area of arctic Greenland, below-normal temperatures were recorded for 19 consecutive months for the first time in 100 years; the Moscow region suffered its worst drought in three to five hundred years; drought occurred in Central America, the sub-Sahara, South Asia, China and Australia; massive floods took place in the midwestern United States.*

The implications of climatic change are staggering. Europe, presently with an annual mean temperature of 12 degrees Centigrade, supports three persons per arable hectare. But, an average temperature of only 1 degree Centigrade less would mean that only two persons per arable hectare could be supported and that more than 20 percent of the population could not be fed from domestic sources. In China the picture is much worse. China presently supports seven persons per arable hectare at the present annual mean temperature. A decline in the average temperature of 1 degree Centigrade would mean, in China, that only four persons

could be supported per arable hectare and that 43 percent of the
population could not be fed from domestic sources.

Dr. J. E. Kutzback of the University of Wisconsin has undertaken
a study on climatic change during the past 1,600 years. He con-
cludes that, *at best*, the world is returning to the climate which
existed from 1600 A.D. to 1850 A.D., the neo-boreal or 'Little Ice
Age', characterized by 'broad strips of excessive and deficit rainfall
in middle latitudes and extensive failure of the monsoons.'

> *What would a return to this climate mean today? Based on
> the Wisconsin study, it will mean that India will have a major
> drought every four years and could support only three-fourths
> of her present population. The world reserves would have to
> supply 30 to 50 million metric tons of grain each year to
> prevent the deaths of 150 million Indians. China, with a
> major famine every five years, would require an annual
> supply of 50 million metric tons of grain. The Soviet Union
> would lose Kazakhstan for grain production, thereby showing
> a yearly loss of 48 million metric tons of grain. Canada, a
> major exporter, would lose over 50 percent of production
> capability and 75 percent in exporting capability. Northern
> Europe would lose 25 to 30 percent grain production
> capability while the Common Market countries would zero
> their exports.*

It must be emphasized that this sort of climatic change is already
occurring. Sub-Saharan Africa, Central America and South Asia
are already suffering abnormally frequent droughts and millions
have already died. Western technological culture, by polluting the
atmosphere, has contributed to the severity and rapidity of a cycle
of climatic change. In fact, atmospheric dust may have stimulated
the onset of cyclical change.

Another of our peaceful activities presents the world with appalling threat: nuclear power generation. In Sweden alone (among
Western nations) there is a moratorium on nuclear power
development until solutions to the problem of nuclear waste disposal
are found. But elsewhere in the West the development of nuclear
power generation 'progresses' in spite of the fact that we will be
faced immediatly with the task of disposing of waste materials which
can poison the environment for 20,000 years. It is known that fish
and shellfish in the North Sea already show signs of radiation
contamination because of the nuclear pollution caused by a French

uranium-enrichment plant on the channel coast. During the winter of 1977-78, a Soviet nuclear-powered satellite re-entered the atmosphere and crashed in northern Canada, leaving radioactive materials in and around Great Slave Lake. In April, 1978, a U.S. nuclear-powered monitoring device was lost in a Himalayan avalanche and its plutonium fuel may eventually contaminate India's 'healing river', the Ganges.

In spite of the assurances of the nuclear power promoters, nuclear power is not, and was never, a safe energy source. Nuclear accidents have occurred, but have been covered up. A Soviet nuclear power station in the Urals exploded in the late 1950's and contaminated large areas with radiation. The Enrico Fermi Reactor outside Detroit experienced a fuel melt-down in the early 1960's but, luckily, the fuel did not achieve the critical mass and configuration needed for a nuclear explosion. Canada's experimental reactor at Chalk River has *twice* experienced difficulties resulting in environmental contamination. A British military breeder reactor near Seascale on the Irish Sea caught fire in October, 1957, and contaminated down-wind areas to such a degree that milk production was banned and some people had to be evacuated.

Yet, in spite of the fact that nuclear accidents have happened, and in spite of the fact that even without accidents we know of no way to dispose of nuclear waste materials, the development of nuclear power generation continues unabated by Western nations.

Nuclear weapons constitute another of the white man's threats against the rest of the world, even if such weapons are never again used in warfare. The testing and development of nuclear weapons in the atmosphere is not done in Western countries. Wherever possible, the West has appropriated some non-Western area of the world to pollute with contaminants from weapons testing. The South Pacific has been a favourite choice for the U.S., the U.S.S.R., and France. It is calculated that 50,000 abnormal births occur around the Pacific Rim for each open-air test in the Pacific. Only China, a non-Western nation with no access to colonial areas outside its own geographic domain, consistently tests nuclear weapons within its own territory.

2

Greek Gifts:
Western Psychology and Philosophy

Perhaps even worse than specific and very real threats which Caucasoid behaviour has posed to the non-white peoples of the world is the world-wide establishment of Caucasoid 'civilization' and 'values' which has transformed almost all of our planet into one dingy monoculture.

Belgian anthropologist Claude Levi-Strauss maintains that the Indians of the Americas died out because of cultural poisoning more than anything else. In *Tristes Tropiques,* Levi-Strauss writes:

> *In what used to be called Hispaniola [today Haiti and Santo Domingo] the native population numbered about one hundred thousand in 1492, but had dropped to 200 about a century later, since people died of horror and disgust at European civilization even more than of smallpox and physical ill-treatment.*

Our progress has succeeded in blanketing the entire world in a dreary and anti-human monoculture which consists of very real threats to human survival as well as mere ugliness. Again, Levi-Strauss writes:

> *Now that the Polynesian islands have been smothered in concrete and turned into aircraft carriers solidly anchored in*

the southern seas, when the whole of Asia is beginning to look like a dingy suburb, when shanty-towns are spreading across Africa, when civil and military aircraft blight the primeval innocence of the American or Melanesian forests even before destroying their virginity, what else can the so-called escapism of travelling do than confront us with the more unpleasant aspects of our history? Our great Western civilization, which has created the marvels we now enjoy, has only succeeded in producing them at the cost of corresponding ills. The order and harmony of the Western World, its most famous achievement, and a laboratory in which structures of a complexity as yet unknown are being fashioned, demand the elimination of a mass of noxious by-products which now contaminate the globe. The first thing we see as we travel around the world is our own filth, thrown into the face of Mankind.

Caucasoid progress, what *we* call 'civilization', is but another Greek gift to the world.

Rampant progress seems to be a racial inclination. History shows that we Caucasoids have by far the strongest penchant for it. Our racial proclivity for progress is so strong that we tend to confuse it with what other men called civilization. A Western reporter once asked Gandhi what he thought of Western civilization. "I think it would be a good idea," replied Gandhi.

That is how others see us. The few specks of objective value in progress, like medicine and literacy perhaps, are magnified out of all proportion in the lens of our racial creator's vanity until they eclipse the truth and the destruction.

And that truth is that progress doesn't really have much to do with technology. Technology is only the means of progress. The motivation is something else. Progress as we have institutionalized it, and as Caucasoids understand it, is a symptom of undisplaced aggression resulting from Caucasoid psychosexual maladaptation: the maladaptation happened long ago. In spite of its terrible and ever-escalating costs to our health and security, progress provides one absolutely invaluable commodity, one utterly priceless necessity: biological and psychological identity. Mankind as a whole wistfully longs for it, but the Caucasoid racial need for it borders on metabolic addiction. We will discover why.

In heroic defense of our delusions, grains come thick and fast, jostling for focus.

If the technical and tangible aspects of Western culture are to be dismissed as a bad bargain, what about Western Philosophy? Freedom for the individual? Democracy? the separation of church and state? Individual dignity?

As we have been repeatedly told, this, Western Philosophy, was the original Greek gift to the world.

If the object of Western Philosophy, as the very etymology of the word 'philosophy' infers, was to structure a just, stable and fulfilling society by analysis of, improvement of, and compensation for the nature of 'Man' ... then Western Philosophy must rank as a conspicuous failure in comparison with all others.

"Peace makes dull reading, but war is rattling good history". It is an aphorism that we might bear in mind as a guide to the objective value of Western Philosophy to the rest of Mankind. Men of other races have kept chronologies, chronicles or satisfied themselves with geneologies when accounting for the past. But so turbulent is the nature of Caucasoid society that Western man has been forced to invent *history*. History is not merely a *listing* of past events in more or less chronological order, a mechanism which satisfies most other races: *our* history incorporates explanation and analysis as justifiable and necessary mechanisms for dealing with the sheer volume of data. Of all human societies, the Caucasoid racial group has managed to structure the least stable. Our small corner of the world has been disproportionately busy making history.

Far from knowing himself, as the meaning of the word 'philosophy' suggests, Western man is quite frankly baffled by his own behaviour. We have not contented ourselves with the mere invention of *history*, our bafflement has demanded attempts to come up with a *history of history*. At least some Caucasoid minds have applied themselves to trying to discover a *pattern* of history. Precisely because we realize ourselves to be so unstable, much effort has been expended in attempts to make sense out of our own apparently senseless behaviour.

Both our history and our peculiar obsession with analysing it must bemuse men of other races.

The Caucasoid domain has had only its fair share of sensible conflicts: there have been naturally expanding populations, migrations and concomitant inevitable conflicts with neighbours; there have been the occasional tyrants and conquerors who've conducted wars of empire and ego. And all that is more or less normal human behaviour exhibited among all races of Mankind.

Perhaps we've indulged in this 'normal' kind of conflict a bit more than other races, but not much more.

It is in the sphere of 'abnormal' violence that we Caucasoids excel among races. The Caucasoid domain has witnessed far more than its fair share of philosophical and religious conflict... waves of competing belief sweeping from the Urals to the Atlantic, from the Sahara to the Baltic, clashing in dins of merciless racial fratricide, and leaving flotsam of broken bodies and swirling eddies of blood testifying to the violence of Caucasoid intellectual paroxysms. Intellectual violence is statistically rare among other races. Intellectual violence is typical of Caucasoids. Our wars of religion, our Inquisition, our philosophical conflicts have no parallel among yellow, red, brown or black men.

It is this kind of violence that makes our history appear senseless to other men, and senseless and baffling even to ourselves.

There are paradoxes in man. In fact, from a biological point of view, man *is* a paradox.

Men of other races have shown themselves capable of accepting the paradoxes of human existence. We Caucasoids possess a uniquely inadequate psychology in this regard. We are unable to accept paradoxes and inconsistencies. For us, they become *conflicts.* We are uniquely incapable of coping with intellectual conflicts and paradoxes within our own minds, and we cannot tolerate dissension in others.

Men of other races are cognizant of the paradoxes of human existence and have responded to them in various ways. Some have responded by embracing asceticism, some have preferred the epicurean solution. But, with few exceptions among non-Caucasoid societies, there has been an almost complete social consensus on the proper response to the human paradox, or opposing solutions have been mutually tolerant and have co-existed side by side.

But not for us. After thousands of years of racial existence we Caucasoids have still not arrived at any consensus as to the appropriate response to the paradox of human existence, nor have we been able to develop any significant degree of tolerance for differing responses.

Our 'abnormal' and uniquely racial history has been characterized by dualistic, antithetical conflicts. At base, *all* our dualistic conflicts are one: a struggle between the 'spiritual' and 'material' aspects of human existence. (Later, we will give the terms 'spiritual' and 'material' meaningful biological definitions.) The history of the

West and the Caucasoids is merely this one struggle endlessly repeated under different guises and labels, different heraldry and different uniforms.

We fought over the spiritual or material nature of Christ. The Church has endlessly fought the Gnosis. The Christians fought the Cathars. Science fought religion. Protestants fought Catholics. The Allies fought the Nazis. The 'Free World' fights 'Communism' yet. Caucasoid history is illuminated by pyres on which the losers, the heretics, writhe. Yet, considering that we will discover that all this violence is merely symptomatic of our psychological inadequacy in dealing with an easily understood and rather mundane biological fact, all the pyres stand revealed as a monstrous vanity.

Since human existence *is* a paradox in biological terms, Western philosophy is inadequate because Western man cannot cope with paradox. The weakness is revealed at all levels of our thought.

This weakness is *alienation*, either from one truth of the paradox or the other. We *have* to separate things.

We have achieved freedom of the individual only at the cost of natural knowledge of belonging in the world, at the cost of being alone in the cosmos. Democracy is a form of government that assumes distrust on the part of the governed, dishonesty on the part of the government. Our checks and balances presuppose no trusting or fitting relationship between leaders and followers, no mutually beneficial pact. And before we become so enthusiastic about exporting democracy to those yet without it, we might pause to consider that it has never been a form of government comparable in longevity to monarchy. Even specifically Western populations have shown a decided penchant for preferring the personal bond of feudalism to the inherent distrust implied by democratic checks and balances. The innate dignity or worth of an alienated individual, to himself, to his society or to his environment, is questionable at best.

This is not to say that there is anything inherently bad about Western philosophy, but there is certainly nothing inherently good about it either. At best, Western philosophy is a rough and ready *modus vivendi* for uniquely Caucasoid psychology. At worst, it can be the justification for unleashing conflicts of dualistic intolerance among people who were previously innocent of them. Generally, when such conflicts have been induced in men of other races they have borrowed some tenets of Western philosophy, one half of a dualism, in order to defend themselves against the missing half, represented by other aspects of Western philosophy, that we

Caucasoids are trying to impose on them.

Western philosophy is inapplicable, irrelevant and unsatisfying to non-Caucasoids. It was developed to cope with our uniquely dualistic intellectual conflicts and it doesn't even do that very well. We've prescribed a dubious tonic for people who don't even share our disorder.

And what is our disorder?

We Caucasoids suffer from an extreme manifestation of what I call 'the cronos complex'. It is a psychological malady unique to our species, but possessing the white race with particular force.

My first book, *The Cronos Compex I*, presented an explanation for the biological origin of human culture and psychology. Man was seen as differing qualitatively from other animal species because of one relatively simple biological fact: we seem to be the only species which conceives of time itself as a "territory," to be asserted and defended according to the dictates of well-known biological behaviour patterns originally developed to assert and defend spatial territory and social position.

Simply, the thesis presented in *The Cronos Complex I* was that Man applied territorial and social dominance behaviour to a new dimension: time. Our attempts to inhabit the new dimension of time, to assert and defend it, demanded new psychological and cultural tools.

We had to learn how to communicate in time if we were to inhabit it. We had to learn how to contact the dead and the yet-to-be-born, the past and the future. We invented religion originally as a way of past-present communication. Somewhat later we invented writing, which allowed present-future communication. We invented tools to permit *non-biological communication* with the past and the future. We began to preserve people who showed special aptitude for forms of non-biological communication within the new dimension of existence we had claimed. We preserved shamans, priests, writers and artists.

Our supra-animal, supernatural culture began when we conceived of time as a territory which could be inhabited and when we began to develop non-biological means of coping with this strange environment in which birth and death seemed insuperable barriers to a mortal creature. At the moment of claiming time we became 'man', as distinct from other animals.

Unfortunately, having just recently been good animals, and highly territorial ones at that, we brought with us into the new dimension means of asserting and defending our territory. It was an instinctual decision. We had for long eons, as terrestrial primates, been accustomed to asserting and defending individual territory (social position) and group territory (the geographical feeding and breeding grounds of our clans) .

We may be excused. It was a new dimension and a strange one. We did not realize until much later that in the territory of time our only potential enemies were our own past and future, our parents and our offspring. Not realizing that tragedy would result from temporal aggression, we set our pickets against the past and future.

Applied to the new territory of time, our instinctual aggression demanded that the uniqueness of each lifetime be protected from both the past and the future. Instinctual territorial defense of identity demanded that the past be surpassed and that the future be limited.

We found that we could surpass the past, and proclaim the unique identity of each successive lifetime, with the invention of the concept of 'progress'. It is immediately obvious that, once conceived, and in the absence of counterforce, progress becomes a geometric function. Progress *is* a geometric function.

The first deliberate human burial, and therefore the first indication of temporal awareness that the living have some relationship to the dead, took place about 50,000 years ago. It was a Neanderthal grave excavated at Le Moustière in France. Progress is a geometric function. Mankind came from that graveside to nuclear technology in 50,000 years. Our line had spent the previous 2,500,000 years refining the hand-axe. We came from Le Moustière to the 20th Century in just two per cent of total hominid history.

Yet, in spite of this dramatic acceleration of human culture, progress has been held in check. The protection of territorial identity demanded also that the future, our offspring, be denied access to progress. Progress in the hands of our offspring would eclipse our own identity, just as we eclipsed our own parents in order to obtain it.

We invented various mechanisms to hold the future back, to limit our offspring's access to progress. We were already familiar with social dominance and we reshaped it so that it would function in the new dimension of time. We invented the caste system and inherited occupations... so that the child would be merely a shadow of the parent, so that differences between generations would be minimized. We were already familiar with 'warfare', territorial clashes with rival clans. We refashioned this relatively bloodless animal activity so that it would serve the interests of territorial identity in the new dimension of time. We found that we could limit the future with more brutal warfare than anything known in the animal world. We could hurt the future, cripple it with casualties and thereby compromise its ability to surpass us.

Surpassing the past and limiting the future. That is the tension and essential pattern of human history.

In the final pages of *The Cronos Complex I* a biological analysis of our contemporary Apocalypse was sketched. In simple biological terms, past-surpassing activities have been united with future-limiting ones. The merger represents a quantum jump in the power of the present. The merger was inevitable at a certain level of technology.

Technology and progress were recently discovered to have inherent future-limiting possibilities. Resource wastage and environmental pollution can cripple the future's ability to surpass the achievements of the present Controlling Lifetime. They are conscious attacks on the future in the interests of present identity-assertion.

Technology has now, for the first time, provided the present with a weapon capable of limiting the future totally: nuclear extermination.

The Apocalypse as sketched illustrates that the 'insanity' of rampant progress and nuclear technology proceeds from the ancient and normal mechanism of territorial defense extended innocently and ignorantly into the dimension of time. But the territory of time isn't 'normal'. It is a tricky and paradoxical environment for a biological creature. Normal animal mechanisms, of which territorial assertion is only one, loom as potential tragedies when instinctively applied within the supernatural dimension of time.

The temporal dimension also dictates paradoxes in psychosexual motivations. We have already noted that future-limitation is demanded by the dictates of temporal territorial assertion and defense. But, if we know that the future threatens us, why do we continue to reproduce? Surely, the temporally territorial creature would suffer psycho-sexual conflicts.

Man, the only temporally territorial creature, is full of such conflicts.

Even the most cursory biological glance at humanity reveals both the conflicts and the solutions that nature proposed to combat them.

We find that those humans who are most committed to temporal communication, those who have the most powerful longing to exist simultaneously in past, present and future, are unable to reproduce at all. Time is a non-biological environment. A biological creature presuming to inhabit it fully can do so only at the cost of genetic oblivion. Priests, nuns, exceptional thinkers, writers and artists have all proved statistically sterile. It is not quite a functional and physical sterility: celibacy is an intellectual decision.

Even the average man is affected by psycho-sexual conflicts arising from the human possession of temporal territory. The average person experiences sexual approach-avoidance. We suffer from sexual fears, uncertainties and inadequacies apparently unknown in the animal world. We appreciate sexual stimulation, but we tend to shy away from reproduction. Nature has done its best to overcome our hesitation with an amazing number of stimulatory sexual adaptations. Nature tempts us to reproduce through the use of pleasure. Our stimulatory sexual adaptations are absolutely unique in terms of both quantity and quality.

We naturally enjoy the stimulation, but we know the psychological implications of reproduction. Offspring are an identity-threat. Our temporal identities are selfish. Therefore, we often voluntarily place ourselves in a position where we are exposed to sexual stimulation but where intercourse is impossible. We watch striptease, we patronize pornography.

If there is guilt, and there is, it comes from the impossibility of serving two masters at once. Once conceiving of time as territory, we cease to be completely natural. Our sexual adaptations and desires are an affront to the non-biological environment of the mind by which we communicate in time. Somehow, once glimpsing the vast spectacle of eternity, our sexual equipment and the act of reproduction seem shameful and irrelevant. The temporal territory, fully inhabited in all three tenses of past, present and future, is nothing more than the 'spiritual' world.

At the same time, we are still very much a natural animal. We are also a biological species like any other. Those who turn away from the 'material' world of day-to-day living also feel guilt. Extreme intellectualism is a 'cop-out' from the natural world to which we also owe partial allegiance. The guilt of the cop-out often becomes insupportable. Suicides among exceptional thinkers, writers, artists and poets are commonplace.

Man is a biological creature attempting to inhabit an environment that is non-biological. This is the paradox of human existence, and the conflict reverberates through every facet of what we, in our arrogance and guilt, in our pride and sorrow, consider to be distinctly human in our culture and psychology.

Pornography and priests, ascetics and perverts alike are products of the realization in a dim hominid brain that time was another territory to be inhabited, asserted and defended.

I chose to call the temporal conception, and the human behaviour produced by it, 'the cronos complex'. Cronos, or 'Chronos', was the Greek personification of time. Greek myths concerning Cronos illustrate very clearly that the temporal personality profile was well understood by the ancients... somewhat better understood, in fact, than by modern psychiatry which is still grappling with red herrings. Cronos (time) was married to Rhea (fertility). But Cronos feared offspring. He knew that he would eventually be deposed by any offspring that reached maturity. Consequently, Cronos developed the nasty habit of eating his children. It was only by trickery on the part of fertility that a viable child eventually escaped the jealousy of Cronos. Rhea, after having had yet another baby, decided to deceive Cronos. Instead of giving him the baby to swallow, Rhea wrapped a rock in swaddling clothes and offered it to Cronos. The temporal personality is so greedy for ultimate identity that Cronos grabbed the object and immediately gulped it down.

Thus Rhea saved one baby. The worst fears of Cronos were realized: the baby was Zeus. The offspring did grow up to overthrow the parent. Cronos was cast down, made impotent. His identity was eclipsed by Zeus.

Thus it is within the human, temporal, psychology. Our sexual adaptations are Rhea's tricks. Our identity-greed and penchant for future-limitation are well symbolized by Cronos' appetite. There can be few more fitting labels for the human condition than 'the cronos complex'.

I wrote *The Cronos Complex I* in terms of 'Man' because it seemed obvious that all men share the salient characteristics of the temporal personality profile, and that this possession is shared with no other species and therefore stands as a functional definition of Man.

On the other hand, it is equally obvious that this "cronos complex" finds its most virulent expression in the psychology of but one kind of Man, Western man, white man. Even the Cronos myth is Western. We have some self-knowledge, however allegorical.

We are an extreme expression of the cronos complex. The apparent desire for total future-limitation is ours. Nuclear weapons, rampant technology, environmental pollution and resource impoverishment are the results of an extreme cronos complex. They belong on the white man's doorstep.

We are human, but in the perspective of the entire human population we are a pathology. We are abnormal, atypical Man.

Thus, *The Cronos Complex I* did not tell the entire story. I knew it before setting pen to paper. There was a second level of understanding to be delved.

And it was racial.

3

Child of Fire and Ice

I do not pretend to be the first person to propose a racial ex-
plantion for the obvious differences in behaviour between white
men and other people. Many have previously tested men of various
colours in order to determine if a racial difference in intelligence,
for example, might conveniently account for Western man's
dominant technology and for the imposition of his culture
throughout the world. Unfortunately for our self-image, and in-
conveniently, tests have never proven that innate intelligence differs
significantly among races. There is a difference in brain size among
races, however. Caucasoid cranial capacities average about 50 cc
more than Negroid cranial capacities... but Mongoloid cranial
capacities have been found to average 150 cc greater than the white
man's and this discovery did not do our egos any good.

Thwarted by objective comparative test results, the Nazis rejected
science and embraced pseudo-science in order to retain some basis
for their mystique of race superiority. For the Nazis, the white man
was uniquely created from cosmic struggle. Hans Hörbiger, Chief
Scientist of the Third Reich, developed his theory of fire and ice, a
theory totally at odds with the view of cosmic and human evolution
developed by contemporary Western science.

Hörbiger taught that all cosmic bodies except the earth are made
of ice. He believed that the earth had four moons during its history,

not just the one that inspires lovers presently. And all the moons, including our present one, were made of ice. According to this theory of fire and ice, the previous three moons had crashed to earth, opening up the planet's volcanic interior and deluging men with lava and fire.

Although three moons have crashed to earth previously, each shone in the night sky for many thousands of years before the inevitable cataclysm. The moons' orbits gradually degenerated over many eons. And, as each moon grew closer to the earth, its gravitational field tended to counteract the gravity on earth. Organisms on earth, including men, freed from the full force of the earth's pull, grew gigantic in stature. Men grew gigantically in spirit, too. Men became gods. Their intelligence and moral power were such that they were even able to postpone the inevitable crashing of a moon. But they were not able to prevent it.

The moons crashed, and human populations were decimated by both fire and ice. Most people dwindled in both stature and spirit because they were once again at the mercy of the full power of the earth's gravity. But some of the survivors took refuge in mountains where they were less affected, and dwindled less in size and spirit. These people were Aryans, Caucasoids.

The Nazis believed that a fourth cycle was beginning. The orbit of the present Moon was starting to degenerate. The Aryan tribes who had escaped becoming subhuman because they had taken refuge in the mountains had become sensitive to a new cycle of growth in their bodies and minds. In fact, the Aryans had become sensitive to this thousands of years ago when they had swept out of their mountain havens to dominate Eurasia. The German people, the purest descendants of these ancient Aryans, were innately attuned to the opportunities for superior growth afforded by the maturing of another cycle. Men could again become gods, but the Aryans, the Germans, had the best chance of all because they had preserved some of their superior qualities from the last cataclysm. In fact, at least some Aryans had already become godlike.

By the 1930's Hitler could say: "The New Man is already among us. He is here. I will tell you a secret. I have seen the New Man. Just seeing him made me afraid."

The New Man would inevitably rule the world because of his superiority and the world must be made ready for him. Those subhumans who lingered from the last moon-crashing cycle would have to be exterminated so as not to affront the New Man. Since the Aryan Germans were the most perfect survivors of the last cataclysm and had at least some chance of evolving into New Men — and some already had — it fell to the Germans to cleanse the world for the New Man's advent in numbers.

To our minds, Hörbiger's theory seems both ridiculous and confusing. Illogical. As strange as it may seem, Hitler and the high Nazis fought World War II in order to please a few examples of the New Man already among them and out of almost abject fear of them... whoever they were, whether real or figments of insanity.

It is unbelievable that a world view of this sort should have been adopted officially by the leaders of a modern, civilized Western nation. We grope helplessly for a rational understanding of the process.

However, it does seem clear enough that Hörbiger's theory was not completely original. It rested on an ancient body of Germanic myth. The first emergence of the fire-and-ice theme was perhaps the story of Niord, the first hunter, who defeated the Worm Oroubourous by the use of fire. Niord chased the Worm deep into the earth where Oroubourous became encased in a prison of ice. But it is said that someday Oroubourous will attempt to escape and his struggles will burst the world.

Wagner, who wrote a number of racist pamphlets, wove the theme of fire and ice deftly into *The Ring of the Nibelungs*, while earlier Strauss had composed a tone poem to Nietzsche's superman philosophy. *Thus Spake Zarathustra* is about the Aryan prophet, Zarthustra or Zoroaster, who kept the Aryan spirit and religion pure while these people preserved their superiority in the mountains of the Middle East, the Caucasus, Zagros and Elburz-Pamir ranges. The Aryan-Caucasoid heartland had been in this mountainous region. Memories of Niord, Zarathustra and the crucible of fire and ice centred in these mountains, which explains why the major Nazi offensive in Russia was a strategically senseless attempt to invade the Caucasus region.

I have dealt with Hörbiger's notion at some length because, even though the Nazi world view was a curious amalgam of nonsense, it did trigger the most tragic paroxysm of racism the world has ever known. And for another reason. In spite of the insanity, there seems to be a whisper of true 'racial' memory.

Almost all European peoples preserve some memory of coming from the east and traditions of 'originating' in the vicinity of the Caucasus-Pamir chain of mountains.

It can be said that the languages of most modern European

peoples do, in fact, seem to have originated in the Caucasus or in south Russia, and it is known that some tribal-lingustic groups emerged from that area and invaded Europe, India and parts of the Middle East.

But this memory, although ancient, is still much too young to stretch back to the beginnings of the white race. The Nazi-Germanic fire and ice myths must be coincidence.

Coincidence?

Strange as it may seem, it can be said accurately enough in an allegorical way that the Caucasoids did develop in the conflict between fire and ice. But it had nothing to do with Hörbiger's pseudo-scientific cosmology.

We will find our inheritance of fire and ice if we return to the beginning of the cronos complex at a grave at Le Moustière. It is not mythical, but too mundane. We will find cave fires which allowed one group of men to survive the ice of Würm I. *The Caucasoids, uniquely among the races of Mankind, evolved in a glacial environment.*

There is an increasing body of scientific data suggesting that this group of men did develop in a narrow zone of life between fire and ice... between the cave fires and the savage cold of the Würm I ice age. I will attempt to show that glacial evolution demanded certain special adaptations of Neanderthal man and that present-day Caucasoids still show vestiges of these adaptations.

These special adaptations had incidental side effects which resulted in an exceptionally aggresssive psychology, an extreme expression of the cronos complex, and a higher level of psychosexual conflict compared to all other races of men.

Not intelligence, nor morality, nor 'spirit', but *aggression,* is responsible for the white man's 'superiority'. Aggression is responsible for the expansion of Caucasoids, both geographically and culturally, at the expense of other races. We witness the final act of this expansion in our own time. It began when the glaciers retreated, when Würm released the white race from its tutelage under fire and ice, when pathological temporal aggression was unleashed upon the world.

This higher level of aggression, which is merely an incidental result of glacial evolution, has fueled extreme manifestations of temporal assertion and defense among Caucasoids. Rampant technology, environmental pollution, resource rapine and the threat of nuclear war are the results.

I will also try to show that the white race's apparent inability to cope well with intellectual conflict, to cope non-violently with paradox, stems from psychosexual frustrations.

We have a low frustration tolerance because glacial adaptation robbed us of sufficiently effective sexual displacement activities. Our philosophical and religious conflicts are the result of a glacial distortion of primate behaviour-patterns. All the pyres are a monstrous vanity.

What about our superiority?

Did our glacial evolution, unique among men, and our responsive adaptations serve to make us 'superior'... however accidentally?

Yes... and no.

There is nothing innate or eternal about superiority and inferiority. Both are dictated by external conditions. External conditions can change. Superiority and inferiority can trade places in an instant. It has happened before. It is happening now.

During the Miocene the earth was largely covered with luxurious forests. Two major lines of advanced primates co-existed: ape-tending pongids and Man-tending hominids.

During the epoch of Miocene green mansions the pongids were, by every objective criterion, superior to the hominids. The apes proliferated mightily and spread all over the globe: hominids were well down the road to extinction. Pongids eagerly adapted to the forest world while we hominids remained stubbornly primitive.

There is little room for doubt that if the Miocene had lasted longer the hominids would have perished entirely.

But it did not last. The Miocene became the Pliocene: neither the pongids nor the hominids had the least responsibility for the change. The world's climate altered.

The earth entered a drought millions of years long. Forests dwindled and the pongids dwindled with them. By the sheerest accident, hominid liabilities in the Miocene became assets during the Pliocene. It is often said that our failure to adapt to the forests left our adaptational options open for the new environmental conditions of the Pliocene. It is truer to say that the conditions of the Pliocene *happened* to favour our primitive characteristics. Man is a primitive and unspecialized primate.

It is natural to assume unconsciously that the hominids possessed some sort of innate 'superiority' which made Man's present pre-eminence inevitable. Nonsense. The hominids merely possessed characteristics which were manifestly "inferior" during the Miocene and which suddenly became "superior" in the Pliocene.

So it is with the superiority and inferiority of racial characteristics. Superior for what? Superior when?

I will propose in this essay that the white race possesses an atypical level of aggression. Whether this characteristic is a 'superiority' or an 'inferiority' depends solely upon environmental conditions.

I suppose that, from about 30,000 B.P.*[2] until now, abnormal Caucasoid aggression must be judged to have been a 'superiority'. The Caucasoids manifestly expanded culturally and geographically, often at the expense of other races of men. That is the objective biological criterion of evolutionary success. Under the environmental conditions of a relatively empty and resource-rich world, Caucasoid aggression proved supportable, viable and successful.

But environmental conditions have changed.

The earth is scarred by 30,000 years of Caucasoid aggression. It is no longer empty, it is too full. It is no longer resource-rich, it is impoverished. Caucasoid aggression has developed weapons capable of destroying it.

It seems obvious that Caucasoid characteristics are no longer supportable, no longer viable. Our proclivities can no longer be judged 'superior'. On the contrary, we seem to be rapidly becoming 'inferior' compared to other races of men. Caucasoid predispositions are too expensive, biologically, in a resource-raped world. Unless Caucasoids manage to destroy the world with weapons created because of their temporal aggression, the future would seem to belong to less aggressive, less identity-greedy kinds of men.

In short, it is my judgment, and the position of this book, that since the end of World War II Caucasoids have become biologically inferior to other kinds of men, given our present environment.

One way or another, the tale of the iceman and his heirs seems to be on its last telling. The history of the future will be told by men with less conflicting elements in their composition.

---

*"B.P." stands for "Before Present," which, in C14 dating, is considered to be 1950.

Part Two

*Race
and the
Neanderthal-Caucasoids*

4

The Concept of Race

... it is highly probable that different human races originated independently of one another and that they evolved out of different species of ape-men. The so-called main races of mankind are not races, but species... the voice of blood and race operates down to the last refinement of thought and exercises a decisive influence on the direction of thought.

Lothar Tirala,
Rasse, Geist und Seele

The human species is a species because all its members have shared a more or less common biological history... those of us who have paid some attention to the character and form of behaviour of peoples belonging to different varieties have satisfied ourselves by every scientific means at our disposal that significantly or innately determined mental differences between the varieties of mankind have thus far not been determined.

Ashley Montagu,
*Man's Most Dangerous Myth:
The Fallacy of Race.*

The above two viewpoints illustrate the abundant truth of

Professor Ashley Montagu's observation that the subject of 'race' has
a unique capacity to inspire extreme emotional responses and that
'racial' conflicts, whether violently social or intellectually academic,
have been characterized by confusion, distortion and ignorance of
facts.

It is only fair to inform the reader, right at the beginning, that
the position of this book lies somewhere between Tirala's Nazi
characterization of 'race' and Montagu's extremely liberal view of it.
Both extremes, Tirala's and Montagu's, ignore certain facts,
and, coming as they do from the minds of white men, may be
nothing more than two sides of one racial coin. It seems that of all
races, 'white' people have been inordinately concerned with the 'pro'
or 'con' of racial differences and their possible social or biological
significance.

Indeed, as Professor Montagu himself has remarked: "The
modern conception of race owes its widespread diffusion to the
white man. Wherever he has gone he has carried it with him."

This is another way of saying that, for some reason, the white
man has been preoccupied with differences among people, has
invented certain conceptions to explain and grade these differences,
or to explain them away, and has taken pains to diffuse these
conceptions as gospel. Tirala was a Nazi missionary of 'race';
Montagu is a liberal missionary of 'non-race'.

Since 'racial' preoccupations, whether 'good' or 'bad', seem to be
characteristic of white people, we will take a short look at the
development of our racial and racist concepts.

Use and value of the term 'race'

During what our historians like to call the Age of Enlightenment
Linnaeus began to analyse the complexity of the natural world and
to reduce the various plants and animals into classifications of
similar types. Linnaeus included Man in the animal world and
recognized only one human species as existing presently. In the
tenth edition of his *Systema Naturae* (1785) Linnaeus listed six
varieties of this one human species, and four of these varieties
(*europaeus, asiaticus, americanus* and *afer*) roughly reflected the
inhabitants of continental masses.

The word "race" itself was introduced into scientific literature by
Buffon in his *Histoire naturelle, générale et particulière* (1749) and
he uses the term in a very general sense to mean 'kind' or 'variety'.

In 1775, Johann Friedrich Blumenbach's *De generis humani*

varietate ("On the Natural Variety of Mankind") set out to classify the various kinds of men and to describe their physiology and supposed temperamental and mental differences. Blumenbach used the term 'race', borrowed from Buffon, but attached no significant biological aspects to it:

> *Although there seems to be so great a difference between nations, that you might easily take the inhabitants of the cape of Good Hope, the Greenlanders and the Circassians for so many different species of man, yet when the matter is thoroughly considered, you see that all do so run into one another, and that one variety of mankind does so sensibly pass into the other, that you cannot mark out the limits between them.*

Blumenbach used the term 'race' merely as a convenience. "Still, it will be found serviceable to the memory to have constituted certain classes into which the men of our planet may be divided."

Originally, then, the word 'race' had no rigid or concrete scientific definition and few, if any, prejudicial connotations. It reflected merely the commonsense observation that all men were of the same species and yet exhibited certain readily discernible physical differences on a more or less geographical basis.

It must be said at once that the term 'race' *still* has no satisfactory scientific meaning. Yet, the word has acquired connotations in the popular mind relating to differences in mental and biological worth, relating to 'superiority' and 'inferiority', and not merely to superficial physical differences in appearance. Because of its lack of definition, and because of the judgments of worth that have become attached to it, the modern trend in anthropology is to discard the concept, and term, 'race' entirely. As we will learn presently, there is justification for this view.

I freely admit that I have used the term 'race' for the very purpose of harnessing the emotionalism of the term toward a different end from that professed by other racists. It is my purpose to turn our Caucasoid prejudice back onto ourselves once we have seen that we do tend to differ from other kinds of men in at least one behavioural parameter: aggression. However, I also realize, and will attempt to show, that our Caucasoid aggression isn't innate and immutable, isn't 'racial' in the sense that the popular prejudice assumes. It results from evolutionary and cultural experiences: our predisposition for aggression is genetic only in the sense that environment and culture have tended to select aggression and preserve individuals exhibiting it. And since the human group possessing this higher level of aggression is sufficiently identifiable on the basis of skin colour, the usual and erroneous criterion of 'race', I have made the decision to try to utilize 'racial prejudice' in the interests of increased understanding of how Caucasoids have brought the contemporary world to the brink of several disasters.

Professor Montagu, in several books, has shown that modern racism stems from two separate fonts: a justification for slave economics, and inherent and erroneous assumptions in systems of classification when viewed in an evolutionary construct following the general acceptance of Darwin's thought. It is ironic that both religion and Darwinism were used to justify racism, since each system, for a while, vehemently opposed the other.

Racism and slavery

When Europeans began seriously to expand in the middle of the 15th Century they immediately came into contact with peoples whom they could enslave. In Europe, as elsewhere at this time, slavery was an accepted, if limited, practice and had always been so. The practice was limited because of the scarcity of material.

The medieval world acquired its slaves through either commerce or warfare. Generally, both commerce and warfare were conducted between neighbouring peoples. By the time of European expansion the world had stabilized to such a degree that neighbouring peoples generally enjoyed a parity of sorts in the matter of technology. Therefore, because of the technological parity and a *de facto* sort of balance of power, slaves acquired in warfare did not represent a statistically large percentage of any European population. And because conflicts occurred between neighbouring peoples the slave population did not differ racially in any significant way from the master population. Before the European expansion of the 15th Century, then, there had not been a racial basis to world slavery since ancient proto-historic and historic invasions — with one exception.

It is ironic that the medieval world knew only one instance of racially based slavery and that that one instance occurred in Africa, imposed by black Africans upon an earlier population. As the Bantu peoples expanded toward the south in the African continent they came into contact with 'Bushmen' and 'Hottentot' peoples, who differed physically from the Bantu and who were promptly enslaved by them. While Montagu would place all Africans under one of four 'major groups' of Mankind, C.S. Coon differentiates two 'races' in Africa south of the Sahara: the 'Congoids', or negroes, contemporary 'blacks'; and 'Capoids', the Bushmen and Hottentots, who represent a distinct and more ancient stock. If Coon's distinction is accepted, then one race enslaved the other, and the Bantus came to equate a 'slave' with the conquered 'race', and a racial justification and equation for slavery developed.

What the blacks imposed upon the Capoids was soon to be imposed upon the blacks by white Europeans.

Portuguese probing to the south along the African coast and Spanish exploration across the Atlantic brought Europeans into contact with less technologically advanced blacks and Amerindians. It was a dual meeting of differing physical types and technological levels, unique in the era of recorded history. The gulf between European technology and black and Amerindian technology presented an opportunity for exploitation which had not been equalled in Eurasia itself for centuries and perhaps millenia on a racial basis. It would seem reasonable that the last parallel of massive contact between men of different physical appearance *and* different technological level took place long before the dawn of recorded history when Caucasoids invaded the Indian subcontinent, when the Mongoloids expanded southward into the Indochinese subcontinent at the expense of the Australoid, and when, as already mentioned, the Bantu 'Congoids' expanded southward in Africa at the expense of the 'Capoids'.

With respect to the European expansion from the 15th Century until the present, it was European technology which guaranteed the exploitation and defeat of blacks and Amerinds. In the beginning, at least, there did not seem to be any 'racial discrimination', at least in a pejorative sense, on the part of Europeans.

Because of the friendly natives, Vasco da Gama could name a coastal district in southeast Africa Terra da Boa Gente, 'Land of the Good People'. Christopher Cloumbus could report that the Amerindians were of "excellent and acute understanding" and describe them as "a loving, uncovetous people, so docile in all things that there is no better people or better country... They loved their neighbors as themselves and they had the sweetest and gentlest way of speaking in the world, and always with a smile."

Writing of the Hurons in 1640, Father Le Jeune said:

I naturally compare our Savages with certain villagers, because both are usually without education; though our

Peasants are superior in this regard; and yet I have not seen anyone thus far, of those who have come to this country, who does not confess and frankly admit that the Savages are more intelligent than our ordinary Peasants.

Yet, only a century later, these blacks and Amerinds, originally described in such glowing terms by European explorers, could be characterized as "lazy, filthy pagans, of bestial morals, no better than dogs, and fit only for slavery, in which state alone there might be some hope of converting them to Christianity". In this statement we can see the beginning of a definite 'racial' or ethnic distinction made between Europeans and their slaves, in which the latter have become 'inferior', and their inferiority is used as a justification for exploitation with religious sanction.

How did this change of attitude come about?

Precisely because we in the contemporary world have come to assume a racial and 'inferiority' justification for slavery, we may find it hard to understand how Europeans could rationalize the enslavement of people whom they freely admitted to be 'good' and intelligent, and often better than the Europeans themselves. The point is that slavery in medieval Europe was not generally considered a mark of biological or moral inferiority, but usually merely a matter of unfortunate circumstance for the individual involved. It was recognized that men of great moral worth and martial valour might become slaves through the misfortunes of war or vicissitudes of finances. Slavery was a *circumstance* which, in theory at least, did not necessarily negate recognition of an individual's moral worth, intelligence or competence. Therefore, originally, the Europeans could enslave these 'good' and 'intelligent' people with no further justification than the technological ability to do so. In addition, the Church supplied a rationale for reducing blacks and Amerinds to the *circumstance* of slavery because, however moral and intelligent they might be, the blacks and Amerinds were not yet Christians and the circumstance of slavery by Europeans offered an opportunity for their conversion and the saving of their souls.

This appears as the worst sort of hypocrisy from our vantage point, after several centuries of an unconscious race-slavery equation, but the judgment may be harsh.

In his detailed discussion of the racist foundation of modern slavery, Ashley Montagu says:

It is of even greater interest and importance to note that as long as the trade was taken for granted and no one voice raised against it, or at least a voice that was heard, the slaves, though treated as chattels, were conceded to be human in every sense but that of social status. This may well be seen in the treatment of slaves in Portugal and Spain, where many of them rose to high positions in Church and State, as was the case in ancient Greece, Rome and Arabia.

What might be called the 'slavery — racial inferiority' psychological complex among Europeans and, later, Southern Americans began in the first instance because blacks and Amerinds were so easy to exploit because of European technology that these "racial" groups were imported or enslaved in enormous numbers. Simply because of their sheer numbers these 'races' became equated with slavery in the popular Caucasoid mind. And, due to the easy availability of slaves, a type of agricultural-industrial complex evolved which, in terms of productivity, had been unknown in the medieval world and, in fact, unparalleled since the very similar slave-based economy of the fallen Roman Empire. The economic foundation of Europe's Renaissance and Enlightenment, and especially the unprecedented speed of that cultural-intellectual evolution, was, in a very real sense, slavery... just as the 'glory that was Greece' and the 'grandeur that was Rome' rested squarely upon similarly sordid foundations.

Yet, the European Enlightenment resulted in the gradual development of 'artificial energy' in the shape of the steam engine. And this invention was first applied to industrial situations rather than to agricultural field work. It is no accident that 'humane' opposition to the institution of slavery took root among urban and industrialized populations who, because of the greater efficiency of alternative steam power, could well afford to begin to despise slavery.

There are geographic, rather than moral, reasons why the humane opposition to slavery began in England, northern Europe and the northern U.S. All of these areas had industrial economies amenable to the introduction of steam power. These areas were geographically and climatically unsuited to agrarian economic emphasis while more nearly tropical regions had to rely longer on manpower-intensive plantation crops for an economic foundation.

Mobile steam power, as required for farm equipment, was naturally a later and more difficult achievement than the stationary plant sufficient for industry. In fact, mobile steam-powered farm equipment was never a truly viable proposition because of the cumbersome nature of external combustion. For tropical regions relying on vast plantations, no really viable alternative to sheer manpower became available until the development of the gasoline internal combustion engine and the modern tractor.

Perhaps it is not too irreverent to suggest that the humane movement toward abolition, which gained momentum rapidly in industrial — as opposed to agricultural — areas, had an economic component which was at least as strong as the moral component.

However this may be, when opposition to slavery and the slave trade began to be important, those who still depended upon slaves for their economic status, southern agrarian planters, had to find some mechanism besides bald practicality to justify the bondage which was the foundation of their wealth.

A 'race-slavery' connection had already been made due to the sheer numbers of blacks and Amerinds exploited. It now remained only to justify bondage by adding an 'inferiority' argument which 'naturally' explained subjugation of some men by others.

Generations of slavery and lack of social and educational opportunities for black and Amerind fulfilment had inevitably resulted in poor development of these people and their offspring in comparison with the whites. The cultural gulf between these blacks and Amerinds and whites was presented as evidence of natural, biological and moral inferiority. Their inferiority, and consequent slavery, was a matter of natural law. Witness the following quotations from 19th Century sources:

The red ant will issue in regular battle array, to conquer and subjugate the black or negro ant... these negro slaves perform all the labour of the communities into which they are brought... Upon this definition, therefore, of the law of Nature, negro slavery would seem to be perfectly consistent with that law.

In mental and moral development, slavery, so far from retarding has advanced the Negro race.

Contact with the Caucasian is the only civiliser of the negro, and slavery the only condition on which that contact can be preserved.

... to prove that all men have equal right to Liberty, and all outward comforts of life... [is] to invert the Order that God hath set in the world, who hath Ordained different degrees and orders of men, some to be High and Honourable,

some to be Low and Dispicable; some to be Monarchs, Kings, Princes and Governors, Masters and Commanders, others to be Subjects and to be Commanded; Servants of sundry sorts and degrees, bound to obey; yea, some to be born Slaves, and so to remain during their lives, as hath been proved.

The spurious reasoning of the 'slavery-racial inferiority' construct was complete. As Montagu observes regarding the evolution of the construct from the mid-15th Century to Emancipation:

Their different physical appearance provided a convenient peg upon which to hang the argument that this represented the external sign of more profound ineradicable mental and moral inferiorities. It was an easily grasped mode of reasoning, and in this way the obvious difference in their social *status... was equated with their obviously different* physical *appearance, which, in turn, was taken to indicate a fundamental* biological *difference... What had once been a social difference was now transformed into a biological difference which would serve, it was hoped, to justify and maintain the social difference.*

Perhaps more to the point, it was also hoped that these supposedly profound biological differences would justify an *economic* system.

The attempt to perpetuate slavery was unsuccessful, as we all know. In the U.S. the civil war ended slavery in 1865. Abolition in English colonies had been decreed by 1833, in French possessions by 1848 and in Dutch colonies by 1863.

But, while the 'slavery' component of the 'slavery-racial inferiority' complex disappeared, the 'racial inferiority' component lingers in continuing discrimination, continuing racism. [3]

Racism and Darwinism

Encyclopaedists like Buffon, Linnaeus and Blumenbach had used the term 'race' merely as a convenience to catalogue physically different kinds of men whom, however, they regarded as members of the same species.

Darwinism, if not Darwin himself, bequeathed to the term 'race' and to the catalogues of men a meaning which Buffon, Blumenbach and Linnaeus never intended. If the Linnaean classification of animal and plant species indicated in many cases an evolutionary relationship between types — and this was undoubtedly so in the light of *The Origin of Species* — was it not therefore possible and even probable that the various kinds of men also existed in some sort of evolutionary relationship to each other?

Did it not seem reasonable that some 'races' were more evolved than others? Or, more radically, was it possible that some races might have evolved from different sorts of primate ancestors?

Evolution offered a seemingly scientific way of explaining the observed physical and cultural differences which were indisputably observed among men.

We have already seen how the economics of slavery required and invented a doctrine of differing racial potential. Evolution quite naturally suggested something very similar, though for completely different reasons.

Slavery was a dead issue, just barely, when the Bishop of Worcester was shocked at Professor Huxley's announcement and defense of Darwin's theory of evolution. The implications of evolution could not be mustered to support a retention of slavery, but Darwin's ideas could be marshalled to lend credence to the 'racial inferiority' construct that slavery's justification had left behind as a social residue.

I have always considered it a sobering thought that had Darwin's *Origin of Species* been published a decade earlier the U.S. might still be afflicted with slavery today. At the very least, racism would be more virulent, if that is possible, than it is now. For there is little doubt that with the economic foundations of their way of life at stake, Southern planters would have at least partially abandoned their total reliance on religious defense of slavery, which was at best a two-edged sword for them, and would have pointed to, if not embraced, evolutionary arguments as well. As it was, pro-slavers were denied Darwinian assistance only by a hair's breadth. A congruence of 'God's Order' and 'Natural Evolution' on the differing potential of races, however antagonistic in other respects, would have rendered pro-slave arguments more convincing. Progressive, humane sociology and anthropology would have been retarded by a century.

If Darwinism came too late to assist in the perpetuation of slavery, it arrived in time to develop and justify the most virulent racism, and the most appalling conflict, that the world has ever known. And, thanks to the opportunities afforded by the theory of evolution, many additional varieties of men, and not only blacks and Amerinds, were accommodated in an apocalyptic racial-inferiority construct. The Nazis carried a pseudo-evolutionary race ethos so far that only *one* small division of but *one* of Mankind's major groups was considered capable of being completely and fulfillingly human.

In addition to the inference that the various kinds of men might bear some sort of evolutionary relationship to each other, the theory of evolution, as another aspect of fluorescing 19th Century materialist science, justified the dispatch of hoards of investigators 'into the field', the world, armed with calipers, to refine and improve upon existing catalogues of men.

In all the corners of the world heads, limbs and teeth were measured and their forms noted, hair colour and form accounted, noses scrutinized and genitalia peered at. Traditions were studied in an attempt to learn some clues about migration routes and 'racial' origins.

'Race'.

The term had never been scientifically defined, but used as a vague synonym for 'kind' or 'variety' below the species level. Now, under the onslaughts of anthropometrics, 'race' was stretched to include both major and minor human populations. Even a moderate anthropologist, C.S. Coon, could write a book called *The Races of Europe* inferring the existence of several types of man on that small continental extension and yet later write another book, *The Origin of Races*, which discusses the origin of but five major divisions of Mankind. Some experts listed as many as twenty-eight 'types' of Man, while others plunked for four, three, five, or 'from six to nine'.

It was the proliferation of races — and the non-definition of them — by anthropometricians that allowed, eventually, Nazi politicians to convince millions that an entity called 'the Nordic race' existed and was superior, more evolved, than others.

Human variation

It cannot be denied that various groups of people differ in physical appearance, the most immediately obvious difference being skin colour. Skin colour has, in fact, been the criterion for most racial distinctions, or at least the label applied to them.

One is surprised to find, for instance, after a lucid discussion of human variation and a consequent balanced judgment that 'race' as a term is meaningless *especially* when used as a foundation for social discrimination on the basis of skin colour alone, that Ashley

Montagu himself defines four 'major groups' of mankind (he will not call them 'races') *on the basis of skin colour!*

> *From the standpoint of a classificatory view of mankind which has due regard for the facts it is arbitrarily possible to recognize four distinctive major groups of mankind. These are the Negroid or black, the Archaic white or Australoid, the Caucasoid or white, and the Mongoloid major groups of mankind.*

Yet, skin colour is only one way in which various human groups differ from each other. Groups also differ in the possession of other physical characters.

> *This* status quo [*i.e. adaptive racial characteristics*] *entails not only the variations in bones and teeth that are evident in fossil men, and those of the surface features of living men, like skin, hair, lips and ears, by which we can distinguish races almost at a glance, but also subtler differences seen only on the dissecting table or through the eyepieces of microscopes. Races differ in the extent and manner in which the fine subcutaneous muscles of the lips and cheeks have become differentiated from the parent mammillian muscle body; in the chemical composition of hair and bodily secretions, including milk; in the ways different muscles are attached to bones; in the sizes and probable secretion rates of different endocrines; in certain details of the nervous system, as, for example, how far down in the lumbar vertebrae the neural canal extends; and in the capacity of individuals to tolerate crowding and stress.*

There are good reasons for taking issue with the *emphasis* Professor Coon, an eminent anthropologist, gives this list of human variations and we will question Coon's objectivity when we come to discuss his theory about the origin of races. For instance, it will become obvious that Coon appears to betray an emotional investment when he refers to a "status quo" in the genetic endowment of races. All humans are interfertile, all races can mix and produce fertile and viable offspring, and therefore no race possesses a genetic "status quo". Races are not immutable entities.

Also, in his list of human variation, Coon neglects to mention that most differences are a common legacy of all races to some degree and that racial possession of most characteristics is a matter of degree, not undisputed ownership. Races may exhibit *statistical* differences in the presence or absence of a given variation, but seldom do human groups exhibit absolute presence or absence of a character. Even a dissecting table will not reveal the racial affinity of any *one* individual with any certainty.

Le Gros Clark, an Oxford anatomist, has said:

At first sight, the contrast in appearance of such extreme types as Negroid, Mongoloid and European might suggest fundamental constitutional differences. In fact, however, a close anatomical study seems to show that the physical differences are confined to quite superficial characteristics. I may best emphasize this by saying that if the body of a Negro were to be deprived of all superficial features such as skin, hair, nose and lips, I do not think that any anatomist could say for certain, in any isolated case, whether he was dealing with the body of a Negro or a European.

Human beings do differ in their physical appearance, but the only reason for studying these differences, and cataloguing men on the basis of them, is to determine whether such differences have some fundamental biological and evolutionary relevance.

It is simply a fact that superficial characteristics like skin colour, the colour and form of hair and the shape of noses — those characteristics which have been used most often to differentiate 'races' — not only have no apparent evolutionary significance, but are not even uniquely attributable to any one "race". An analogy most understandable to the Western layman would be the situation of trying to compare car performance on the basis of paint job, presence or absence of hubcaps, the form of the hood ornament. There may indeed be real and significant differences in the comparative 'motivation' of automobiles... but the place to look is under the hood, in the suspension and transmission. Road performance isn't relevant to the paint job and the chrome.

Perhaps it is not stretching this analogy too far to observe that those who have been concerned with finding the comparative worth of races in terms of 'road performance' along the path of evolution have pinned their hopes on superficial characteristics that would not influence an experienced car buyer.

There are human differences in skin colour, nose shape, hair form, etc., but these differences are not concordant. A certain nose shape isn't always correlated with a certain skin colour, a certain type of hair isn't always correlated with either skin colour or nose shape. Cranial capacity, the size of the brain, doesn't vary consistently with skin colour, nose shape or hair form.

The non-correlation of those characteristics which we have learned to believe are 'racially diagnostic' is called 'discordance'. As W.L. Brown says:

> *Applied to the wealth of data on the variation of modern* Homo sapiens, *the "no race" idea seems worth considering on this basis [the discordance of characters], even though the value of the race concept in studies of man has already been challenged widely on other grounds by anthropologists themselves. In the face of such obvious discordance as, for instance, human skin pigmentation with blood type factors, or hair form with cephalic index [taken on a world basis], the wildly varying opinions of anthropological schools on the racial classification of our species show up as irrelevant and unnecessary.*

Perhaps more to the point, anyone who still finds it convenient to suspect that some important characteristic, like brain size, must be however vaguely correlated with the almost-ephemeral geographic races and therefore explain statistically the white man's supposed superiority, should plot the following cranial capacities on maps: a Negroid average cranial capacity of 1,350 cc; a Caucasoid cranial capacity of 1,400 cc; a Mongoloid average cranial capacity of 1,570 cc. Those figures represent average figures for major groups, but the 'discordance' (discordance with prejudice) is even more revealing. Thus we find that the Amahosa tribe of Africa has an average cranial capacity of 1,490 cc, well above the 'white norm', while Buriats (1,496 cc), Iroquois (1,519 cc) and Eskimos (1,563 cc) enjoy a decided advantage in cranial capacity.

And, should one be tempted to say that human performance is dependent upon the 'quality and not quantity' of the brain, Professor W.E. Le Gros Clark, one of the foremost neuroanatomists of our time, and one who was called to testify earlier, observes:

> *... in spite of statements which have been made to the contrary, there is no macroscopic or microscopic difference by which it is possible for the anatomist to distinguish the brain in single individuals of different races.*

Dr. Otto Klineberg, perhaps the leading expert in the field of comparative 'racial' or ethnic studies in psychology, writes: "We may state with some degree of assurance that in all probability the inherited capacities in two different ethnic groups is just about identical."

It is becoming obvious that the characteristics which obviously vary among human groups, and which have confidently been used to distinguish race (a term which has never been satisfactorily defined in any case), are found to be superficial, discordant in worldwide distribution and, more importantly, irrelevant in terms of explaining the relationship of evolution to the realities of the contemporary human world.

None the less, most anthropologists, and even 'liberal' ones like Ashley Montagu, are willing to divide the world's population up into 'major groups' if not 'races'... even though few are agreed on the number of 'major groups' or 'races' and the reason for making any distinction. If the characteristics which distinguish races are superficial and irrelevant in terms of evolution, why bother to distinguish between men at all?

The origin of races

It seems rather incongruous to me to enter into a discussion of the origin of something, 'race', which most scientists agree does not exist in any functional, evolutionary sense or even in a concrete classificatory sense. Yet, since most anthropologists are willing to grant the existence of 'major groups' for some reason, there has been continuing debate as to how these groups came into being. And, since the 'origin of races' has been used by racists to infer the superiority of one group in relation to others, and by others to rebut racist claims at the same time, it is necessary to say something about it.

There are two major and opposing explanations for human raciation: first, the one embraced by most anthropologists today, that man was a single species that migrated into different geographical environments promoting raciation by the selection of certain characteristics; second, the view in disrepute nowadays, that *Homo sapiens* consists of races that evolved from dissimilar hominid types.

I think that I should say immediately, for what it is worth, that I tend to favour the second explanation... but consider both explanations irrelevant.

Those of us holding to the second explanation for human

variation are an endangered species, but not quite extinct. In 1962, Carleton Coon, of the University of Pennsylvania, published a work entitled *The Origin of Races,* and the waves have not yet subsided. Coon's views brought thundering replies from Montagu, S.L. Washburn, and almost every other modern anthropologist. It seemed that Coon's construct too nearly paralleled racist doctrines, like that propounded by Tirala. Not only have Coon's facts been disputed, but his motivations have been suspected. I must confess that I, too, suspect Coon's motivations.

In *The Origin of Races,* Coon purported to be able to distinguish five major races of Mankind and to trace their evolution from somewhat differing hominid ancestors. Coon considers that the species we call *Homo sapiens* is more nearly a 'state', not so much a biological species, and that different groups of hominids passed over the *'sapiens* threshold' at different times and *essentially* separately (but with some genetic help from neighbours).

Coon says:

> *At the beginning of our record, over half a million years ago, man was a single species,* Homo erectus, *perhaps already divided into five geographic races or subspecies.* Homo erectus *then evolved into* Homo sapiens *not once but five times, as each subspecies, living in its own territory, passed a critical threshold from a more brutal to a more sapient state.*

As if this were not enough, Coon goes on to state:

> *Each major race had followed a pathway of its own through the labyrinth of time. Each had been molded in a different fashion to meet the needs of different environments, and each had reached its own level on the evolutionary scale.*

At best, and being charitable, it must be said that Coon indulges in the use of terms which are scientifically incautious and emotionally charged, and does so with dubious justification.

Montagu, in criticizing Coon, observes that it is something of a non-sequitur to say that Man has passed from "a more brutal to a more sapient state" since modern man is manifestly more 'brutal' than even the bad-tempered Cynocephalia and, one suspects, enormously more brutal in his behaviour than primitive man.

At worst, and not being so charitable, one can point to passages in Coon's work which reflect the author's apparent belief in the superiority of some races: "and each has reached its own level on the evolutionary scale" is one example of such a statement, while the following statement is another:

> ... *it is a fair inference that fossil men now extinct were less gifted than their descendents who have larger brains, that the subspecies that crossed the evolutionary threshold into the category of* Homo sapiens *the earliest have evolved most, and the obvious correlation between the length of time a subspecies has been in the* sapiens *state and the levels of civilization attained by some of its members may be related phenomena.*

Coon's five races are the Caucasoid, the Mongoloid, the Australoid, the Congoid and the Capoid. Of these, the Caucasoid and the Mongoloid races passed over the supposed *'sapiens* threshold' the earliest and are the most evolved, the Australoids are closest to this threshold and Coon rather obviously refrains from stating his belief that some Australoids are straddling it, while Coon's Congoids are something of a recent and mysterious development which can't be explained. Coon says: "The origin of the African Negroes, and of the Pygmies, is the greatest unsolved mystery in the field of racial study." (I disagree with Coon in that I feel that the white man's peculiar obsession with racial study is the greatest unsolved mystery in the field of racial study.)

Coon's Congoids, then, are a mystery, but Coon is certain that they're a recent and therefore less evolved development:

> *As far as we know now the Congoid line started on the same evolutionary level as the Eurasiatic ones in the Early Middle Pleistocene and then stood still for half a million years, after which Negroes and Pygmies appeared as if out of nowhere.*

And elsewhere Coon remarks: "If Africa was the cradle of mankind, it was only an indifferent kindergarden. Europe and Asia were our principal schools."

My judgment of Coon's thesis is that he gives reasonable support for the existence of an Australoid-Pithecanthropus line, for a Mongoloid-Sinanthropus line... and not much else. I believe that Coon can be accused of special pleading when he constructs an argument for an early *sapient* state among 'Caucasoids' on the basis of one skull (Steinheim) and three cranial fragments (Swanscombe), more so when he admits that he did not examine the skull itself, but only a cast. Since the Steinheim skull is incomplete, and the Swanscombe fragments consist of an occipital and two parietals *found at three separate times* in Thames river gravels, the evidence is dubious at best.

But by attributing these fragments to a *sapient* level, Coon provides the Caucasoids with a pedigree boasting *sapiens* emergence in Europe as early as the Great Interglacial, or 300,000 years ago. Thus, on the basis of three fragments and an injured skull Coon makes the Caucasoid race the earliest to cross the *sapiens* threshold and, therefore, in his words the "most evolved". One cannot escape the feeling that Coon has abused the evidence to arrive at a preconception.

However, as I said, it may be fair to say that Coon does give reasonable support for the existence of an Australoid-Pithecanthropus line of evolution and a Mongoloid-Sinanthropus line of evolution. And, if this is so, Coon's argument that at least two "races" evolved over the *sapiens* threshold separately from somewhat differing ancestors deserves detailed analysis... which hasn't been forthcoming. And it may be germane to remark here that Chinese anthropologists, at least, consider Sinanthropus to have been *their* evolutionary ancestor, but apparently don't hold out the opportunity of an identical ancestor and antiquity for the rest of us. In this attitude, whether flattering to other kinds of men or not, contemporary Chinese anthropologists echo the initial statement of Weidenreich that Sinanthropus was not only a man, but a Mongoloid one.

Coon's Australoid-Pithecanthropus evidence cannot be wished away, although it may be undermined by cogent investigation and argument, nor can his and Weidenreich's argument about the existence of a Mongoloid-Sinanthropus continuity be wished away, especially in view of Chinese anthropological concurrence, although, again, the Mongoloid-Sinanthropus evidence may evaporate with further investigation and theorizing.

Such is the nature of racial investigation that Coon said much more than he could support with facts, but what he did say *and* did reasonably support has not received truly critical attention by his opponents. If Coon can be perceived to exhibit some emotional investment in determining the most evolved races, and making sure that the Caucasoid gained entrance into that elite by somewhat nefarious means, Coon's critics have been no better in arguing from an essentially emotional 'one species' article of faith.

Coon relied completely on comparative anlysis of purely skeletal material in supporting his thesis in *The Origin of Races*. He adhered rigidly to anatomy and took no cognizance at all of the functional importance of culture in Man's elevation to the *sapiens* estate.

Coon has been criticized *both* for relying on purely biological factors *and* for being ignorant of the process of evolution.

Montagu says: "(Coon's theory) is far-fetched because it is out of harmony with biological facts. Species and subspecies simply don't develop that way."

S.L. Washburn dismisses Coon with a terse: "I think that great antiquity of human races is supported neither by the record nor by evolutionary theory."

Again, Montagu:

> *The specific human features of the evolutionary pattern of man cannot be ignored. Man is a unique product of evolution in that he, far more than any other creature, has escaped from the bondage of the physical and biological into the integratively higher and more complex social environment.*

If we look at the entire 'origin of race' issue, while firmly bearing in mind that there do not seem to be any significant *racial* differences among men living in the contemporary world, we will meet several ironies, the least of which is that Coon, castigated as a reactionary by opponents, may have opened the door to a truly modern concept of 'Man'... and one we may have desperate need of soon.

The first problem to tackle is that Coon's opponents may be adamant about the 'one species' theory because of a deluded notion of the concreteness of the term 'species'. Under investigation, 'species' may be seen to be as ephemeral as Montagu and others argue 'race' to be.

A species is thought to be 'the unit of evolutionary change', a distinct breeding population. In spite of the fact that the higher animals, at least, are very definitely individual organisms and show a great capacity for individual variation, Montagu insists that a species *'evolves as a unit'*. This is patently absurd. A species is an assemblage of generally similar animals, or, more correctly, *groups of animals* with different genetic possibilities, but sufficiently alike to interbreed. It is precisely group and individual variations, permitted to recombine because of interfertility, that allow 'a species to evolve'.

Montagu's notion that a species evolves 'as a unit' implies the somewhat ridiculous vision of say, Canada geese, getting together one day and, somehow, hopping 'up' one more scale on the evolutionary ladder in concert. In reality, of course, there are different kinds of Canada geese, different races if you prefer, but they can all breed together if the opportunity or necessity arises. In practice, although the different kinds or races of Canada geese can interbreed, they do not generally do so to an excessive degree. Each group represents a gene pool exhibiting one or more characteristics which distinguish it from other kinds of Canada geese. *It is the varieties within species that are tested by selection.* If one set of racial characteristics prove especially 'survival-prone' the interfertility of the species makes it possible for that set of characteristics to be transmitted and enjoyed by the remainder of the species through interbreeding.

A species does not evolve 'as a unit'. Rather, a species in process of evolution may be regarded as something of an amoeba exploring its surroundings. The species, like the amoeba, puts out feelers... 'races', geographic 'races', subspecies, varieties, kinds, whatever you want to call them... and if one or more explorations prove particularly successful, the remainder of organisms, under the pressure of selection, gradually shift in the new direction. It seems reasonable that *this* is evolution: the testing of variety on the subspecific level, not on the specific level. It is difficult to imagine any other process which could account for sufficient genetic flexibility, and sufficient genetic stability, to result in 'new species' evolving (which is to say 'having a relationship') with an ancestral one.

Therefore, it does not seem unreasonable to suppose that the human species, like animal ones, might 'evolve' through the expression of its races.

In fact, this appears to have happened.

While saying that "Genetics shows us that typology must be completely removed from our thinking if we are to progress" in the process of criticizing Coon-type thinking, S.L. Washburn gives evidence to the contrary. He says:

> *If we are concerned with history let us consider, on the one hand, the ancestors of these Bushmen 15,000 years ago and the area available to them, to their way of life, and, on the other hand, the ancestors of the Europeans at the same time in the area available to them, with their way of life. We will find that the area available to the Bushman was at least twice that available to the Europeans. The Bushmen were living in a land of optimum game; the Europeans were living close to an ice sheet. There were perhaps from three to five times as many Bushmen ancestors as there were European ancestors only 15,000 years ago... If one were to name a major race, or*

a primary race, the Bushmen have a far better claim in terms of the archeological record than the Europeans.

Yet, as we observed earlier, the Bushmen were killed off by Bantu advancing southward and by whites advancing northward in Africa. The Bushman, as a type or kind of Man, is on the road to extinction. Because of changing conditions and inter-specific competition, the Bushman's type has yielded its primacy in Africa to the Congoids, or Blacks. There are some whites in Africa south of the Sahara and *they* are witnessing a reduction in their primacy in competition with the blacks. This 'loss of primacy' is a euphemism for conflict and extermination. We may judge such conflicts to be social and cultural ones, and they are, but they also have a direct bearing upon the composition of the gene pool in a geographic area. If Washburn's construct is correct then, during the last 15,000 years Africa has witnessed a reduction in Bushman typology and an increase in Congoid typology. In Africa, the human species has 'evolved' away from the Bushman stock, and toward the Congoid stock. The human species as a whole has therefore shifted toward the Congoid expression in terms of its genetic potential.

Similarly, Coon presented evidence which indicated a previous Australoid habitation of much of the Indochinese peninsula. Mongoloids inhabit the area now. The area has 'evolved' toward the Mongoloid expression and away from the Australoid expression and the entire human genetic potential has shifted accordingly.

Therefore, according to Washburn's own argument, a major human type 15,000 years ago, a primary race, that of the Bushmen, has been almost entirely replaced by another human type, the Congoid.

It is difficult to see, therefore, how Washburn can maintain that "genetics shows us that typology must be completely removed from our thinking if we are to progress." It seems that evolution is the testing of types on a subspecific level.

In the last 15,000 years, as Washburn would have it, two of Coon's five major races have been drastically reduced in number and in terms of influencing the human species genetically, while the other three major races have expanded from their original respective bailiwicks. Compared to the situation 15,000 years ago, the human species has altered its genetic composition through the agency of change on the subspecific level.

Rather than try to explain the relative extermination, or 'selecting out', of Bushman and Australoid genes on the basis of inferiority in comparison with other kinds of men, it is perhaps enough to suggest that their elimination was more or less inevitable given the geography of our planet.

A quick glance at any map or globe (see Figure 1) reveals the fact that the earth's land masses are arranged in triangles with bases to the north and apexes pointing southward. The two major groups under discussion, the Capoids (Bushmen) and Australoids, apparently had the misfortune to develop in the two south-pointing apexes of Old World land masses, the Capoids in the southern half of Africa and the Australoids in the Indochinese peninsula. The other three major groups of mankind happened to develop in the larger land areas representing the basal portions of our huge geographic triangles: The Caucasoids in Eurasia; the Mongoloids in the heartland of Asia proper behind the barrier of the Alai Tag, Tien Shan and Tannu-ula mountain chains; the Congoids in the vast expanse of Africa north of the equator (and their domain was extended by a then-fertile Sahara).

The Caucasoids, Congoids and Mongoloids thus had much more room in which to develop and build up their respective populations before expanding from their indigenous areas. By the time the Mongoloids expanded south to contact the Australoids, and the Congoids expanded south to establish contact with the Capoids, the black and yellow men doubtless outnumbered their respective adversaries by wide margins. It is likely that the Australoids and Capoids were swamped by numbers and no one has to postulate relative 'inferiority' to explain their defeat. The precarious position of Australoids and Capoids was aggravated by the fact that, being in the apex of geographic triangles, neither race had room for retreat. Most were exterminated.

Some few Bushmen were able to escape into the Kalahari desert of South Africa, while some few Australoids managed to cross the water barrier to the harsh haven of Australia.

The primitive culture of these peoples in comparsion with that of other men, remarked on by the Europeans at the time of contact with them, is readily explained by the fact of near-extermination and the harshness of the foster-environments imposed upon them. That these races were not always so primitive seems to to be indicated by extensive mining works recently discovered in Rhodesia, dated to about 47,000 B.C. and attributed to the indigenous Capoids; and also, perhaps, indicated by the very recent dwindling in stature among Capoids.

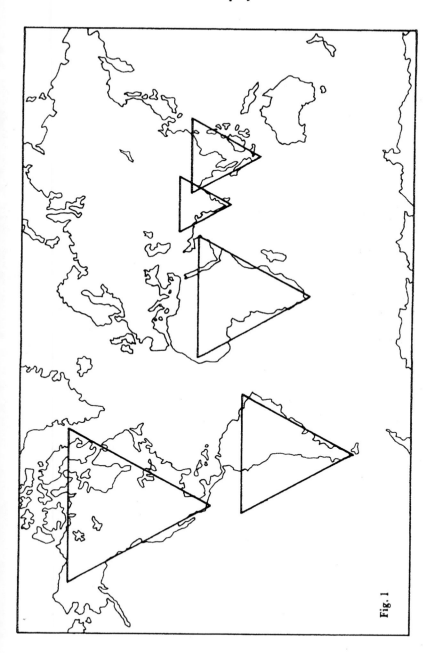

Fig. 1

Australian tribes hauntingly refer to their dim past as 'Dreamtime' and the richness of their memory argues for a fuller cultural life in that lost epoch than they enjoyed at the coming of Cook. Then, too, the Australoids must have reached Australia somehow and yet, when discovered by the Europeans, no Australian tribe possessed watercraft capable of crossing the Wallace Line. Their life, like that of the Bushmen, had dwindled.

Before leaving this subject, because I do not want to be accused of patronizing and apologizing for people whom anthroplogists have almost universally labelled 'primitive *races*', something should be said about the artistic life of Capoids and Australoids *before* they were exterminated or immediately after they reached their havens. They have been characterized as a generally artless people in comparison with other races of mankind, and they were when first discovered by whites. But it seems that they had not always been so. Bushman paintings have recently been discovered in Rhodesia and South Africa and they rival the cave art of France in both naturalistic and abstract expression. Surviving Bushmen know very well that their ancestors once painted, but, as some of them told Laurens Van Der Post, they now lack the spirit to do so.

Similarly, there are cliff drawings in Australia which must have been executed by the ancestors of present-day aborigines, yet the tribesmen themselves have forgotten. Places where such figures occur are merely 'holy' in some poignant fashion relating to the forever-lost 'Dreamtime'.

It may be worth mentioning here that with the Capoids human potential may have taken a somewhat unique direction, a direction which would be precious today and whose loss is bitter. Van Der Post was told by several different Kalahari tribesmen that the Bushmen "could speak the baboon's language" until about a century ago, but no longer, and that they used to be able to communicate with many other animals and plants. Van Der Post saw no reason to doubt this assertion, and neither do I, especially considering recent experiments with such diverse creatures as dolphins and philodendrons which indicate sentience of some sort. All peoples have preserved legends about a time of human-animal communication, but the Capoid traditions seem both more recent and more vital. The white man's way of doing things, as illustrated by our cumbersome experiments with dolphins' communication and our shock at discovering philodendron sentience, appears to be significantly inferior when compared to Capoid abilities.

But returning to the original point being made, whether one attributes Capoid-Australoid extermination mainly to geographical factors, as I do, or finds it convenient to chalk their extermination up to their inferiority as expressions of Mankind, these two races offer an example of how the human species has altered its genetic potential by *subspecific* activity.

Like Canada geese, the human species evolves by activity of its component parts. The species doesn't evolve "as a unit", as Ashley Montagu would have it, but through the medium of its 'races'.

If that is so, the concreteness of the term may be questioned to some degree and we are left with the idea that a species is an assemblage of individuals, or groups of individuals, sharing genetic characters and varying, but sufficiently alike to be interfertile.

Under this construct of species-dynamics, C.S. Coon's theory loses much of its titillating controversy for supporters and opponents alike. Why shouldn't a species, *Homo erectus,* have consisted of five or more subspecies or 'races' representing slightly differing genetic expressions and being mutually interfertile? And what is so odd about the possibility that these advanced primates, all of whom were on the verge of 'human' emergence, would have taken the same general path toward Man? Coon says that these 'races' of the *erectus* species independently crossed the *sapiens* threshold and merged into the 'species' called *Homo sapiens.*

Montagu holds that five independent crossings into the *sapiens* domain is "expecting too much from convergence", but this comment betrays a curiously biological outlook for a man who has always stressed the *cultural* aspect of human evolution.

Montagu, being an anthropologist, has perhaps fallen into the error of accepting too trustingly pedantic biological definitions of 'species'.

The definition of species, applied to man, has always been something of an exercise in circular thinking. Basically, the human passion for cataloguing required some sort of separation between modern, *cultural* man and more primitive man. We have dubbed primitive man 'Homo erectus' because, by virtue of erect posture and consequent cranial development, the creature was irrevocably on the road toward Man and was sufficiently morphologically distinct from other hominids to warrant a separate specific status.

But it is at least arguable that the purely *morphological*, physical differences between ourselves and *Homo erectus* are not sufficient to warrant a conference of separate specific status. We unconsciously recognized this truth when we decided to label the undoubted difference in some fashion. We called ourselves *sapiens*. Sapient man is reasoning man, man capable of culture. But reason is an abstract, not a morphological character. Reason cannot be understood by dissection. Moreover, even most of the ways in which we do differ from *Homo erectus* are due to the cultural selection we impose upon ourselves, and not to natural selection that environment imposes on us.

Modern man is not a biologically and morphologically distinct species from *Homo erectus*. In fact, as I have stated previously, Man, insofar as he is a cultural creature, is not *essentially* a biological creature at all. The *sapiens* state is a threshold, not a species in the purely biological sense, because it is the doorway through which we have passed into the non-biological environments of time and culture.

Therefore, in a sense that Coon might not appreciate, we find that his use of the term *'sapiens threshold'* is not only descriptively satisfying, but also reflects reality. At the same time, and for reasons and a philosophical posture that Montagu would probably appreciate, we find his adherence to the idea that *Homo sapiens* is a species erroneous.

Viewed in this light, the controversy over Coon's *The Origin of Races* dissipates and the impassioned arguments 'for' and 'against' the theory seem to be based on uncritical assumptions, unexamined definitions, blinded perspective and a good deal of sheer bad will.

Modern man is a creature resulting from the fact that five (or four, or three, or 'between six and nine') geographic races of *Homo erectus* evolved through a threshold which transcends biology... including most considerations of both 'race' and 'species'.

The substitution of a 'threshold' for a 'species' in defining sapience is of immense philosophical importance, and perhaps of equal practical importance in the not-too-distant future.

If we define our sapient and 'humane' characters in terms of biological speciation *we are by definition incapable of extending recognition of culture and intelligence to creatures who are not, biologically, earth-type hominids.* In other words, if we attribute our intelligence and capacity for culture solely to biological speciation, we cannot so easily discern intelligence and culture in other creatures in this world or others.

Our biological blinders seem already to be operative in our

dealings with the toothed whales. Because we have attributed our intelligence to hominid speciation, we have difficulty recognizing it in 'non-human species'.

Coon's concept of a *sapiens* threshold is a valuable tool for structuring a more cosmopolitan (literally) and less parochial world view. The threshold concept makes it easier for us to accept the possibility that intelligence and culture may exist in creatures other than hominids. We may more easily confer the rights, privileges and dignity of 'Man' on creatures who may not be even remotely hominid. And it is not altogether unlikely that we will face the necessity of doing so within the next decade. 'Man', insofar as he inhabits the environment of time and thought, and survives within that environment by non-genetic, cultural means, is not a biological creature... and it follows that any creature which partially inhabits time and thought must be considered a 'Man' by us. The term 'Man' is not so much biological as it is cultural.

It seems reasonable enough to sum up this way: that however many varieties of men there are, and whatever the origin of these varieties, 'racial' characteristics do not seem functionally significant in terms of evolution. Original racial traits which might have been significant, if any, have been dissipated by migration and interbreeding. All men apparently boast the conceptual capacity to participate in the cultural habitation of time and thought. We attribute this capacity to an ill-defined entity called 'intelligence'. And, to the degree to which we have defined it, and have devised tests to measure it, all men possess an equal amount of it on a 'racial' basis.

Yet.

It is my contention that one kind of Man does indeed possess an attribute not shared to the same degree by other kinds of Man. And it is my contention that this attribute is significant in terms of evolution. My authority for this assertion is not an 'expert', nor a mass of laboratory data.

My authority is history. It is the ultimate laboratory in the testing of human behavioural psychology.

We witness a contemporary world largely dominated by the values and works of one kind of Man. This is so obvious that it does not need to be commented upon further except to say that even those who are rebelling against 'Western' dominance use Western values and weapons against us. As but one example — one topical in many parts of the world just now — even those non-Western peoples who are busy trying to throw off the yoke of European economic, cultural and military imperialism do so by invoking merely another aspect of Western culture — Karl Marx.

Western culture so thoroughly permeates the world that even opposition to it relies on Western philosophies.

Western culture, white man's culture, is almost totally and exclusively the product of the mind and motivation of one 'race' of Mankind — the Caucasoids.

Because we constructed this edifice in our own psychobiological image, we naturally considered it both 'good' and 'superior', and once coming into significant contact with men of other races we searched about for some mechanism to explain our 'goodness' and 'superiority'. Quite naturally, we assumed that we must have superior amounts of some good characteristic. We banked on a superior intelligence, but the concept is bankrupt.

It has only been since the end of World War II that Western man has come to doubt, seriously and sincerely, his values and his works, and only because both have evolved to the point where they threaten his own survival. We are suffering from resource shortages, pollution, nuclear, racist and sexist traumas and nightmares. They are spectres of our own Caucasoid psychobiology. That cannot be denied, even to ourselves, because just before these aspects of the contemporary world passed some threshold of "critical mass" and became threats, we proudly took credit for the attitudes and technology which spawned them.

Precisely because we are threatened by our own works and values, and are slowly beginning to remove our rose-coloured spectacles in the interest of survival and clear vision, we may now be ready to accept the fact that we Caucasoids are neither 'good' nor 'superior'. In fact, perhaps we have reached the point where we might be able to reach agreement among ourselves that we may possess superior amounts of a 'bad' characteristic compared to *all* other men.

This book is racist because I believe that history shows that men can be divided into two divisions on the basis of one significant characteristic.

There are Caucasoids... and everybody else.

The significant characteristic shared unequally by these two groups is *aggression*.

Our works and our values reflect aggression. Our technology is aggression directed against the natural world. Our unexcelled military technology is aggression directed against our fellow human beings. Much of our art and our culture reflects sexual aggression.

We were always right. We *are* different, just as we always suspected. Only now, the results of this difference don't seem so good, intelligent, or superior. Our conceit is bankrupt, or at least seriously overdrawn, and maybe we're ready to do some objective 'racial' accounting.

The significant difference between ourselves and other men, our 'racially' higher level of aggression, must be explained if we are to deal with it.

We differ from other men in one other respect: of all major groups, only Caucasoids crossed the *sapiens* threshold in a glacial environment.

It is my contention that the rigours of this *rite de passage* traumatized us.

5

The Neanderthal-Caucasoids

I have postulated a significant and possibly crucial distinction between Caucasoids and all other kinds of men. I have contended that this difference has to do with the characteristic or capacity we call 'aggression',[4] and I have cited the pattern of history, culminating in our endangered contemporary world, as my authority.

I find it difficult to believe that any objective observer, or even a subjective one, viewing the world's history, can deny that there *is* this difference between Caucasoids and other kinds of men.

Having proposed it, I am obligated to try and explain it. But perhaps it would not be stretching the limits of 'racial' difference to suggest gently that this 'obligation of explanation' is itself a Caucasoid notion. Other men might more readily and simply accept the fact of a difference, and not feel a pressing need to explain it, but consider it most important to simply ameliorate any inconvenient behaviour generated by it.

But I'm at least mostly Caucasoid myself and prey to the intellectual dissatisfaction seemingly always inspired in 'our' race by an unattacked, unknown, exploitable conception... and perhaps these words drive home a certain message.

Since most of my readers (if any) can be expected to share the almost physical ache of an unexplained, 'undefended' assertion no matter how patently obvious, I will try to offer some defensible construct to account for our abnormally high level of aggression.

And in proffering this explanation I would like to try to generate as much good will as possible, in advance, by freely admitting that it is going to be tenuous, barely defensible, and maybe not much more satisfying than no explanation at all. But, after saying this, I will also maintain that it will be much more defensible than theories about our 'moral superiority' and-or 'higher intelligence' resulting from 'earlier evolution into the sapient state.'

The explanation will be somewhat thin simply because our knowledge about prehistoric man is threadbare. Worse, especially in the West, the fabric of human evolution is adorned with confusing and sometimes conflicting patterns. The mind is easily led astray and I can only hope that the thread I've followed has any real continuity. Anyone who thinks I've picked on the wrong thread, or lost it somewhere in the warp and woof of skeletal and cultural material, is free to choose another which, perhaps, holds more promise of unraveling the secret of obvious Caucasoid behavioural differences.

I will begin by dismissing Coon's evidence for a very early Caucasoid emergence into the sapient estate. Coon does not commit himself about the species of the Heidelberg jaw (450,000 B.P.), but says only:

> As a single bone, the Mauer mandible [i.e., Heidelberg jaw] belongs to the expected grade, considering its antiquity, but because there is no Mauer cranium we do not know to which species, Homo erectus or Homo sapiens, Heidelberg man belonged... Mauer therefore stands on a base line of its own.

Elsewhere, Coon does not hesitate to damn a cranium-less jaw to the category of *Homo erectus* and there are few anthropologists who would hesitate very long about putting Heidelberg in that category.

For reasons outlined earlier, I consider the Steinheim cranium and the Swanscombe fragments much too dubious to be of any assistance whatsoever in ascertaining when the *sapiens* threshold was crossed in Europe. These bones date from the Great (Second) Mindel-Riss Interglacial about 325,000 years ago. To some degree, the Steinheim-Swanscombe material is apparently related to the Fontéchevade crania which are some 100,000 years younger.

H.V. Vallois says of the Fontéchevade skull material:

> The essential fact is the absolute absence of a supraorbital

torus: the glabella and the brow ridges are less developed than in the Upper Paleolithic Europeans, or even in the majority of Europeans living today.

According to Coon, "Fontéchevade 2 (the more nearly complete skull) resembles Swanscombe closely." But we must recall that 'Swanscombe man' (actually the bones are believed to have belonged to a woman) consists of three separate fragments discovered at three separate times *in river gravel*. Swanscombe was not recovered from a stratified site, there is no proof that the fragments belong together since they were not found at the same time, and even if they belong together the disjointed skull may have been intruded into faunal association which dates it.

It would seem that a hypothetical evolutionary line based on Fontéchevade-Swanscombe is a very tenuous support for immensely ancient sapience in Europe.

Perhaps the most that can safely be said is that the Fontéchevade people seem to have crossed the sapient threshold about 225,000 years ago as far as morphology is concerned, bearing in mind the fact that physical characteristics are only the roughest indication of the possession of cultural sentience. The age of Fontéchevade is not in too much disagreement with W.W. Howells' opinion that *Homo sapiens* appeared in Europe "almost certainly... some 150,000 years ago." The age of Fontéchevade and its very ephemeral relationship with Swanscombe may be in at least inferential accord with LeGros Clark's grudging acceptance that Swanscombe *might* be considered as a *very primitive* expression of *Homo sapiens*. If *sapiens* 'may have' appeared at Swanscombe, it should have 'almost certainly' appeared in Fontéchevade.

A note of caution is sounded by S.L. Washburn's opinion that "the species *Homo sapiens* appeared perhaps as recently as 50,000 years ago." Washburn's doubt seems to stem from an uncertainty about the place of the Neanderthals in the scheme of things. This is a problem to which we will turn presently, but not quite yet.

While feeling compelled to record other experts' disagreement with his theory of a 300,000 or 400,000 year old antiquity of sapience in Europe, Coon does so with a trace of petulence:

As no one in the Anglo-American world knows more about Steinheim and Swanscombe than these four experts [i.e., LeGros Clark, W.W. Howells, Clark Howell and S.L. Washburn], who are well aware of the date of these skulls, the disagreement is rather obviously a matter of how one defines Homo sapiens.

And that is the crux of the problem.

In terms of morphology, Coon seems determined to tie the *sapiens* estate intimately to the modern European head form, and in spite of the fact that there are human beings alive in the world today who don't share that skull form. A morphological emphasis of Coon's sort virtually guarantees that some men will have difficulty joining the *sapiens* club. And, it simply cannot be doubted that Coon seems unwilling to grant *sapiens* status to some living people. In his chart 'Grades and Lines of Fossil Hominids' on page 335 of *The Origin of Races*, Coon brings both the Congoids and the Capoids right up to the present as 'HE' (i.e., *Homo erectus*).

We are getting a bit ahead of ourselves, and being drawn a bit prematurely into the inevitable confusion, but it is necessary to point to a paradox in Coon's values. While hesitating to grant sapience to skulls stubborn about becoming 'modern European', Coon willingly confers sapience on Neanderthals whose head shape is wildly divergent from the modern European form.

As it happens, I not only agree with Coon and most other anthropologists that the Neanderthals and their 'brutal' skulls were fully sapient, but also maintain that the Neanderthals were the first people, of whatever head shape, to show indisputably and *culturally* that the *sapiens* threshold had been crossed.

The words of Sonia Cole are very pertinent here: "The line dividing man and apes is so arbitrary that considerations other than anatomical features have to be taken into account... We depend upon his mental attributes more than the shape of his bones."

And the line becomes exceedingly arbitrary when it comes to dividing man and man, whether living or extinct.

There can be no doubt that cranial morphology and capacity are guides to increased cultural capacity, but the guide is treacherous. People with more nearly modern skull shape and capacity existed in Europe long before the Neanderthals. Yet, it was the Neanderthals with their brutal crania and larger-than-modern brains who first exhibited the symptoms of culture in a truly and definitively human sense.

So, to conclude this part of the argument being prepared, perhaps it is enough to say that sapience in the treacherous and more or less meaningless morphological sense appeared "about the time of Fontéchevade" around 225,000 years ago... but, as far as the cultural record is concerned, 100,000 more years elapsed before a group of men would prove their functional humanity by suffering from the cronos complex. And they would be the 'wrong' men.

Before turning to the mysteries and ironies posed by the Neanderthals, one more step in the physical development of modern *sapiens* characteristics should be mentioned. Between 1895 and 1906 some 649 pieces of bone fragments and teeth were recovered from a sandstone rock shelter near the town of Krapina in Yugoslavia. Most of these pieces have remained unstudied, but the collection resolved itself into five skulls that show undoubted development of modern, *sapiens* morphology which emerged at Fontéchevade. The Krapina collection dates from the end of the last Riss-Würm interglacial, roughly 125,000 years ago. Flint implements were found in association with the skeletal material and B. Skerlj states that the cultural styles represented were Acheulean and pre-Aurignacian... something of a non-sequitur. The 'Acheulian' culture was a refined hand-axe culture which replaced the older 'Abbevillian' style about the beginning of the Mindel-Riss Interglacial. The Acheulian culture thus began about 350,000 years ago. On the other hand, the Aurignacian culture was a much later development and only began *after* the onset of Würm and after the date given to the Krapina people.

The conclusion seems to be twofold: first, the site had been used and disturbed by later cultures; and second, for all their physically developed traits, which Coon compares to fully modern Central Europeans in every essential respect, the Krapina people had a very primitive culture. The morphologically *sapiens* Europeans had stood still culturally for a quarter of a million years. Once again, morphology had revealed itself to be an untrustworthy reflection of human cultural capacity. It is about to be discredited again.

The Neanderthals

By the time Joachim Neander died in 1680, at the age of only thirty, he already had some seventy-seven published hymns to his credit. The family's name had originally been Neumann, but, around 1580, one of Joachim's ancestors had changed the name, translating the German 'Neumann' into the Greek 'Neander'. This sort of name-changing was common practice among North European bourgeoisie of that period because of a faddish appreciation of all things classical that followed from the popular publication of Greek and Roman writings rediscovered during the Renaissance. 5

Joachim Neander's reputation as a minor literary figure was honoured in the name of a small river valley near Düsseldorf, the Neanderthal.

In this small valley, in 1856, a human skullcap was discovered. A similar cranium had been found in Forbes's quarry on the Rock of Gibraltar in 1848, but the importance of this skull wasn't recognized until 1864. Following the publication of Darwin's *The Origin of Species* in 1859 "these two pieces, figuratively swept under the table, suddenly became significant for a serious study of human evolution by means of the fossil record". Dr. H. Schaaffhausen examined the skull found in the Neander valley and pronounced it to be a relic of one of the barbarous tribes that inhabited Europe before the Celts and Germans, or perhaps a relic of one of those wild races of north-western Europe described by Tacitus.

Schaaffhausen seems to be responsible for coining the term 'Neanderthal man', with the implied meaning of a 'type' or 'race' of Man... to the sorrow and confusion of more than a century of anthropology. But it is worth noting that the most famous pathologist of the time, the great Rudolf Virchow, disagreed with Schaaffhausen. Virchow doubted that 'Neanderthal man' was the representative of a separate type or race of human being. For Virchow, the brutal skull was evidence of an individual human pathology. The skull was the remains of a human freak, the unfortunate victim of acromegaly.

During the early 1860's someone noticed that the Gibraltar skull was very similar to the Neanderthal cranium. The similarity of the two skulls, their wide geographical separation, and the 'monkey wind' generated by Darwin's theory of evolution... all combined to force the consensus that these skulls were representative of a type of Man that had existed before modern man and was now extinct. The theory of evolution more or less required a 'missing link', some very primitive type of creature somewhere between 'ape' and 'Man', and the Neanderthal skull seemingly supplied him very quickly following *The Origin of Species.*

Neanderthal's massive brown ridges, his low, broad cranial vault and his prognathous jaw distinguished him from modern man, were more apelike, and suited the theory of evolution. For a long time, almost thirty years, Neanderthal was the most primitive fossil man known, and in the absence of competing 'missing links' his brutality was emphasized. As Dr. Harry L. Shapiro says:

Thus, the primitiveness of Neanderthal man was overstressed

*because for a long time he was our only ancestral form.
Although his differences from modern man were visible and
real enough, they were exaggerated in a way that might not
have been the case if we had found the earliest types of man
first and worked our way up to the Neanderthal type.*

But it was not until 1891-92 that the much more primitive
Pithecanthropus erectus was found in Java by Dr. Eugène Dubois,
and not until 1911 that the Piltdown skull, hoax aside, was found by
Charles Dawson in Sussex. The major discoveries which have given
anthropologists some perspective on human evolution did not come
until the decade 1925-1935, and included: *Australopithecus*
(1924), *Sinanthropus* (1926), Swanscombe man in 1935 and
Steinheim man shortly afterwards. Von Koenigswald's discovery of
additional *Pithecanthropine* material, including an even more
primitive *Meganthropus*, did not come until the later 30's.

Description and analysis of these finds lagged far behind their
initial discovery, of course, and study was impeded by the war. The
upshot was that a satisfactory consensus on the general outlines of
human evolution was not achieved until the 1950's and 1960's by
scientists themselves and this working model has still not percolated
down to the layman.

Neanderthal's brutal characteristics, and his isolation as a fossil
human type for so many years, allowed an erroneous impression of
human evolution in general, and Neanderthal's place in it
specifically, to become thoroughly entrenched in the popular mind.
But, while saying this, it must be admitted that the contemporary
consensus achieved by the anthropologists about the general outline
of human evolution still leaves Neanderthals somewhat up in the
air. This is particularly unfortunate for us since the Neanderthals
very recently occupied the part of the world which is the cradle of
the Caucasoid race, and the most extreme Neanderthals occupied
the part of Europe which has produced the most extreme
manifestations of Caucasoid aggression (see Figure 2).

Since this is true, and since it did not happen so very long ago in
terms of human evolution, it is very tempting to assume that
Neanderthal traits must have had something to do with Caucasoid
aggression in general and its apparent concentration in Western
Europe. And this is the direction we will pursue... while fully
recognizing that professorial dictum which warns that "correlation
isn't necessarily causation."

It is only fair to point out that there is no scientific consensus

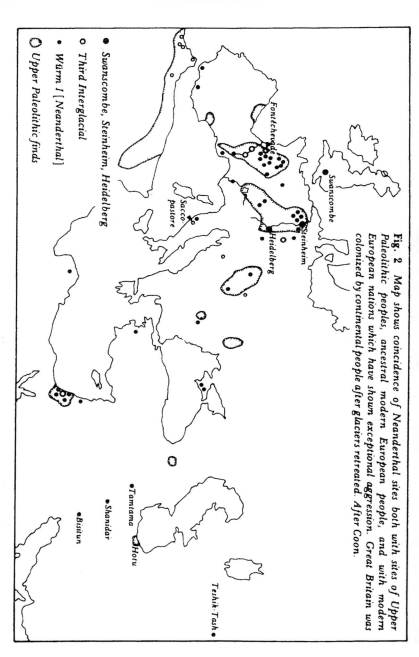

Fig. 2 *Map shows coincidence of Neanderthal sites both with sites of Upper Paleolithic peoples, ancestral modern European people, and with modern European nations which have shown exceptional aggression. Great Britain was colonized by continental people after glaciers retreated. After Coon.*

- ● Swanscombe, Steinheim, Heidelberg
- ○ Third Interglacial
- ● Würm I [Neanderthal]
- ◑ Upper Paleolithic finds

about the nature and significance of the Neanderthals. The Neanderthals have become evolutionary orphans where once they were our undisputed, if unpleasantly primitive, ancestors. The Neanderthal morphological traits appear to be primitive, but there is disagreement among scientists as to whether the Neanderthal were primitive relics of *Homo erectus*, or merely *looked* primitive.

Perhaps it is fair to say that most anthropologists now believe that the apparently primitive morphology of the Neanderthal was the result of special adaptation, not vestiges of *Homo erectus*. This view has been increasingly adopted because of a curious circumstance : the older Neanderthals were less brutal than the later ones. The Neanderthals appear to be a unique example of regression or 'evolution in reverse'. They started out being closer to modern man in appearance and ended up being far removed from him. The Neanderthals of 100,000 years ago were apparently less brutal and more modern than the Neanderthals of 40,000-50,000 years ago.

In the light of our present knowledge, which is admittedly scanty, only one environmental factor can be correlated with the backward evolution of the Neanderthals. The last glacial period, Würm in the European sequence, began 100,000 years ago, deepened into intense cold, and moderated about 40,000 years ago before returning once more to savagely cold conditions which ended only with the last retreat of the glaciers about 8,000-10,000 B.C. The period of moderate climate about 40,000 years ago is called the Göttweig Interstadial.

The Neanderthals apparently 'died out' with the warmer weather of the Göttweig Interstadial, and more modern kinds of men migrated into Europe. The last Würmian cold snap, from about 30,000 to 8,000 years ago, was endured by essentially modern men who were the ancestors of Europeans of today.

So, in Europe, there is a confusing sequence. Fairly modern-tending types existed in Europe from about 250,000 years ago until 100,000 years ago, but there is no evidence that these *sapiens* achieved any high degree of culture. With the onset of the Würm glaciers, these *sapiens*-tending Europeans, who at least at Krapina closely resembled modern Europeans, were replaced for 60,000 years by a more primitive morphological type, the Neanderthal. The Neanderthals, in spite of their brutal skulls, have left the first indications of indisputable human culture. During the Göttweig Interstadial of 40,000 years ago, the Neanderthals were replaced by peoples who seem to have *returned* to Europe since they show affinities with both modern man and with the pre-Neanderthal populations of Krapina and Fontéchevade.

In Europe, then, there was a 60,000 year 'regression' of Man's physical evolution, but this regression mysteriously coincides with a significant advance in cultural development. In the light of our present knowledge this cannot be satisfactorily explained. It must simply be accepted for the moment.

Scientists are divided in their opinions about the origins of the Neanderthals. There is evidence that the Neanderthals moved into Eurasia from elsewhere as the advancing Würmian glaciers drove more modern men out, but there is also some evidence that at least some Neanderthal traits developed in Europe itself, particularly in Italy. Like everything else about the Neanderthals, their origin is in dispute.

Saccopastore

In 1929, Sergio Sergi found the skull of a thirty-year-old woman in the gravel pit of Saccopastore just outside the walls of Rome. Seven years later, Baron A.C. Blanc and the famous Abbé Breuil found a second skull, a male's, in the same location.

These skulls are the first to indicate the appearance of Neanderthal morphological characteristics in Europe, even though they are not classically Neanderthal.

A comparison of the Saccopastore skulls with those from Krapina reveals the one trait which immediately distinguishes Neanderthal cranial form from that of modern man. In the Krapina crania and in modern ones the brain case approximates the shape of a sphere or ball atop the spinal column, whereas the Saccopastore brain cases (and later fully Neanderthal ones) are more like a cylinder balanced horizontally on the spinal column. Coon describes the Saccopastore brain cases as "barrels laying on their sides". The cranial capacities of the Saccopastore skulls are not impressive compared to roughly contemporaneous "round-headed" skulls. Saccopastore 1, the better preserved female cranium found in 1929, has a calculated volume of about 1,200 cc., while the more fragmentary male skull in 1936 is perhaps 100 cc larger. By comparison, Fontéchevade and Krapina crania have a capacity of about 1,450 cc.

In both size and shape, the Saccopastore skulls recall Eastern *H. erectus* crania, and there is one other point of similarity. Saccopastore 1 has no less than 16 Wormian bones, a world record. Wormian bones are extra bones, separated by sutures, in the area of

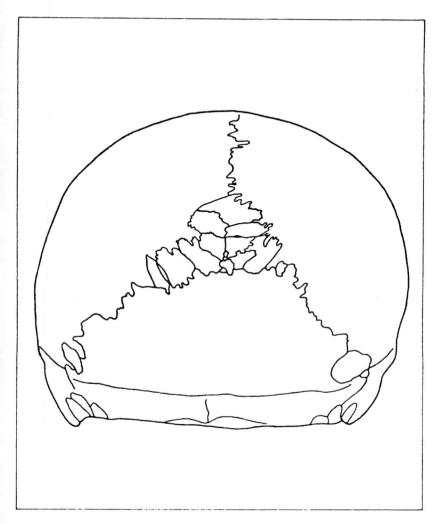

Fig. 3 *Saccopastore Wormian Bones*

Rear view of Saccopastore skull shows round section and numerous Wormian bones at the junction of the parietals and the occipital bones. These extra bones are found in modern Mongoloid skulls, Ancient Andean ones, and in the Sinanthropus series. They are also characteristic of Neanderthal crania, of which Saccopastore may be a racial ancestor.

Drawn after Coon. Reprinted with permission of Alfred A. Knopf, Inc.

lambda (see Figure 3). Sometimes called 'Inca bones', these extra
cranial bones are characteristic of Mongoloid crania and are rare or
always absent in other races. Wormian bones were found in the
Sinanthropus skulls and are frequent in Neanderthal crania.

It would seem, then, that the Saccopastore skulls are evidence for
a *Sinanthropus*-Mongoloid presence in Europe, a genetic presence
on some level lower than modern man and not much above the
grade of *homo erectus* in brain size.

The Saccopastore skulls are generally agreed to be 'proto-
Neanderthal' and to reflect Eastern *Homo erectus* characteristics. It
is *possible* that interbreeding between round-headed Krapina-type
people with cranial capacities in the order of 1,400 cc, and
Sinanthropus-type evolved *erectus* people with cranial capacities in
the order of 1,100-1,200 cc *might* result in something like the
Saccopastore crania. The *erectus* skull form was pentagonal in
section and long, whereas the Krapina skull form was round. A
mixture of the two might very well result in the 'barrel on its side',
round in section and long, that we see in Saccopastore. The Saccopastore cranial capacity of 1,200-1,300 cc is mid-way between the
Krapina and Eastern *Homo erectus* values. The Wormian bones of
Saccopastore 1 and the later Neanderthals can be accounted for by
proposing a 'Sinanthropoid' admixture.

One theory concerning the origin of the Neanderthals is therefore
that they resulted from *Sinanthropus* genetic input into the
European stock represented by the Swanscombe-Steinheim-
Fontéchevade-Krapina sequence.

Carleton Coon appears to favour this hypothesis, more or less. He
believes it possible that some of the European stock, which he
already labels 'Caucasoid', expanded into the Mongoloid-
Sinanthropus domain, picked up some Eastern genes useful for cold
adaptation which were passed on back to the West, and donated
some Western genes which helped the *Sinanthropus*-Mongoloid
stock pass over the *sapiens* threshold. In fact, it does appear that
there was some European migration toward the East. According to
Bushnell and McBurney, flint artifacts found at Ting-tsun are
typologically similar to Mousterian flints.

Mousterian is a culture characteristic of the Western Eurasiatic
realm in general and of the Neanderthals in particular. Therefore,
while it seems that there is some support for the idea that the
Neanderthals originated as a mixture of Coon's 'Caucasoid-
European' stock with Far Eastern *Sinanthropus*-Mongoloid stock,
there are a few problems. First, the notion that *Sinanthropus* was

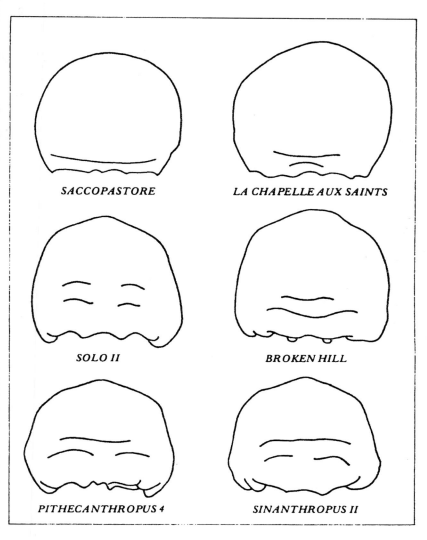

SACCOPASTORE

LA CHAPELLE AUX SAINTS

SOLO II

BROKEN HILL

PITHECANTHROPUS 4

SINANTHROPUS II

Fig. 4 *Comparison of Neanderthal skulls* [*Saccopastore and La Chapelle*] *with skulls of Eastern and African* Homo Erectus. *Neanderthal skulls are round in cross-section, whereas* erectus *skulls are markedly pentagonal. Coon believes that Neanderthals are not* Homo erectus *because of this difference in skull shape, but Neanderthals might have resulted from a mixture of* Homo erectus *and round-headed Third Interglacial people like those of Krapina.*

Drawn after Carleton Coon. Reprinted with permission of Alfred A. Knopf, Inc.

particularly cold-adapted just isn't supported by any fact. Second, Bushnell and McBurney may be in error in holding that the Chinese flints at Ting-tsun are typologically Mousterian. Third, by about 100,000 B.P. it is possible that the *Sinanthropus* line had already crossed the *sapiens* threshold and needed no 'help' from hypothetically *sapiens* 'European-Caucasoids'.

However, the Coon hypothesis *is* an explanation for Neanderthal origins, however tenuous, and in fairness it must be said that Coon exhibits no great investment in it, but merely offers it as a suggestion.

There is another theory of Neanderthal origins which rests upon cultural and skeletal discoveries of Baron A.C. Blanc, who traced the Mousterian tool-making culture back to the Riss glacial period in Italy, or, in other words, back to about 200,000 years B.P. Mousterian is associated with, and very nearly inseparable from, the Neanderthal genotype. Thus, if Blanc's evidence is to be accepted, the Mousterian beginnings in Italy are of great antiquity and complement the discovery of the proto-Neanderthal skulls in the Saccopastore quarry outside of Rome. Neanderthal man and his cultural assemblage may therefore be indigenous to Europe and of an antiquity comparable to the supposed *sapiens* morphological emergence. On the basis of Blanc's evidence, it is at least possible that the Neanderthals' resemblance to Eastern man with respect to skull form, Wormian bones and teeth is purely superficial and shows no evolutionary relationship. Blanc's research indicates that there may have been two separate strains of Man in Europe... 'sapiens' and 'Neanderthal'... as early as 200,000 years ago.

So, in conclusion, we may summarize by saying that the Neanderthals originated in one of the following ways:

1. By mixture of "European-Caucasoid" stock with Eastern Sinanthropus-Mongoloid stock.

2. By indigenous evolution in Europe itself from "sapiens" stock, or from some more ancient stock, due to selction for cold-survival qualites. [6]

Whatever their origin, it is enough to know that the 'Neanderthals' represent a fairly distinct type of human, fairly obviously cold-adapted since they flourished during a glacial epoch. They dominated Europe from 100,000 to about 40,000 years ago and occupied what later became the 'Caucasoid' racial domain. Further, we may add that the most extreme Neanderthals inhabited the part of Europe which later manifested extreme Caucasoid aggression, reflected in incessant warfare and eventual cultural and geographic expansion at the expense of other races.

Neanderthal characteristics

However elusive Neanderthal origins may be, both the physical characteristics and the geographical distribution of the genotype are well-known. As of 1962 Carleton Coon could say:

> [*there are*] *some eighty-two true Neanderthals, found in forty-two sites... Their geographical distribution follows a distinct pattern. For the most part they favoured the portions of western and southern Europe now lying south of the present-day January frost line...*

And elsewhere:

> *Their time span is Early Würm or Würm I, from about 75,000 years ago to the beginning of the Gottweig Interstadial, about 40,000 years ago. Its* lebensraum *was Europe, western Asia, and central Asia as far as the Altaï Mountains and south to the Hindu Kush. Its culture was Mousterian, itself a complex of earlier tool-making techniques.*

By 1971, the amount of Neanderthal material had increased dramatically. Ralph Solecki writes:

> *We are not exactly sure at this writing how many Neanderthal skeletons or individuals have been found in the world, nor how many archeological sites are involved. However, using some recent counts, and some scattered references, there are at least 44 sites with 86 Neanderthals in Europe; 12 sites and 45 individuals in the Near East, and 12 sites and 24 individuals elsewhere...*

For the first time in our dealings with fossil men, there is abundant skeletal material (though some bones are not well represented) and even some significant cultural remains. Our physical and cultural pen portrait of the Neanderthals as a group cannot be far off... at least, nowhere near as problematical as our vision of other fossil hominid populations.

There is one problem in assessing this material, however, and it stems directly from a pedantic and outmoded zoological concept of 'species', the concept we have discussed before. The classic taxonomic practice was to define a 'species' by a so-called 'type specimen' to which all other individuals of the same species, or different ones, were compared. Very often, and especially in the case of relatively rare animals, this all-important 'type specimen' might be the *only* specimen, or it might be the most complete specimen out of a very small collection. In many cases, this type specimen was not a typical example of the 'species', but a representative of one of several subspecies or races. Consequently, when other specimens of a similar kind were found they were often not identical to the type specimen and a new species had to be invented to accommodate them.

Sometimes, under the rules of classical taxonomy, things could get a little out of hand. New species were created because of whisker counts that differed from the whisker count of the type specimen or slightly different colouration, with no regard for individual variation. As an example, until recently (1953) zoologists considered that there were nine separate species of lion in Africa distinguished by mane length and colouration. Yet, representatives of all nine species of lion can be found in the Kruger preserve, sharing the same habitat, behaviour and apparently all happily interfertile. Most authorities now prefer to include all the lions in Africa under one species, and some authorities grant that the Indian lion, restricted to the Gar forest, is different enough to warrant separate specific status.

Ratels in Africa seem to be in a similar muddle with the different species apparently reflecting only sexual and age differences in colouration, and the bears of both Tibet and North America share the ratels' taxonomic problems.

It is becoming increasingly clear that very few species can be truly represented by a 'type specimen'. Rather, a species is usually the *averaging* of individual and group variations to arrive at a statistical 'type specimen' which may not exist, and usually doesn't in reality. Just as it would be difficult to capture, skin and mount an 'average man', it is equally difficult to get hold of an 'average ratel', 'average lion' or 'average brown bear'.

Unfortunately, however, classical taxonomy was in full swing when 'Neanderthal man' was studied. A type specimen was chosen, the most complete skeleton available. This skeleton is known as La Chapelle aux Saints (see Figure 5) and is a French Neanderthal. 'La Chapelle' is the Neanderthal usually studied and the template

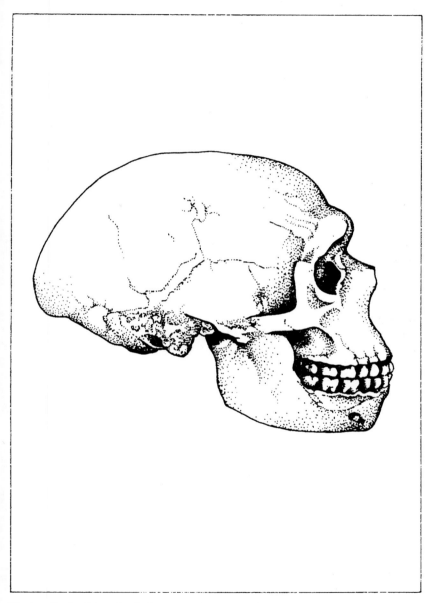

Fig. 5 *Skull of Neanderthal type specimen, La Chapelle aux Saints.*

generally in mind when sweeping generalities about 'Neanderthals' are made. Yet, 'La Chapelle' is not a 'typical' Neanderthal: he is a very extreme individual variation on the basic Neanderthal scheme of things. La Chapelle boasts the most beetling brows and the most chinless jaw of any Neanderthal specimen. The use of La Chapelle as the Neanderthal 'type' by several generations of writers has rather naturally tended to emphasize the real physical differences which do exist between the Neanderthals and ourselves. The choice of La Chapelle as the type specimen was somewhat unfortunate because of his rather extreme individual characteristics but even more unfortunate because La Chapelle's departures from the basic Neanderthal plan are aggravated by senile degeneration and arthritis, and because, according to Coon, his skeleton was faultily mounted in the first place.

Therefore, unlike many writers, we will not rely on the Neanderthal type specimen in our discussion of the genotype's characteristics, but mentally create an 'average Neanderthal', as it were, from an amalgam of many slightly varying individuals. When this is done, our view of the Neanderthals will require some revision. As Coon says:

> In the last century the fame of Neanderthal man has increased. He is pictured as a crouching, stooping, squat and brutal creature, with huge jaws and little or no forehead, and a low grade of intelligence. Flesh reconstructions of his face make him look like an ape. In this guise he has become the prototype of innumerable cartoons, in which a slant-browed man, clad in a skin, hits a woman over the head and drags her unconscious body into a cave. This, the popular image of Neanderthal man, will probably be with us for decades to come, because it is picturesque, exciting, and flattering to ourselves. But it is wrong, and so are most of the elements in the total Neanderthal concept.

If anything, the erroneous image of Neanderthal brutality became even more vivid after the discovery of Crô-Magnon man. For some years we somewhat shamefully accepted Neanderthal as our ancestor. Then the Upper Paleolithic Europeans were discovered in quantity, including 'Crô-Magnon' man and our joy was unbounded at the discovery of Crô-Magnon's art and chin. Crô-Magnon, then, was quickly adopted as the 'true' ancestor of modern man and the more primitive Neanderthals suffered by comparison. Crô-Magnon was eulogized, just as Neanderthal was despised... and both emphases are myths. Crô-Magnon has been presented as a physically giant and perfect specimen of humanity, one to which modern man might even suffer by comparison. Yet, the average stature of twelve Crô-Magnon skeletons is just five feet eight inches (173 cm.), shorter than modern Americans, whose average height is now over five feet ten inches.

During the height of the Crô-Magnon adoption, from about 1900 to 1920, H.G. Welles could write in his *Outline of History* that Crô-Magnon man would have disdained interbreeding with Neanderthals because the odour of the Neanderthals would doubtless have been offensive to Crô-Magnon's evolved sensitivities. Needless to say, a modern man would probably find the stench of the Neanderthal cave and a Crô-Magnon one equally offensive.

Compared to the individual variation present in collections of most fossil hominid groups, the skulls and postcranial bones of Neanderthals are remarkably similar. Coon observes that some very strong selective agency must have rapidly pruned off individuals who deviated excessively from the basic Neanderthal blueprint, and this is especially true of the Neanderthals of Western Europe where the cold of the Würm glaciation was at its height. Somewhat more deviance was apparently permitted in areas of more moderate climate further removed from the ice sheet. Neanderthals of the Zagros, the Levant and of central Eurasia were less extreme than the Neanderthals of Western Europe who lived in the heart of Würm. But, in spite of some West-to-East decrease in 'brutality', the Neanderthals were an exceptionally cohesive genotype in terms of both morphology and culture.

Neanderthals had low, broad skulls which curved outward over the ears and which overhung the area of muscle attachment at the back of the neck. Neanderthal foreheads sloped sharply backwards from large brow ridges and the skulls have definite depressions at both major sutures. But even though they are low and broad, Neanderthal crania are round in section, and not pentagonal in section as in *Homo erectus.*

Neanderthal skulls were very large compared to the size of skulls in modern man, being an average of 30mm longer and 20mm wider (see Figure 6). The cranial capacities of Neanderthal skulls ranged from 1,525 to 1,640 cc. in six male skulls and from 1,300 to 1,425 cc. in three female skulls. This is from 100 to 250 cc. larger than the average cranial capacities of modern Caucasoids, but the sexual differentiation with respect to cranial capacity was much greater among Neanderthals than among more modern populations.

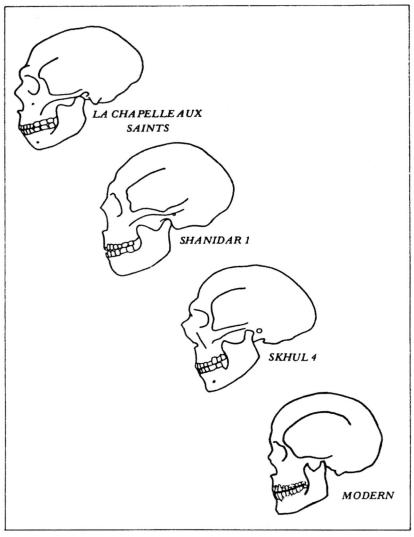

Fig. 6   *Difference Between Neanderthal and Modern Man*

Longer and fuller Neanderthal skulls contrast with more spherical form of modern crania. Nasal profiles indicate that Neandethals had over-sized noses.

Neanderthals drawn after Coon,
Reprinted with permission of Alfred A. Knopf, Inc.

Modern male Caucasoid skulls average about 1,400 cc., while female skulls are about 100 cc. smaller. But the sexual difference in cranial capacity among Neanderthals averaged 200 cc. and could approach 350 cc.

Most Neanderthal jaws are prognathous, but it is a different sort of prognathism than that encountered among apes. Although evidence of tooth wear testifies that the Neanderthals were constant and energetic chewers and used their teeth for softening skins as well as food, the prognathism in Neanderthal jaws is not due to any environmental need for massive chewing apparatus.

Coon argues persuasively that the prognathism of the Neanderthal j. resulted from the jaw being stretched forward in order to 'catch up' with an overdeveloped nose. The entire face of the Neanderthal was dominated by a projecting and beaky nose, like a prow, and other facial elements have accommodated to this unusual nasal development.

For all their prognathism, Neanderthal jaws are not exceptionally massive, as is the gorilla's which is designed for extra-heavy chewing. The bone in La Ferrassie's mandible is thinner than in many modern jaws. The Neanderthal jaws are prognathous because they are stretched to accommodate nasal development. This is illustrated by a characteristic peculiar to Neanderthal mandibles. The ascending ramus begins to rise well behind the third molar, in La Ferrassie by as much as a full centimeter. In most modern and fossil human jaws, the coracoid process of the ascending ramus begins even with the rear edge of the last molar or overlaps it, and in the Australopithecines the ascending ramus may extend as far forward as the second molar. Thus, the Neanderthal prognathism isn't a primitive trait, but, on the contrary, results from an extreme development of a modern one. This stretching of the Neanderthal jaw, resulting in a 'gap' between the last molar and the beginning of the ascending ramus (see Figure 7), was actually a hindrance to powerful chewing because the length of the jaw decreased the leverage of the temporal muscles. Thus, although the Neanderthals were heavy chewers, like most fossil men, their prognathous jaws were not an adaptation reflecting a particularly massive chewing apparatus.

Neanderthal jaws are also notable for the number and size of mental foramina, the holes in the mandible through which veins pass bringing blood and warmth to the lower face. Neanderthal mental foramina are either so large or so numerous that six or seven times more blood could flow through them than is the case in

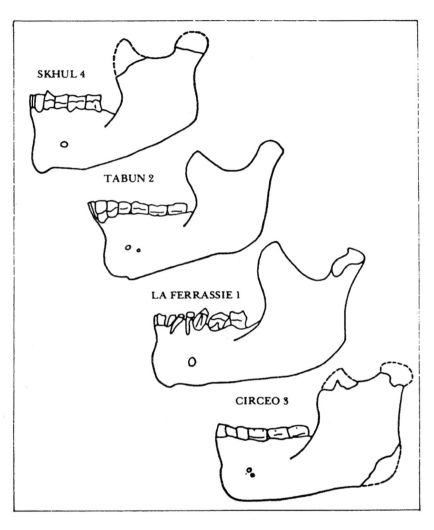

Fig. 7   *Neanderthal Jaws*

The Neanderthal type specimen, La Chapelle, is the most nearly chinless of Neanderthal mandibles as these profiles show. Other Neanderthals boasted at least a hint of chin. Note the gap between the last molar and the upward rising part of the jaw bones [coracoid process of ascending ramus]. This gap is characteristic of Neanderthals and shows how their jaws had been 'stretched' forward to match extreme nasal development.

After Coon. Reprinted with permission of Alfred A. Knopf, Inc.

modern jaws.

The remarkably developed nasal profiles exhibited by Shanidar 1 and Skhul 4, the characteristic stretching of the mandible, and the number and size of mental foramina were all components of one adaptive package. Neanderthals were cold-adapted, as their time and habitat would suggest.

Coon advanced the idea that the Neanderthal nose was a special cold-weather adaptation, a massive 'radiator' to warm incoming air and remove incoming cold air as far from the brain as possible. Neanderthal sinuses are also remarkably well-developed for the same reason. Coon therefore disagrees with the generalized image of Neanderthals as reflected in classic flesh reproductions which emphasize the prognathous jaws. Coon's reconstructions emphasize the nasal development of which the stretched mandibles are only a secondary and concomitant feature.

On a bone-by-bone basis, the postcranial skeletons of the Neanderthals compare in size and shape with modern man. Some of the bones are stout, but none are so massive that they cannot be matched among living people. The feet and hands were broader than is usual among living people, but fully human. Coon says that "no evidence yet produced indicates that Neanderthal hands were notably different from those of hardworking modern Europeans." Of the feet he says: "They looked like Russian rather than English feet."

I think it can be fairly said that Coon is seeking to minimize certain differences between ourselves and the Neanderthals. Neanderthal hands and feet *can* be matched among living people, but not easily. The Neanderthal footprints found in the moist clay floor of "The Witch's Cave" near Toriano, Italy in 1948 show a very broad short foot. The plantar index of these prints is around 1.61 which, translated into modern commercial shoe sizes, is an "EEE" and isn't manufactured.

The curvature of Neanderthal ribs testifies to very deep chests and a couple of preserved sternums, extremely concave on the inner surface, emphasize this. Some Neanderthal ribs are either round or triangular in section, a departure from the modern European ribbon-like form. In addition to being deep, the lower part of Neanderthal rib cages appears to have been unusually large, almost flared, as shown in Skhul 5 and Skhul 4.

The Neanderthal pelvis was within the modern size range for Europeans, but the ilium had a tendency to flare upward and outward above the sacrum. Coon calls this condition 'super-

Caucasoid' because it occurs in about 22 per cent of modern Europeans, but is entirely absent in other races. Neanderthal pubic bones differed consistently, but in detail only, from those of modern people.

La Chapelle stood five feet four and a half inches tall (164 cm). In life, Neanderthal, Spy 2 and La Ferrassie 1, all males, were about five feet four to five-five in height. But a female, La Ferrassie 2, stood only four feet ten inches.

Thus, the most extreme Neanderthals, the ones inhabiting Western Europe, were relatively short, at least compared to modern man, and exhibited a much greater relative difference in stature between the sexes than is the case presently in Europe.

In the East, among the Neanderthals of the Levant, there was an increase in stature, especially toward the end of the Neanderthal period, and much morphological evidence of mixture with a non-Neanderthal, more modern and more or less 'Krapina-like' stock. The significance seems to be that during the worst of Würm the pre-Neanderthal population of Europe, as reflected in the Krapina skeletons, retreated from the glaciers at least as far to the south and east as the Levant. They left glacial Europe to the Neanderthals, but in the Levant the two types overlapped and interbred.

Neanderthal culture

Just as the Neanderthals present a remarkable degree of morphological homogeneity throughout their geographical range, they also present an equal amount of cultural solidarity. From central Asia to the coast of Western Europe, Neanderthals are associated with the 'Mousterian' type of artifact assemblage, which varied little.

Neanderthals also apparently invented deliberate interment, burial. It is among Neanderthals that we find the first indisputable awareness of a past-present-future continuum and the notion that the dead have some relationship to the living. Neanderthals were the first humans to leave evidence of care for the dead, the first to supply the dead with artifacts against future need in the afterlife.

It is even possible that the Neanderthals had developed some religious sophistication. Graves in Europe and Asia alike were oriented in an East-West direction and this may indicate 'sun worship', or at least some idea of cosmic relationship to human life and death.

And not only footprints were found in the cave near Toriano. The

Neanderthals enjoyed a game similar to darts where clay balls were thrown at a graduated circular target on the wall.

Many Neanderthal skeletons show these people must have had a co-operative society and showed as much solicitude for the injured and aged as for the dead. La Chapelle had only two teeth at the time of his death and someone must have prepared his food for him. Several individuals, crippled through accident or congenital defect, lived to a relatively old age even though they could not have been fully productive. At Shanidar there was evidence of a deliberate amputation of an injured arm, an operation from which the patient fully recovered and lived to a ripe old age.

Though supposedly so much more primitive, the Neanderthals enjoyed greater longevity than Upper Paleolithic Peoples and this must have been due, at least in part, to co-operation in their society. According to figures tabulated by Henry Vallois, the Neanderthals' population included a fairly large percentage of individuals from thirty to sixty years of age at any one time (35.8 percent), while the percentage for Upper Paleolithics of the same age group was only 26.7 percent and for Mesolithics a still lower 12.7 percent. The truism that primitive man's life was 'nasty, brutish and short' seems to hold less for the Neanderthals than for supposedly more advanced men.

Evidence from Shanidar proves that Neanderthal man had some appreciation of beauty and, perhaps, emotions closely paralleling our own in some respects. Pollen analysis of soil samples from Shanidar burials, undertaken by Mme Leroi-Gourhan, showed that the Shanidar Neanderthals had adorned the graves of their dead with varieties of flowers obviously selected for decorative appeal. It is possible that all Neanderthals used flowers during interments, but, unfortunately, pollen analysis wasn't applied before the excavations at Shanidar.

In our brief and superficial study of the Neanderthals we have none the less progressed far beyond the popular vision of a shambling ape-man. As Ralph Solecki says of the Neanderthals:

> ... *while we may still have the privilege of ridiculing him, we are not actually rejecting him. For what person will mind having as an ancestor one of such good character, one who laid his dead to rest with flowers?*

Neanderthal-Caucasoids

The Origin of Races was a massive and detailed work in which Carleton Coon set out to identify, isolate and trace the evolution of five primal human groups, 'subspecies' or 'races', as each progressed towards modern man and the *sapiens* threshold. In spite of the philosophical and emotional objections of liberal anthropologists like Ashley Montagu, Coon seems to have been largely successful with at least two of his five primal groups.

Relying on the work of Weidenreich, Coon reiterated Weidenreich's argument that, in the Far East, Man was Mongoloid before he could be called *sapiens*, that race was older than species. And if Montagu, Washburn, Hogben, Hiernaux and many others reject this contention as an affront to humanity, there are others of equal stature who find Coon's and Weidenreich's evidence objectively compelling. Harold L. Shapiro says:

> *That the living Chinese tend to regard Sinanthropus as at least one of their ancestors would be strongly justified by these [Weidenreich's] comparisons. That Peking Man looked like a primitive version of the present day Chinese would seem to be equally borne out by the available data.*

Coon and Weidenreich seem to have presented a defensible argument for a *Sinanthropus-Mongoloid* racial line.

I think that any fair-minded reader would admit that Coon presents an only slightly less defensible argument for the existence of a distinct *Pithecanthropus-Australoid* racial line.

It may be accurate, or at least defensible, to refer to these lines as 'races' in the manner in which people seem to use that ill-defined term: a *strain* or kind which had a distinct origin and which has remained relatively isolated and identifiable.

But the term 'race' cannot be used in this sense for Coon's other three groups, and especially it cannot be used in this sense for Caucasoids.

With respect to Coon's hypothetical Congoid and Capoid racial lines there are simply not enough data to support his contentions.

But with Coon's 'Caucasoids' the situation is much worse.

If the term 'race' is to mean anything, it must be used in the context of some cohesive genetic origin and continuity. It is perhaps permissible, therefore, to refer to the Mongoloid and Australoid races in this context.

But if there is anything which is characteristic of human evolution in the West, it is a lack of cohesion and continuity. The Neanderthal genotype apparently intruded upon the evolutionary pattern of an indigenous European genotype. It is commonly said that the Neanderthals 'died out', or 'became extinct'. But what does this mean? It used to mean that most anthropologists believed that the Neanderthal disappeared from the Eurasian scene without contributing to the modern Europoid gene pool. But this view is losing ground. Coon, Solecki, Shapiro and an increasing number of anthropologists now tend to think that the Neanderthals were absorbed by people migrating into Eurasia (or 'returning').

If the modern Eurasian population is an amalgam of Neanderthal genes and genes possessed by the 'returning' primal Eurasian population, then the term 'race' cannot be applied to Caucasoids in the same way that it can be applied to Mongoloids or Australoids. For Caucasoids 'race' cannot mean a genetic continuity; at most the term 'race' can only refer to a 'state'. The Caucasoids are merely the result of a complicated genetic amalgam, not the result of genetic continuity. The word 'race' cannot be applied to *both* situations with any justification or honesty.

Yet, the word 'race' seems to have a magnetic hold on Coon and he applies it to the people of Eurasia with the label 'Caucasoid'. It is an exercise in circular thinking.

The pre-Neanderthal population of Eurasia is not well enough represented in the fossil record to enable determination of any common genetic origin or significant shared traits. The Mauer mandible, the Steinheim skull, the Swanscombe fragments come down to us as *individuals*. There is simply not enough material to establish a 'racial line'. The 649 bones of Krapina do show some degree of genetic continuity with the Fontéchevade cranium, but Krapina material *also* shows Mongoloid admixture and the 'line' thus becomes fuzzy at best. Then, for 60,000 years, this racial 'line' disappears altogether, the Neanderthals dominate Eurasia and disappear, and the original 'line' returns and absorbs Neanderthal genes. No one knows where the original Eurasian people went during the 60,000 years of Neanderthal dominance in Eurasia, and no one knows what other 'racial' genes this original Eurasian population absorbed while it was elsewhere during Würm.

There has only been one race in Eurasia in any strict sense, the Neanderthal race. And rather than try to fit Neanderthals into the Caucasoid race, as Coon continually does, it seems more resonable to wonder how much *Neanderthal racial traits* contributed to the *state* we now call 'Caucasoid'".

Coon's original Eurasian and pre-Neanderthal people went 'elsewhere' during Würm, most likely to Africa, and there they probably picked up 'Capoid' and 'Congoid' racial traits. In fact, the Upper Paleolithic Grimaldi skeletons, which represent examples of these 'returning' original Eurasians, show strong negroid traits. In Palestine, some skeletons of this period (i.e. 30,000-40,000 years ago) reflect influence of Coon's 'Capoids'.

In short, even before leaving Eurasia, Coon's Caucasoids were something of a mixture. After 60,000 years in Africa and elsewhere, and genetic interchange with all manner of people, it is highly doubtful whether the 'returning' people could claim any significant racial continuity with those who had left.

Upper Paleolithic people migrating into Europe and Asia after the worst of Würm simply cannot be considered to belong to any race at all, at least not in the sense by which the Mongoloids' and Australoids' genetic cohesiveness and continuity are recognized by the term.

However, it could be said that these people *did* widely mix with a very distinctive and cohesive race — the Neanderthals — as they migrated into Eurasia. The Neanderthals were numerous and 60,000 years of rigourous selection had made them genetically distinctive and consistent throughout their range. To the extent that the discordant migrating peoples attained a degree of similarity granted by the term 'Caucasoid race', they probably did so through the medium of a significant admixture of distinctive and cohesive Neanderthal genetic traits.

Coon's emphasis, viewed in this light, appears curious at best. Neanderthals were not 'Caucasoids'... rather, the reverse.

In the absence of expert opinion, I somewhat apprehensively suggest that the highly variable peoples now inhabiting Eurasia can be collectively considered as belonging to one 'race' only because they share, and only to the extent that they share, genetic traits once characteristic of Neanderthals. It is my view that the dissimilar typological bricks of the 'Caucasoid' 'racial' edifice are held rather loosely together by a mortar of Neanderthal genes.

6

Fire and Ice: Psychobiology

The 'pendulum swing' of judgment seems to be an intellectual institution in the West. In the interests of objectivity, we may presume to anticipate a pendulum swing in the judgment of Neanderthals. We have seen that the last hundred years have been dominated by writers too ready to consign Neanderthals to irrevocable bestiality and unpardonable brutality. Since about 1960 there has been a Neanderthal re-think, perhaps culminating in, and aptly illustrated by, the title of Ralph Solecki's recent book: *Shanidar, the first flower people*. The Neanderthal 'ogre' has become transmuted into an acceptable Man of Destiny in human evolution. Only a few short years ago he was an unconscionable brute: now Neanderthal is likened unto a flower child.

Neanderthal's new image has not yet percolated down to become part of the intellectual repertoire of the average man — *that* will take a little longer — but there is little doubt, humans being what we are, that by the time the average man becomes adjusted to the New Neanderthal, a re-re-think will be catching hold in academic circles.

In the interest of short-circuiting this sorry and inevitable development, I offer the following re-re-think in advance.

Everybody agrees that Neanderthal skulls differ radically from ours. Above and beyond morphological details, Neanderthal skulls were, simply, huge. Neanderthal faces were twice the size of modern ones and their heads were about an inch bigger in every direction but up.

On a bone-by-bone basis, we have learned that almost every single Neanderthal skeletal characteristic can be matched among living people. The operative word here is 'can'. It would be very difficult to match Neanderthal hands and feet among living Europeans.

The bone-by-bone analysis of Neanderthals tends to disguise the truth of the Neanderthal gestalt. We are talking about people with faces twice as large as ours, heads an inch longer and wider, and postcranial bones which *can* be matched, after a lot of hard looking, with modern people... and all this on a creature about five feet four inches high. Neanderthal women were quite a bit smaller, barely within the normal European range, and yet their bones *can* be matched by living Europeans.

The Neanderthals were exceedingly squat, heavy little people and *grotesque* by our standards. There is no way to get around the fact that the Neanderthals differed considerably from later Eurasians.

But, as great as the skeletal differences are in terms of gestalt, I think that the flesh appearance of the Neanderthals would likely be more shocking to us yet... and I think that some skeletal details point to this.

In Neanderthals the lower rib cage was very full, or even flared, and this on a chest that was already very deep by modern standards. Then, add to this the fact that Neanderthal pelvic bones, though similar to modern man's in shape, had a tendency to be a bit higher and more flaring. We are left with low flaring ribs and high flaring hips, and these skeletal structures must have had some function. And this function can only have been to support a very round and full trunk, I'm inclined to believe that the Neanderthal body type was, *in the flesh*, almost absurdly round.

There is some theoretical support for this notion. 'Allen's Rule' states the general principle that cold-adapted animals tend to adopt a spherical form while tropical animals tend to be elongated. The rule is more complex than that, but that's what it boils down to for all practical purposes.

Being cold-adapted animals, the Neanderthals, like Eskimos, would tend to be short and stocky, but the Neanderthal skeletons argue that they were excessively so compared with modern Eskimos. There is good reason why Neanderthals should have been even rounder than Eskimos according to the dictates of Allen's Rule.

Anthropology texts are fond of saying that by the time of the Neanderthals man's culture had evolved to the point where survival under arctic conditions was barely possible. Before the Würm glaciation it is believed that hominids fled south with the onset of 'ice ages', but that the Neanderthals held their ground because their Mousterian technology was enough of an advance to permit their survival.

It sounds good if you say it fast, but there is something spurious about it.

There is nothing easier to borrow than culture traits. If the Neanderthals' Mousterian was the crucial difference, it is difficult to explain why other men did not borrow their 'Mousterian' tool kit and remain to face Würm also. We have seen that there were other kinds of men in Eurasia just before the onset of Würm.

Yet, other kinds of men did not adopt the Neanderthals' Mousterian tool kit. They fled. The worst of the Würm glacial period is correlated with a genotype, not with Mousterian tools. This circumstance leads one to suspect that the Mousterian tool kit alone was insufficient to guarantee human survival and that the rigours of the Würm ice age demanded a specialized kind of Man. Perhaps *any* tool kit that could have been developed at the human level of evolution 100,000 years ago would have been insufficient to permit survival.

There is no doubt that Neanderthal man was much poorer culturally and technically than contemporary Eskimos. Therefore, Neanderthal man survived and flourished during Würm because he was adapted to cold more completely than modern Eskimos and *this* compensated for this relative cultural and technological poverty compared to them.

I believe that Neanderthals must have been a more extreme example of Allen's Rule in operation and they must have been rounder than even our modern Eskimos. I think it is reasonable to conclude that Neanderthal ribs and hips reflect this, Yet, I'm not altogether sure that increased roundness, by itself, would have been enough. I think that there is at least scanty evidence for more dramatic adaptations, but I don't want to go into this yet.

Perhaps the assumption that physical adaptations, rather than cultural ones, made the difference during the last ice age can offer some insights into apparent discontinuities.

Sapiens in the modern morphological form had appeared in Eurasia before the onset of Würm, but there is no evidence for a comparable cultural advance. Because we've more or less automatically assumed that culture made survival possible during the last glaciation, and since we know that *sapiens* forms didn't inhabit Eurasia during Würm, it has been natural to conclude that the cultural wherewithal simply wasn't there.

But, in paleontology, negative evidence means nothing. It is entirely possible that Fontéchevade and Krapina peoples had a cultural level comparable to, or even higher than, 'Mousterian'. And it is also more than likely that such hypothetical cultural parity with, or superiority to, Neanderthals would have made no difference whatever in their practical ability to survive Würm.

Fontéchevade and Krapina people were warm-weather animals. They may very well have had a respectable culture, but since there was no reason for them to live in caves, because the weather did not demand it, they may have preferred to live in open camps. If that is the case, all traces of their technology may have been erased. If they fled from the ice, it may have been because they did not have the genetic characteristics capable of being stretched to accommodate the adaptations demanded by Würm... and human culture in general, by itself, was at that stage too primitive to give the necessary survival edge.

Eurasia was bereft of *sapiens* morphology for only 60,000 years. When modern peoples returned to Europe they brought with them flake and blade cultures which were much more sophisticated than the Neanderthal Mousterian. It is always possible that Upper Paleolithic techniques did develop, as most experts believe, while the Eurasians were 'waiting out' Würm in the sunnier south, and perhaps these techniques were partially borrowed from peoples with whom these future Europeans came in contact.

But it is also just possible that the genesis of the Upper Paleolithic dates from open camps of Krapina-like people, or even earlier, and that the evidence was destroyed and scoured away by Würm. Skerlj's assertion that 'Aurignacian' flints occurred at Krapina may be a mistake, of course, or evidence of later occupation of the same site by more advanced people, but it may be a valid observation indicating that cultures more sophisticated than Mousterian existed 125,000 years ago. The point is that cultures of even proto-Upper Paleolithic level may not have given a survival edge comparable to the Neanderthal's unique physical adaptations.

I'm inclined to believe that our view of ourselves as a 'cultural animal' has tended to prejudice the value of good old physical adaptations in our eyes. And I think that there's reason to believe that a bona fide Upper Paleolithic level of technology was hard-pressed, by itself, to ensure survival and that Man fell back on his genetic resources, and Neanderthal ones at that, during Würm II and even during Würm III.

It seems that the 'Venus figurines' represent a Neanderthal-influenced body type, at least in a general way, something that could either be called 'refined Neanderthal' or 'extreme Caucasoid' depending upon the perspective in time. The evolutionary scenario may have been as follows.

At the end of Würm I about 40,000 years ago, more modern peoples began migrating back into Eurasia and began assimilating the "indigenous" (by this time) Neanderthals. This went on all during the Göttweig Interstadial, about 11,000 years, and we must realize that although the Neanderthals had been a remarkably distinctive and cohesive genotype, they were probably nowhere near as numerous as the newcomers. The Neanderthal physical type rapidly disappeared, especially in the area of the skull, but left its mark genetically in a refined form in the new composite European population. But just as the Neanderthal genotype seemed likely to become swamped altogether, the moderate weather of the Göttweig Interstadial ended and Würm II brought another onset of ice. Europeans went back into caves and glacial conditions again tended to select what was left of Neanderthal cold-weather adaptations. Of these, we are concerned here only with the tendency toward a round body and relatively short limbs. And this is the body type reflected in the 'Venus figurines' (see Plate I).

Most art experts doubt that the Venus figurines represent a real physical type. The prevailing opinion is that the round women represent "a generalized type of childbearing woman and stress fertility." There are several reasons for doubting this and we will examine them more fully later.

For the moment, it is enough to suggest somewhat tentatively that until very recently the Neanderthal genotype, in an attenuated form, has probably been at least as useful to modern man's survival as Upper Paleolithic cultures and flint industries. And it is important to realize that the Neanderthal genotype has never been given an opportunity to die out altogether. Würm II and Würm III revived the credit of lingering Neanderthal characteristics, although by now these are little more than vestiges... but one such vestige may very well be the typically wide hips of European women, shown during a cold period in more extreme form in the Venus figurines of from 15,000 to 10,000 B.C.

There are other vestiges which I suggest came from our Nean-

Plate I *Semi-relief 'Venus' figure from Laussel, Dorgogne, 15,000-10,000 B.C. Fertility symbolism or naturalistic image?*

derthal ancestors, and which serve to characterize us 'racially'.

Assuming for the moment that Neanderthals may have been 'extremely round' little people, and perhaps it will be granted that their skeletal material hints at this, I don't think that roundness by itself was enough. I'm inclined to believe that the Neanderthals boasted a thick, woolly fleece, a pelt, and there is some reason to believe that the dominant colour of this fleece was a reddish brown.

Before going into 'evidence' for a Neanderthal fleece, and it is embarrassingly threadbare and perhaps even unacceptable to any remotely reputable anthropologist, something should be said about the theoretical support for this notion... such as it is.

We have noted the observaion of Vallois that the Neanderthals had a fairly high percentage of "geriatrics" in their population. About 35 percent of the Neanderthal population was represented by the age group thirty to sixty. Surprisingly, considering the comparative levels of technology and comparative environments, Vallois found that the technically more advanced Upper Paleolithics could support about 30 percent fewer geriatrics, and the even more advanced Mesolithics could support 60 percent fewer geriatrics compared to the Neanderthals.

There must be some reason for this discontinuity. We know that the Mesolithics, at least, could sew clothing because we have found their awls which were used to punch thread-holes (or, more likely, sinew-holes) in skins. We may suspect that the Upper Paleolithics sewed too, although we have no proof, and it might even be granted that the Neanderthals used their characteristic Mousterian 'burins' for worrying thread-holes in skins. However, no one doubts that the Mesolithics enjoyed a richer material culture than the Neanderthals. Why, then, could the Mesolithics not support their senior citizens in greater numbers?

Since *the* significant environmental and survival challenge was identical for all three peoples, that is to say 'ice' of the various phases of Würm, one is led to conclude that the Neanderthals were better equipped to meet this challenge. Since their better equipment cannot reasonably be ascribed to culture, it must have been supplied by nature. A natural pelt is more efficient than a man-made coat and it is just possible that the Neanderthals lived longer because they had better protection from the elements. Perhaps it is not carrying this line of reasoning too far to suggest that the Upper Paleolithics were able to support a greater number of geriatrics than the Mesolithics because the Upper Paleolithics were closer to the Neanderthals in time, possibly reflected Neanderthal cold-adapted genetic characteristics in a less vestigial form and therefore 'naturally' coped with a glacial environment more efficiently.

Now, with considerable diffidence, I present the evidence for Neanderthal hairiness. Since I fully realize that what follows will be unpalatable to our North American school of anthropologists, I will take the opportunity to stress, defensively, that most of the evidence has been extracted from *official* Soviet *scientific publications* and therefore, whether we like it or not, must be given the same respect due our own scientific journals. These Russian publications include: *The Reports of the Special Commission to Study the Snowman of the U.S.S.R. Academy of Sciences, under the Direction of Prof. B.F. Porshnev and Dr. A.A. Shmakov (Reports* 1 and 2 were published in 1958, Reports 3 and 4 were published in 1959, in Moscow); reports to the Soviet (then "Imperial") Academy of Sciences by Dr. V.A. Khakhlov, 1914; medical report of V.S. Karapetyan, Lieutenant-colonel, Medical Service, Soviet Army, 1941, courtesy the Russian Information Service; and several articles in *Tekhnika Molodyozhi.*

It is necessary to refer briefly to the 'abominable snowman', but only because 'it' inspired the Soviet Academy of Sciences to put four separate expeditions into the field in 1957 and to conduct much bibliographic and historical research on the subject of living and fossil hominids in Eurasia. Of these, the creature we call the 'abominable snowman' proved to be the most ephemeral and probably the least important... in spite of the fact that Western scientists and laymen are mesmerized by it to the exclusion of rational thought by either group.

Of much greater interest to the Soviets, and probably of much more importance to the study of Man's evolution, was evidence that a few Neanderthal-type creatures apparently still exist in central Asia, or have only *very recently* become extinct. This evidence includes the inevitable 'eyewitness reports', but it also includes a footprint cast, the official medical report of a Soviet Army doctor about an examination performed on one of these creatures, the anatomical analysis of a mummified hominid forearm and the report of a Soviet zoologist.

And it cannot be said often enough that these Neanderthal types have nothing whatever to do with the 'abominable snowman', 'Yeti', or whatever it is that is pounding about in the Himalayas.

These apparently Neanderthal-type hominids inhabit the mountain fringes *north* of the Pamirs-Hindu Kush-Elburz-Caucasus 'chain', and mostly *western* fringes of the Altai Tag-Tien Shan-

Tannu-Ula-Sayan 'chain'. This is to say that these Neanderthal-type creatures now occupy the fringe areas of what is usually regarded as the 'Caucasoid racial cradle'. In a number of instances, evidence of surviving Neanderthals in this area comes from locations which are just a stone's throw from established Neanderthal-Mousterian sites, and this is particularly true of the Zagros-Caucasus area.

Admittedly, none of this 'evidence' is 'hard'. We have no surviving Neanderthal in captivity, nor do we have a freshly skinned pelt. However, Soviet scientists could have had both, at least once, since one of these Neanderthal creatures fell into the hands of an Army medical team in Dagestan in 1941. The Soviet Army was busy with other problems at the time, however, and the Nazi invasion may have seemed more important. Lieutenant-colonel V.S. Karapetyan reports:

From October to December of 1941 our infantry battalion was stationed some thirty kilometers from the town of Buinaksk (in the Dagestan A.S.S.R.). One day the representatives of the local authorities asked me to examine a man caught in the surrounding mountains and brought to the district center. My medical advice was needed to establish whether or not this curious creature was a disguised spy.

I entered the shed with two members of the local authorities. When I asked why I had to examine the man in a cold shed and not in a warm room, I was told that the prisoner could not be kept in a warm room. He had sweated in the house so profusely that they had to keep him in the shed.

I can still see the creature as it stood before me, a male, naked and bare-footed. And it was doubtlessly a man, because its entire shape was human. The chest, back, and shoulders, however, were covered with shaggy hair of a dark brown colour [it is noteworthy that all the local inhabitants had black hair]. This fur of his was much like that of a bear, and 2 to 3 centimeters long. The fur was thinner and softer below the chest. His wrists were crude and sparsely covered with hair. The palms of his hands and the soles of his feet were free of hair. But the hair on his head reached to his shoulders partly covering his forehead. The hair on his head, moreover, felt very rough to the hand.

The man stood absolutely straight with his arms hanging... his mighty chest thrust forward. His fingers were thick, strong, and exceptionally large.

His eyes told me nothing. They were dull and empty — the eyes of an animal. And he seemed to me like an animal and nothing more... I gave the verbal conclusion that this was no disguised person, but a wild man of some kind. Then I returned to my unit and never heard of him again.

Karapetyan, in retrospect, gives the man's height as 180 cm, or about five feet ten and a half inches, which is outside the range of pure, classical Neanderthals. But Karapetyan stresses its massiveness compared to the body type of local people and his estimate of the creature's height, in retrospect, may have been slightly exaggerated to match the man's outsized proportions in other respects.

At any rate, similar creatures reported by other observers in the Caucasus area are stated to be about five feet in height. They are called *Kaptar* by the modern inhabitants. In July, 1957, Prof. V.K. Leontiev, a biologist with the Ministry of Hunting of Dagestan A.S.S.R., was conducting an official survey of the Gagan Sanctuary at the head of the Jurmut River when he saw a *Kaptar*.

It should be said here that the Jurmut River valley is a particularly wild area, uninhabited by modern men. Its fauna includes moose, some surviving European Bison or 'Wisent', Red Deer, mountain sheep, brown bear, wolf, lynx and leopards. Tigers do not range quite as far as the Jurmut, but occur in the Elburz Mountains not far to the south. Carleton Coon reported tigers in the vicinity of his Bisitun Cave excavation in the Elburz (Neanderthal skeletal material and Mousterian flints were recovered at Bisitun).

Leontiev's report is long, detailed and objective. It is too long to reproduce in full here and the reader is referred to the source: No. 120, *Report 3, "Special Commission to Study the Snowman of the U.S.S.R. Academy of Sciences, under the Direction of Prof. B.F. Porshnev and Dr. A.A. Shmakov"*, 1959, Moscow.

Leontiev saw his *Kaptar* at a distance of "approximately 50 to 60 meters" and it was in view for "5 to 7" minutes. The sighting occurred in the late afternoon under generally good weather conditions, although a light snow was falling. According to Leontiev, the *Kaptar* he saw tallied perfectly with descriptions of the creature current among local mountain folk. It was about 1.6 meters in height (about five feet two or three inches), and had an unusually wide body covered with dark hair. Its feet were very heavy, broad and about nine inches in length. The head was 'massive'. The *Kaptar's* back was slightly bent and its shoulders were slightly stooped. Leontiev described the creature as a massively built man with a heavy growth of hair on the head and body.

After viewing the *Kaptar* for some time, Leontiev took a shot at it, but missed. Leontiev traced and measured the Kaptar's footprints (in light snow), but acknowledges that these prints do not represent the true shape of the foot because the creature had been walking away from him, uphill, and put most of its weight on the toes. The heel part of the prints was not well defined. But the prints were of generally human shape. The *Kaptar* made several cries, but Leontiev could distinguish no words.

Travelling east along the Elburz, we find that Danial Dotson repor'ed that a 'gorilla' had been killed in Iran during the 1940's. Dotson was an engineer with an American oil company. There is no further information on this report.

Continuing east across Afghanistan, the Uzbek, Tadzhik, Kirghiz and Kazakh S.S.R.'s, and across the Badakshan Autonomous Area, there are literally hundreds of reports of creatures similar to the Caucasus *Kaptar*. Most of these reports were collected by the 1958 Russian expedition. Depending upon the local language, these creatures are called *Gul-Biavan, Dev, Almas*. In general, witnesses say that they are the size of a small man, covered with reddish brown hair or fur, have very broad and heavy feet and seem to have a primitive form of language. Caves are their favourite homes and they have been seen to use simple tools.

Porshnev found a footprint of a *Guli-yavan* in the mud in Kirghiz S.S.R. Porshnev's sketch of this print shows it to be almost identical in both size and shape to the Neanderthal prints found in 'The Witch's Cave' near Toriano (see Figure 8). If anything, the foot of the *Guli-yavan* seems a bit more modern and less brutal than the Neanderthal one which left its mark at Toriano.

Along the great Altai barrier which runs northeast from the Pamirs and separates the 'Caucasoid' realm from the Mongoloid one, the Russian expedition of 1958, and Khakhlov half a century earlier, collected reports of a *Kaptar-Almas*-type creature which is merely regarded as a primitive human by the peoples of Dzungaria. These *Almas* are hairy, short and squat, have a language unintelligible to modern humans, will suckle human babies on occasion and will carry on trade by barter with the nomads. Prof. Rinchen of the University at Ulan Bator, Mongolian D.R., asserts:

> *There was a lama in the Lamin-gegen monastery who was famous for his scholarship, and known under the name of 'a son of an* Almasska'. *The father of this lama was captured by* Almas *and begot a boy with an* Almas *woman. Both father*

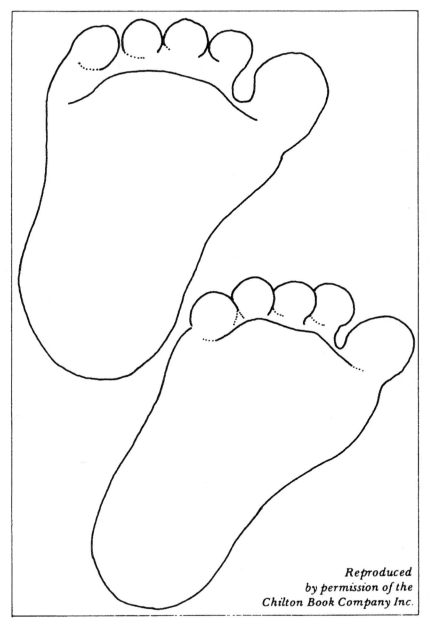

*Reproduced
by permission of the
Chilton Book Company Inc.*

Fig. 8 *Neanderthal footprint from Italian cave [left], after Blanc, compared with footprint of a 'Guli-yavan' found in mud in U.S.S.R., after Porshnev.*

and son managed to escape by joining a caravan. The boy was allowed to become a pupil in a monastery and achieved scholarly fame.

But perhaps the most persuasive evidence that Neanderthals still linger, or at least survived until recently, is the desiccated hominid hand of Pangboche, Nepal. This hand was examined and photographed by Prof. Teizo Ogawa in 1957; the photograph has been studied by Porshnev and Shmakov and by Dr. W.C. Osman Hill of the Zoological Society of London. The two Soviet scientists consider this hand to be 'almost definitely' Neanderthal, while Osman Hill concedes that it 'possibly' looks like the hand of a Neanderthal. The hand is perhaps as much as 500 years old.

It only remains to be said that zoologist Vladimir A. Khakhlov carried out a survey of allegedly living primitive hominids from 1907 to 1913 and came to the conclusion that Neanderthals were extant in some of the more remote mountainous areas of Eurasia. This report was presented to the Imperial Academy of Sciences in 1914, and was shelved. But Khakhlov's report was re-studied by the Soviets during the early 1950's, when the Western press was full of the 'abominable snowman', and his research formed the basis for the decision to send four expeditions into the field.

I think it should be noted that the Soviets seem to have a more mature perspective on this whole business of 'unknown humanoids'. Of the four expeditions, only *one* Soviet team was sent to the Himalayas in pursuit of true 'abominable snowman' evidence. The other three teams, the major part of the Russians' effort, were directed toward a different goal entirely. And that goal was to ascertain whether Neanderthals had perhaps lingered later than previously suspected, and to clarify the implications of this possibility in the study of human and racial evolution. The major thrust of the Soviet effort was based on Khakhlov's earlier research and the Russians spent little time on that which obsesses us, the Yeti. The three other Russian teams went to the Caucasus, the Pamir-Elburz and the Altai barrier respectively.

And the reason for the Russian interest in these regions is the fact that Neanderthal-Mousterian sites had recently been uncovered in lowlands overlooked by these interconnecting mountain chains: Kiik-Koba (1924) in the Crimea; Starosel'e (1952) in the Crimea; Teshik-Tash (1938) in Uzbekistan; Musa Dagh teeth (1954) in Northeastern Turkey; the Mousterian industry at Bisitun (1949); and the first Shanidar finds in the Zagros in 1953.

Since it was obvious that the Neanderthals had inhabited the fringes of these mountains only 30,000 to 40,000 years ago, and since living creatures apparently resembling Neanderthals were reported continuously from these mountains, there was a suspicion that the two phenomena might somehow be related.

It has not been proved that Neanderthals in a more or less pure form survive yet. But there is at least some provocative evidence that they may. And, if so, it makes sense that isolated survivors would have been forced, by the pressure of modern man, to retreat into uninhabited areas of the Caucasus, Pamir-Elburz and Altai overlooking their former homes. It is possible that not all the Neanderthals were assimilated. It is likely that some Neanderthal groups, those living in cultural backwaters like the Zagros and the Pamir-Elburz which were far removed from the initial and major migration routes of the Upper Paleolithics into Eurasia, retained their genetic purity for a long time... too long. It is possible that by the time modern man got around to inhabiting these backwaters there was too much cultural difference between Neanderthals and the newcomers to permit interbreeding. If that occurred in places, then, the Neanderthals would have been forced to retreat to extremely inaccessible environments where they could barely survive, but where modern man could not... at least not in any numbers. And if the *Almas* and the *Kaptar* seem a bit too primitive to be Neanderthals it may be that they have suffered the refugees' regression as other peoples have.

My point is not to try to prove the continued existence of Neanderthals. The issue at stake is their hairiness. If it is at least arguable that Neanderthals, or their degenerated descendants, may survive and have been reported by Eurasian people we must note that these creatures are always reported to be hairy, and the bulk of descriptions insist on a reddish brown colour.

Before concluding the argument for Neanderthal hairiness *per se,* and before proceeding to the much more important question of Neanderthal sexual dimorphism, I would like to recall, for a moment, those geriatric ratios. There is a subtlety in these ratios which very nearly proves the case for a substantial Neanderthal pelt.

A number of Upper Paleolithic and Mesolithic Eurasian peoples were sturdily built, short and stocky, and especially those peoples who were big-game hunters and who followed the arctic fauna north as Würm glaciation retreated. Indeed, in an effort to explain the rather bewildering multiplicity of body types in Europe, it used to be thought that there were three distinct 'races' which migrated into, or differentiated after arriving in, Europe. This naive anthropological 'cliché', as Coon calls it, maintained that the Crô-Magnons were Caucasoid, the Grimaldis Negroid and the Chancelade people Eskimoid.

Some of the European people were as stocky as Eskimos, and probably almost as stocky as the Neanderthals. An 'Eskimoid' race was proposed to explain them.

So, in Upper Paleolithic and Mesolithic Europe we have people who, like the Eskimos of today and the Neanderthals of the further past, were 'roundly' cold-adapted according to the tenets of Allen's Rule. Yet, even though these 'Eskimoids' were adapted almost as much as the Neanderthals in 'roundness', they had a decreasingly significant percentage of old people in their populations. They did not live as long as the Neanderthals and were less well adapted. It is obvious that a stocky body type was not the only Neanderthal adaptation to cold. The fact that the Neanderthals could support *three times* the number of elderly as Mesolithics, and one third more elderly than Upper Paleolithics, strongly suggests *another* dramatic adaptation to cold conditions. As we have said, this adaptation could not have been cultural because Upper Paleolithics and Mesolithics had a richer cultural assemblage than the Neanderthals' Mousterian. This additional cold adaptation was supplied by nature. And everything we know about arctic adaptation in other kinds of terrestrial mammals insists that this additional adaptation must have been fur.

And, in passing, there is no need to postulate three 'races' in Europe in order to account for great variations in body types at different times.

The modern men who came into Eurasia at the close of Würm I, during the Göttweig Interstadial, came from the south. There is no reason why some of these men should not have shown strongly Negroid characteristics, but there would have been absolutely no reason for *any* of them to have been stocky and squat. Coming from the warmer south, these men too would have reflected Allen's Rule. In general, *all* of them should have been taller and thinner than the Neanderthals.

I suggest that the range of body types in Europe can be very easily explained by the degree to which these newcomers interbred with Neanderthals, and the degree to which climate and geography tended to favour Neanderthal characteristics in the resulting composite population. This picture has been considerably muddied by even more recent migrations undertaken by men with the cultural and technological adaptations allowing them to live in almost any climate or geographical location, but the basic outline is clear enough.

We will conclude our Neanderthal re-re-think by summarizing that Neanderthal's purely skeletal differences form modern men do not truly reflect the extent to which he departed from modern man's appearance *in the flesh*. We know that Neanderthal was squat and powerfully built, that he had a huge head for his size and a prognathous face. We have also seen that he almost must have been covered with a heavy growth of hair, perhaps even approaching furriness, all over his body, including his face. If *Almas* and *Kaptar* descriptions are at all relevant, Neanderthal was a reddish brown creature.

Any modern man would consider Neanderthal 'bestial' and 'primitive' enough. It was this very bestiality and primitiveness which allowed Neanderthal to face oncoming Würm, and stand his ground, when more refined and modern men had to flee. Neanderthal provides another example of how sudden environmental changes can make a mockery of 'superiority' and 'inferiority'.

For all his bestial and primitive appearance, Neanderthal seems to have been human enough culturally and emotionally. He was the first human to bury his dead and therefore conceive of some past-present-future relationship bridging the twin abysses of birth and death. He seems to have oriented his graves in an east-west direction and demonstrated by this that he took cognizance of the cosmos, the movements of the heavenly bodies, and conceived that his kind had some place in it. He took care of his aged and his ailing, and in the face of death he affirmed the fragility and beauty of life by the sacrifice of blossoms.

Neanderthal was human, but it is absurd to call him 'Caucasoid'.

It is my feeling that Carleton Coon was led astray by his view of race. It is my suggestion that Coon got the relationship between 'Caucasoids' and Neanderthals backwards. Neanderthals were not 'Caucasoids'. It is the other way around. 'Caucasoid' is the label we apply to the present and historical inhabitants of Eurasia because they can be roughly differentiated from other kinds of men on the basis of Neanderthal vestiges they retain. This otherwise very variable Eurasian population, that of the 'Caucasoids', just barely retains sufficient traces of very distinctive Neanderthal adaptations to justify regarding it as a group.

We differ from other men in our hairiness, in the width of our pelvis, in the proportions of our limbs, in the heaviness of our wrists and hands, in our straight hair, in our tendency to exhibit brown and red hair. Those are the significant differences if 'significant' means 'giving a clue about evolution'. All these seem to be faint echoes of once-extreme Neanderthal characteristics.

Both Ashley Montagu and Ivan T. Sanderson have observed that Caucasoids, far from being the most refined 'race', are actually the most primitive-appearing and least refined race.

Montagu says:

> *If racists would take the trouble to visit their local zoo and for a moment drop their air of superiority and take a dispassionate look at one of the apes, they would find the hair of these creatures lank, that their lips are thin, and that their bodies are profusely covered with hair. In these characters the white man stands nearer the apes...*

Sanderson says:

> *The Negro so-called 'race' is apparently the newest and is the least pongid-like of all. (Apes have no lips and the straightest of hair, the shortest legs and the longest arms, and a host of other features that are the exact opposite of those of Negroes). The most pongid-like are the Caucasoids which have non-everted lips, straight hair, and so forth. The Mongoloids are really very different from both. Their long head hair, round in section, and their absence of body hair is very odd; so also are the proportions of parts of their limbs, with small hands and feet, short lower limbs and long upper.*

It is clear that insofar as the word has any meaning, the Caucasoids are the most 'primitive' of human races and not the most evolved if we choose to regard human refinement as Man's distance from ape-like physical traits.

It seems reasonable to suppose that we Caucasoids are an identifiable group because of the 'primitive' and 'bestial' physical characteristics we inherited through Neanderthal genetic input. And, just as an aside, our Eurasian fossil hominid history clearly shows that 'Caucasoids' are probably the most mixed and least 'pure' of any human group.

Sexual dimorphism

There are two more or less distinct schools of anthropological thought when it comes to explaining Neanderthal characteristics.

One school, generally older and flourishing a few decades ago, maintained that Neanderthal primitive characteristics reflected the traits of eastern *Homo erectus* stock which migrated into Eurasia from southeast Asia.

That is, that Neanderthals looked primitive because they *were* primitive hominids.

The newer school of anthropological thought, represented by the thinking of Coon and, perhaps, Solecki, maintains that the Neanderthals were only primitive-*looking* and that their distinctive traits resulted mostly from special adaptations.

It may be that both emphases are somewhat correct. Perhaps the Neanderthals began as relatively primitive hominids compared to people living in Eurasia during the last Interglacial, and that their more primitive characteristics were reinforced by glacial adaptation until reaching an extreme form.

If the Neanderthals were originally somewhat 'closer to the apes' as a relatively primitive hominid, it might be justifiable to speculate that our Caucasoid aggression may mirror the apes' lower frustration tolerance. But I think that this would be a far-fetched explanation. The hominid line is not all that new, as was once thought, and our separation from ape-like ancestors is receding ever further into the past.

I believe that we can find adequate explanation for our behaviour by going only a relatively short distance back into our evolutionary history.

If it is granted that the Neanderthals were squat and hairy, and that we Caucasoids retain vestiges of Neanderthal traits, then it must also be granted that the sexes do not share these vestigial traits equally. I think it can be fairly said that one additional Caucasoid characteristic that serves to distinguish us from other kinds of men is the degree of sexual dimorphism in our race. We Caucasoids all have a tendency to be hairy, and all men of whatever race have a tendency to be hairier than women, but our men are *much* hairier than our women. Likewise, we Caucasoids have a tendency toward heavy bones and a certain broadness of body, but our women have broader pelves than women of other races. The Caucasoid difference in height between the sexes is somewhat greater than is the case in other races.

We recognize this sexual dimorphism in phrases like 'the fair sex' in comparing our women to our men, or when a woman is called a 'broad'. This rather unusual degree of dimorphism, this 'sexism' to use a modern word, is a Caucasoid character.

Perhaps this sexual dimorphism is another vestigial inheritance from the Neanderthals.

We recall that Neanderthals exhibited a relatively great degree of sexual dimorphism in height and in cranial capacity. Neanderthal women were somewhat disproportionately short. Yet, these women had to give birth to children of a race which had bigger heads than modern man. It is likely that Neanderthal infants had somewhat larger heads than modern babies.

Neanderthal infant skeletal material is scarce. We have two skeletons: one from Shanidar and one from Starosel'e and both are badly crushed. However, the skull of the Starosel'e infant is more massive than the skulls of modern babies. Coon says that "the vault is thick for an eighteen-months-old baby, especially the lower part of the forehead" and that "The forehead is high and steep, and somewhat bulbous... It is even more strongly rounded and bowed forward than most modern baby skulls of the same age." Yet, in spite of its massiveness, the Starosel'e infant was a very late Neanderthal, if wholly Neanderthal at all, and shows evidence of intrusion of more modern stock. "It is either an early example of modern Caucasoid *Homo sapiens*, a product of mixture with local Neanderthals, or the end result of an evolutionary progression from Neanderthal to modern man."

It would seem reasonable, therefore, that infant skulls of classically extreme Neanderthals would have been even more massive than that of the transitional infant of Starosel'e.

And yet, these infants had to pass through the pelvic bones of exceptionally small women.

It would seem that there had to be some sort of pelvic adaptation to permit birth. First, of course, the Neanderthal women were stocky, and had visibly wide hips for their size. But hips can only become so wide before the articulation of the legs becomes exceedingly clumsy. We may conclude that the *interior* of the pelvic bone, the 'rim of the pelvis', had to be widened without widening the gross dimensions of the bone too much. This can be accomplished by a different configuration of the interior of the pelvic bone and by thinner bone, and this is the direction Neanderthal female pelves take. Stewart found that the Shanidar pelvic bones, especially the pubic bones, were thinner than in modern man.

Modern European women have internal pelvic dimensions that are larger than those of women of other races. In Europeans, the 'rim of the pelvis' may be up to an inch larger in diameter than the norm for other races. We have inherited our women's hippiness from adaptations necessary for Neanderthal birth mechanics.

Actually, it has always seemed to me that Neanderthal and Caucasoid hips should be wider than they are. Especially, Neanderthal women should have had wider pelves than they do. But, as already noted, stockiness combined with short stature can only be carried so far without imperiling the efficiency of basic hominid erectness. Some other adaptation may have been at work to ease Neanderthal birth.

Carleton Coon says of Wormian bones:

> *Wormian bones are so called because they are found in ancient Andean skulls. They are found principally in Mongoloid crania, in both the Old and New Worlds. The skull of Saccopastore 1, a Caucasoid Italian of the Last Interglacial, has sixteen Wormian bones, possibly a world's record; eleven major and five minor. Later on, Wormian bones were also characteristic of Neanderthal skulls. No one knows their function.*

While doubting that this Italian of the Last Interglacial was 'Caucasoid' in any meaningful sense, we can propose a function for Wormian bones. Perhaps they gave flexibility to a long, large skull during birth. The facial skeleton and the forward part of human skulls are well supplied with joints which would allow some 'play' during the rigours of birth, but the rear part of the human skull is composed of just three major bones which meet at lambda (the meeting of the occipital and the two parietals). There would be less 'play' in the rear portion of the skull because there are only three major joints, or sutures. The Wormian bones may serve the purpose, in large skulls, of widening these sutures and rounding out the joint between these large bones during birth. The extra Wormian bones give 'play' to the rear of a large skull, just as the more numerous bones of the face give natural play to the forward portion of a head.

The increased elasticity afforded the rear of the head by Wormian bones may have been necessary to assist the birth of large and-or long-headed babies. The Neanderthals had such heads and the modern Mongoloids have the largest average cranial capacities of all major groups. Thus we should not be surprised that Wormian bones are characteristic of both Mongoloid and Neanderthal skulls.

From this look at Neanderthal birth problems we have sufficient explanation for the width of female Caucasian hips, and we have good reasons to suspect therefore that during any cold period, when

Plate II *'Venus of Lespugue', rear view, carved from mammoth tusk about 20,000 B.C. Note naturalistic treatment of string skirt hanging below buttocks.*

Neanderthal-like traits would tend to be re-selected, European women would have appeared to be extremely large-hipped. We may therefore take issue with the opinion of paleolithic art experts who tend to believe that 'Venus figurines' were symbolic and abstract rather than naturalistic. All of these figurines date from cold periods during Würm II and Würm III when Allen's Rule and inherited Neanderthal characteristics would have combined to produce European women of disproportionate stockiness and hippiness.

Art experts often say that these figurines cannot be naturalistic representations because the extremities, the hands and feet, appear 'perfunctory', to use the word of Andreas Lommel. But the hands and feet of an excessively fat woman *can* appear perfunctory. Then, there is a curious detail in most of these figures that is definitely not perfunctory and seems to be faithful naturalism. The hair shown on most of these figurines, and especially on the "Venus of Willen-dorf", is faithfully reproduced and hints at purposeful styling. The faithful reproduction of a hairdo would seem most unnecessary for a purely abstract figure of fertility. Human beings *have* made abstract fertility figures, of course, but the 'Venuses' of the Upper Paleolithic would not seem to be of that genre (see Plate II).

The cronos complex

If we have possibly given a satisfactory explanation of Caucasoid female hippiness, we have not yet offered any reason why Caucasoid men should be so much more hairy than Caucasoid women. Nor have we given any reason for the large breasts characteristic of Caucasoid women. Perhaps it is time to try this, but it will require a detour into philosophical biology. I believe that when we return to the discussion of our sexual dimorphism we will have a greater insight into the causes of Caucasoid aggression.

Man has always realized that he, too, is an animal in some ways... and yet different. Human observation, even on the lowest level of culture, leaves no room for doubt that Man seems to be unique in the animal world. Some men, and perhaps this would include most of the world's population, are capable of accepting this difference and have proposed explanations for it which appear to be truly satisfying.

But other men have proved not so easily sated — the Caucasoids by and large belong in this group — and have continued to wonder why Man differs from other species in the purely natural world. I don't think that we have to go deeply into the various explanations that we Caucasoids have embraced in order to account for Man's uniqueness. We have been created in God's image; we have descended from space travellers, according to a more recent explanation proffered by von Däniken and others; since Darwin, Wallace and Haeckel our official Western explanatory institution, 'science', has held that we evolved from lower primates.

It was fashionable a few years back to believe that science had increased our uncertainty and alienation because it destroyed mythic explanations for our origins which were psychologically satisfying. But our notions of special creation were never truly satisfying. The creative powers ascribed to the Titans and Olympians did not prevent Anaximander and Aristotle and Archimedes, and many others, from doubting. And Churchmen could not regard Jehovah's creative powers as sufficiently definitive because they continued to debate the nature and rank of various angels, their size and weight, the dimensions of heaven, whether God had supplied souls to other animals, and whether the Christ was essentially a material or a spiritual entity. Von Däniken's offering of space-travelling ancestors does not solve the problem of our uniqueness, but merely postpones it... what made *them* unique in whatever world they originated?

We have, therefore, never really accounted for our undoubted uniqueness in the animal world in a way which puts our minds at ease and which truly satisfies our curiosity.

It must be admitted that the scientific explanation, 'evolution', is probably a bit less satisfying than others because evolution does not recognize *a* difference, but only numberless degrees of difference between ourselves and other animals. Scientists have offered the explanation that we have large brains and more intelligence than other animals, that we have a more complex culture than other animals, that we have a greater 'consciousness'.

And this may indeed be true, and an adequate explanation for our uniqueness in the natural world, but not one of these terms has been adequately defined *in biological terms*... and we began as a purely biological animal, according to evolution.

A dictionary may define intelligence as 'the ability to learn and understand or to deal with new or trying situations', and consciousness as simply 'awareness'. The English anthropologist Edward Taylor defines culture as: "that complex whole which includes knowledge, belief, morals, custom, and other capabilities acquired by Man as a member of society."

But not one of these definitions tells us what the quality under discussion *is*. These definitions are merely lists of symptoms, lists of the behaviour these qualities *result in* when they are possessed. Culture *results in* 'a complex whole of knowledge, belief, morals, etc.'; intelligence results in the ability to deal with new situations; consciousness results in 'awareness', which isn't much help. As definitions they are not satisfying because, basically, they are tautologies.

Science insists that Man was once merely an animal like others, a small primate resembling living tree shrews, or, as one primatologist maintained, a tarsier. Man was once wholly biological.

Then, if Man is unique in the animal world, and that is recognized by us, those qualities which make him unique must have some definition which is acceptable *biologically*. If Man was once purely biological then there must be a biological mechanism which could somehow let him achieve culture, intelligence and consciousness. We need a definition bridging biology and metaphysics when we talk about the qualities which make Man different from other animals.

There is one trait which does not seem to be mirrored in the animal world and seems to be the unique possession of Man and not a matter of degree: religion.

There are many types, kinds and forms of 'religion' but all of Man's religions have at least one thing in common. All include the notion that living men have some relationship to those of their kind who came before and have perished. Some religions, but not all, include a present-future relationship, an afterlife.

Religion is acknowledgement of time beyond birth and death. Religion is a symptom that Man has claimed a territory which is larger than a single life.

There is one mechanism, very well known in the animal world, which can be stretched to explain Man's unique situation. This mechanism is territoriality.

It has been observed by many naturalists that some animals claim a piece of territory, defend it, and derive 'identity' from their possession. A robin claims about a half-acre of ground and chases other robins off, all except his mate. A bull seal claims a bit of beach as his own and chases all others off, except his mates.

There is another type of territory in the animal world. There is the territory of status in a group. This is called 'dominance' by zoologists, but it is merely another form of territory. A barnyard hen claims and asserts social territory in competition with other hens.

The relative success of competing hens results in a pecking order, but this pecking order is merely a manifestation of the size of social territory. Number 2 hen may peck anyone but Number 1. Number 2 hen has the right to food and choice roosts before any other hen... except Number 1. In a barnyard, then, Number 1 hen has the biggest territory of all, Number 2 has the next biggest territory, Number 3 the next biggest, and so on, down to the luckless hen at the bottom who is pecked by all and can peck no one in return, has the last access to food and the worst roost. Many animals compete for social territory: jackdaws, platys are examples.

Some animals are more complex and assert both kinds of territory at once. Primates tend to do this. A group of monkeys, or men, will claim and defend a geographical territory and will simultaneously compete among themselves within the group for social territory. The group will show aggression against other groups which approach its territory too closely, and, while this is going on, individuals within both groups exhibit aggression against each other in defense of social status. Most animals which are territorial have developed mechanisms to display and release aggression in relatively harmless ways. Howler monkeys provide an excellent example.

When howler monkeys want to display aggression in defense of group territory or individual social status they do not come to blows or bites. They yell. Howler monkeys are specially adapted to yell and their throats boast cartilaginous resonance chambers which enable them to produce an incredible volume of sound. Howlers push each other around by sheer force of decibels.

What is the significance of territoriality? In what way does it assist survival?

Territory, either geographic or social, affects reproduction.

It has been observed that males compete for territory, as a general rule, and females compete with each other to mate with the males who have the most valuable territory. A bull seal will claim a bit of beach and the size of his territory will depend upon his energy and aggressiveness compared to other bull seals. When female seals arrive, they go up onto the beach and perforce end up on some bull's territory. There they mate. It is obvious that the bull with the most territory will therefore mate with the greatest number of females. The bull's relatively greater energy and aggression will be reflected in a relatively greater number of offspring. His superior survival qualities are passed on to a large number of offspring and the species is well served.

The same mechanism is operative in social territory. Female

jackdaws compete to mate with high-ranking males. Jackdaws are monogamous and mate for life. The males compete for relative dominance early in life and establish a rank order much like the pecking order of barnyard hens. After the males have sorted themselves out through the mechanism of aggression, the females compete for marriage with high-ranking males. This process insures that superior males will mate with superior females, average males with average females, inferior males with inferior females. Because jackdaw dominance confers very definite material advantages, just as the pecking order confers the same in the barnyard, lower-ranking pairs, the least successful in the jackdaw world, will tend to die off and therefore leave fewer progeny. The 'best' jackdaw genes are preserved and favoured, because the best breed with the best and because the best get the most of life's requirements.

Territory, usually claimed and defended by aggression, is a selective mechanism designed to allow favourable characteristics to assert themselves.

If we take a biological look at the behaviour which makes us unique in the animal world, I believe that we can explain it by territoriality expressed in a unique dimension: time. Like other primates we indulge in group defense of territory and we indulge in struggles for social status and the benefits it confers. But, unlike other primates, and unlike any other animal, we do this in the past, present and future.

As a very simple example, a scientist, artist, writer or musician may compete with someone who is already dead by seeking to create a better theory of mechanics than Newton, paint a better picture than Rembrandt, write 'the great American novel' and displace Melville's *Moby Dick,* or a musician may wish to express something more profound than Strauss's *Also Spracht Zarathustra* and perhaps come up with five notes that more dramatically express human searching.

At some point a hominid conceived the notion that his dead fellows still had a relationship with him. If we wish to pinpoint *the* significant difference between ourselves and other animals we only have to say that 'Man conceived of time'. Our true specific name should be *Homo temporalis.* I do not pretend to know how or why this happened. Perhaps it has something to do with 'intelligence'. Perhaps the conception is only possible with a certain size of brain, a critical number of synapses. But whatever 'intelligence' has to do with it, the recognition of a past, present and future of one's kind *beyond the twin barriers of birth and death which delineate any one lifetime...* that *is* consciousness. Non-genetic communication across these barriers *is* culture.

When I first offered this explanation of basic human beginnings in *The Cronos Complex* I, published in 1973, I was forced to *assume* that early man did, indeed, possess the capacity to conceive of time. My assumption was based solely upon the existence of purposeful burial among Neanderthals and the metaphysical implications of interment. During the years of my research, 1967 to 1972, I had come across no one who had discovered hard evidence of time-factored activity among the cultures of early man. There was no such evidence at that time.

Ironically, that evidence was supplied in the same year that *The Cronos Complex* I was finalized in manuscript form and was in the process of publication. But I remained ignorant of this evidence for almost six years... something which I bitterly regret because that evidence, if it had been included, would have strengthened considerably the structure of sheer speculation that was *The Cronos Complex* I. And the evidence could have been included.

In 1972, Alexander Marshack's *The Roots of Civilization* was published and it provided the proof that early men, even as early as the Neanderthals, had been capable of conceptualizing time and capable of recording it.

As so often happens with an important breakthrough, the research Marchack originally undertook was intended for something else and directed toward a different goal entirely. He was initially writing a book for NASA about space travel, which is about as far as it is possible to get from paleontology. Marshack's task was to explain Man's progress from the 'beginnings' to the space age. The developments of recent specific technology permitting space travel posed no particular problems for Marshack, but the 'beginnings' of technology and civilization did. Marshack found himself doubting the established view of both the date of human civilized 'beginnings' and the established time-table of civilized development.

The established view was that Man made very little conceptual or technological progress until he settled down to experiment with farming and town life, until the time of 'The Neolithic Revolution'. According to the contemporary view of human development, Man's civilized and cultural start began in the Neolithic. The trouble with this view, and the cause of Marshack's doubt, is that the Neolithic was not so very long ago and, when some men turned to farming and town life about 7,000 B.C., they did so with a fairly sophisticated knowledge of time, measurement and technology. The foundations of this knowledge must have been manifest much earlier, Marshack suspected, perhaps even as early as the Middle Paleolithic... 40,000 to 100,000 years ago.

Armed with his suspicion, Marshack took another look at Paleolithic artifacts and the cave art of Europe. He was able to demonstrate that the scratches and dots on many artifacts were not mere decoration, but corresponded to notations of lunar cycles. Early man had noted and recorded the phases of the moon. The oldest time-factored notation that Marshack discovered dated from the Neanderthal period of about 50,000 years ago... about the same time as the Neanderthals exhibited deliberate interment.

Marshack was able to prove by brilliant and imaginative statistical analysis of art and artifacts what I had had to assume on the basis of the metaphysical implications of burial. Early man had conceptualized time, was aware of time, and recorded it.

Marshack's immense contribution amounts to a revolution in our understanding of Man's cognitive development. The beginnings of Man's culture and civilization must now be regarded not as a mere technological progression, but as *effects* proceeding from Man's psychological response to his discovery of time. The roots of civilization are firmly planted in a matrix of time-factored living.

No other animal has given evidence of conceiving of time-factored living transcending individual birth and death.

But human beings are not only, or perhaps even mostly, metaphysical and time-factored creatures. We are, morphologically, related to the ground-living omnivorous apes, like drills and baboons. Such apes are highly territorial and highly aggressive.

Being from a territorial family, it was natural and inevitable that we would apply territorial behaviour to the newly conceptualized dimension of time. It was to become a new field for the display and development of dominance.

Our first requirement, once having conceived of this new type of territory, was to 'claim' it. Somehow, we had to establish contact with others of our own kind who inhabited the past. We had to contact our dead. We invented religion. It was our first symptom of temporal assertion and, as we have noted, it is a unique symptom in the animal world. We began to bury our dead, to take care of them and send them through the barrier of death with adequate supplies and equipment for their 'future' afterlife. We buried food and implements with them. We buried them, or otherwise disposed of them, in ways which were symbolic and reflective of cycles rather than of merely an ending. The Neanderthals buried their dead with east-west orientation. True, the sun was born this morning and died this evening, but, somehow, it would be born again. Days were like lifetimes, separate, yes, but part of an endless continuity that stretched far back into the past and would extend into the future. The Neanderthals chose the east-west-oriented burial, but other peoples may have chosen scaffold burials (to elevate the dead closer to the cyclical heavens) which have left no trace.

Doubtless, very soon after we began burying our dead and sending them to their future prepared, we began paying attention to those who claimed to understand this strange territory of time. They could better tell us where the dead had gone, where we ourselves would someday go, and they could make the dark journey of death somewhat less frightening. They understood time and they could affirm the continuity of life which remained undefeated by individual death. They were shamans, later priests.

If these people understood time and death better, they were probably a bit more intelligent than their fellows. Perhaps their brains were a bit bigger, or had a few more cells, or happened to possess some abnormal cellular circuiting which permitted the recognition of more — and more subtle — relationships. And, because we needed them to communicate with our dead, and ease the fear of our own inevitable death, we supported them as best we could and ensured their survival if possible. When we invented religion we structured a 'haven' from biological selection and we began to preserve exceptional intelligence.

The shaman could contribute to group survival because of his intelligence. Although the shaman might not have been an exceptional hunter, for example, he might be aware of patterns of animal behaviour and assist the hunters to become successful. He might have conceived the idea of disguise in an animal skin which would allow the hunter to approach his prey more closely. The shaman's magic of shape-changing, assuming the form and behaviour of an animal, taught to the hunters through ritual hunting dances, may have significantly increased the number of kills. If the survival of the group became more secure because of this, the group had a bit more margin to support yet more exceptional intelligence.

This is a greatly simplified schematic of the process. A fuller presentation was the subject of *The Cronos Complex* I and it is necessary here only to draw an outline.

But it can be seen that this preservation of exceptional

intelligence, once begun, tends to become a geometrical function. In time, we began to structure other havens besides religion for exceptional intelligence. Shamans became priests and priests invented writing so that we could not only communicate with the dead, but leave messages for the yet-to-be-born. Probably, persons of exceptional temporal awareness broached the idea of growing food and raising animals against *future* need. Eventually, we could support artists, musicians, writers and people who could supervise our labour and administer the group for still greater efficiency, greater opportunity for existing in the intellectual world.

It is not difficult to see how we came from the first graveside, the Neanderthal burial at Le Moustière, 50,000 or 60,000 years ago, to the present level of technology.

The non-genetic way in which we communicate with past and future, and bind them into a continuity with the present, is culture.

We think of culture as 'good', but it is not wholly so. It is a remarkable biological adaptation allowing the communication of minds and hearts across the barriers of birth and death and it is precious insofar as it allows us to love more fully and more deeply.

But culture is also the medium of communication of aggression, and across the same biological barriers.

We are territorial animals. Having claimed time and established contact with the past and the future, our territorial behaviour demanded that we invent ways of protecting ourselves from both. The territory of each human generation, each 'present tense', had to be asserted with respect to the past and defended with respect to the future. Each generation must strive for a place in the 'pecking order' of history, each generation must strive to be unique.

Each generation must progress with respect to the past, and prevent the younger generation from progressing with respect to itself. The past must be surpassed and the future must be held back. As was said many pages ago, we developed mechanisms to 'hold the future back' and prevent its being significantly different from ourselves in order to protect our 'present tense' identities. Warfare, morals, custom, caste systems and the tradition of hereditary occupations are, or can be, 'future-limiting' mechanisms. It is obvious that we surpass the past through technological and cultural progress. We develop those things which the past did not and assert our unique identity.

And I gave my opinion many pages ago that the crises of the contemporary world have the following psychobiological profile: activities which were once wholly 'past-surpassing', like industry and technology, were found to have inherent future-limiting possibilities. These, allied to traditional future-limiting possibilities. These allied to traditional future-limiting mechanisms, have brought the world to the brink of several simultaneous disasters. We live in a world where the future is not only threatened by war, it is threatened by progress.

I maintained in *The Cronos Complex* I that all men share temporal aggression and the penchant for progress, although it is obvious that we do not all exhibit the same degree of temporally motivated behaviour. I believe that there are two major factors which can modify this behaviour: environment and sexual-sensual adaptation.

Some groups of men had the misfortune to be indigenous to — or were forced to migrate into — geographical areas which offered harsh environments generally or which posed special problems. In these cases, the difficulty of physical or cultural survival was a limiting factor to the preservation of a 'critical mass' of intelligence. Some environments, either through harshness and lack of resources, or because of geographical peculiarities, kept human groups too small to achieve the division of labour necessary to a sufficiently large intelligence pool which would lead to high culture or 'civilization'. Australia and Tasmania are examples of exceptionally harsh environments. Aborigine groups are very small and are forced to be nomadic because the land will support very few people per square mile. Under such conditions, Australoid culture could never get off the ground and the full human potential for temporal communication was never reached. The Aborigines remained restricted to a very primitive past-present orientation. They never had an opportunity to develop the present-future communication that comes with writing.

The Polynesians represent a human group thwarted by a sufficiently rich environment, but one with restrictive geographical characteristics. The Polynesians were apparently forced to migrate out into the Pacific where numerous islands, some of which were extremely favourable for human habitation and some of which were marginal, dispersed this people into relatively small groups. Communication was maintained between the islands, thanks to an immensely complex navigational culture, and a certain degree of linguistic and cultural cohesiveness was preserved against all odds, but the diffused population never reached critical mass in any one place. The Polynesians were, however, considerably more fortunate environmentally than the Australian Aborigines and were able to develop a very sophisticated past-present culture. If the Easter

Island *rongo rongo* are any guide, some Polynesians may have been on the verge of establishing present-future communication through writing.

Woodland Amerindians present some similarities with the Polynesians. They entered into an immensely challenging environment of virgin forest, evolved agriculture and sophisticated culture and politics, walled towns, and were apparently on the verge of inventing writing when the white man arrived. It has recently been discovered that the Hurons had birchbark scrolls of what might be called proto-writing. [7]

The Benin and other West African nations developed high technological and artistic cultures after having recently entered a virgin and challenging environment. The ruins in Rhodesia, called 'Zimbabwe', are evidence of a 'Capoid' or 'Congoid' culture equal to, or slightly superior to, the culture of Catal Huyuk which stands near the base of Caucasoid civilization.

Migrating into a new environment, as the Amerindians, Polynesians and many Africans did, or being forced into marginal environments, a fate suffered by Australoids and Capoids, can retard culture or cause it to regress.

Another factor which modifies the common human tendency toward temporal assertion and a full three-tense continuum of culture is sexual-sensual adaptation.

If we are temporally territorial and must assert our present identity against both past and future we must also have reservations about bring the future into being if it is going to surpass us. Temporal awareness, as we saw illustrated allegorically in the Cronos myth, makes humans realize that offspring will be an identity-threat. Why bring such a threat into existence at all? Why reproduce?

As we know, some extremely intelligent people, or those who wish to live in the purely spiritual and mental world of time, *do not*, statistically, reproduce. Geniuses are statistically sterile, some religious functionaries are celibate. There are two opposite biological explanations for this non-reproductive behaviour. First, just as a seal who does not assert its personal territory is likely to have less biological relevance, so it may be that a person who isn't chauvinistically assertive of his own lifetime will be less likely to leave a genetic imprint. Or, this non-reproductive behaviour may be a purely intellectual decision: the demands of the material world, exaggerated by offspring, keep one from being able to inhabit the world of Mind fully. Both factors may be operative on different levels.

But even the unexceptional average man experiences approach-avoidance when it comes to sex and reproduction. Nature has provided human beings with a number of sexual-sensual adaptations which compensate for the normal reproductive hesitation of us temporally territorial creatures. These adaptations were outlined in titillating detail by Desmond Morris in *The Naked Ape.*

Alone among animals our females' breasts stick out all year round, and not just when nursing. Rare among mammals, we are more or less naked in the interests of greater tactile sensitivity. Our sexual organs are proportionally the largest by far among primates. The gorilla, which may reach 6 feet in height and weigh 600 pounds, has a penis only an inch long. And our larger sex organs are richly supplied with nerve synapses for increased sensitivity. Primate periodicity works to ensure that sexual intercourse has maximum chance of resulting in offspring.

Nature tempts us to get together and, when we do, works to ensure that conception will likely result. Nature combats our temporal territorial approach-avoidance, and attendant frustration, with pleasure. Our natural temporal aggression is dissipated by sexual adaptations unrivalled for pleasure-giving in the animal world.

It may be mentioned here that primate frustration and aggression have generally been absorbed by sex. Especially ground apes, like drills and baboons, almost invariably have intercourse after or during squabbles for dominance. Both males and females seek sex after frustrating or aggressive situations.

Nature apparently supplied us with very sophisticated sexual adaptations in order to absorb and displace temporal aggression in general and our unique hesitation about reproduction, also occasioned by temporal awareness. Perhaps the depth of these frustrations and confusions and aggressions can be gauged by the fact that baboon intercourse lasts for about five seconds, whereas ours requires some minutes.

In addition to these generalized sexual adaptations common to all people to a lesser or greater degree, Nature has evolved certain racial adaptations for some 'major groups' of people. The Mongoloids have less body hair than any other race. Perhaps this increases their tactile sensitivity. The Bushmen and Hottentots are supplied with an enlarged labia minora, the 'Hottentot apron', and with a continually semi-erect penis. Negroids have large sex organs.

And what about us Caucasoids?

Perhaps, after this long bio-philosophical detour, it will be easy to see that Nature's sexual adaptations conflicted in large measure with Neanderthal glacial adaptations... and easy to see the grave implications of this.

We may assume that the Neanderthals were not naked apes, like other men, or at least not nearly so naked. They needed their pelt for sheer survival. Neanderthals were robbed of some tactile sensitivity. In the interests of cold-weather survival Neanderthals could not sport vulnerable extremities. No larger penises for them, no Hottentot aprons.

Still, I believe that Nature did what it could. Insofar as was possible, I think that the women became less hairy and perhaps, in compensation, even a little rounder. Breasts, on this body-type, would have to become greatly exaggerated in order to fulfil their tactile and stimulatory function. Neanderthal men were hairier by far than their women, while the women may have been extremely plump and large-breasted. We will note in passing that female *Kaptar* and *Almas* are reported to have very large breasts for their size and to be less hairy than the males.

If this was the case, and Neanderthal sexual adaptations followed my train of logic, then it is easy to see how we Caucasoids look the way we do. Our sexual dimorphism is great and affects the *general appearance* of the sexes and not just the sex organs. To hark back for a moment to the 'Venus figurines', we now have more theoretical reason to believe that they truly reflected glacial female bodies.

We retain vestiges of Neanderthal dimorphism. Our men are considerably hairier than our women. Our women are shorter, hippy and large-breasted.

Nature did what it could considering survival characteristics that could not be altered, but I think that our inadequate sexual-sensual adaptations caused another problem while only partially alleviating the original one.

The Neanderthals already had a high degree of sexual dimorphism and the patchwork sexual adaptations only emphasized it. I'm inclined to believe that the sexes looked different enough that each tended to regard the other as something of a distinct species. I think that there may have been grave difficulties in each sex recognizing the other to be completely human. Among the Neanderthals there could not have been as much sexual solidarity as among other races of Man.

Even our lesser Caucasoid degree of sexual dimorphism has

resulted in a noticeable amount of sexual conflict. Long before *Lysistrata* and Aristophanes, Caucasoids must have been aware of a continual, low-grade war of the sexes. Caucasoid sexes have never really got used to each other, never really completely trusted each other. Given the delicate balance of approach-avoidance generated by temporal territorial behaviour, and the aggression surrounding sexual encounters, it is obvious that a high degree of sexual dimorphism would tend to heighten the very aggression and frustration that sexual adaptations were intended to absorb.

I remember listening to an interview with Susan Brownmiller, author of *Against Our Will; Men, Women and Rape*. Brownmiller was describing rape, accurately, as a crime of violence and power. Rape is sexual aggression. If I remember correctly, the interviewer was Barbara Frum and the show was CBC Radio's 'As It Happens'. Frum asked Brownmiller at the end of the interview, "What have men got against women?" Brownmiller answered, "I wish I knew". I think that the temporal aggression surrounding human reproduction is the answer. Because males have generally been more territorially assertive, it would seem reasonable that males would be more temporally aggressive than females and would approach the act of reproduction (and the consequences) with a greater degree of anger and frustration. This might be 'normal' to all human males, but increased sexual dimorphism could be expected to provoke greater sexual aggression. Therefore, it might be a valid assumption that rape within major groups would likely occur most frequently among Caucasoids, while rapes between major groups in time of conflict would be more common.

It is relevant, if disturbing, to note here that Marshack's study of European cave art uncovered much evidence of violence directed toward females, and especially *pregnant* females, in company with time-factored notations. A drawing of a pregnant mare in the cave of La Pileta (Malaga) shows several sets of double-wound marks painted on the mare's stomach. These marks were made at different times and may represent ritual violence practised at seasonal ceremonies.

Marks corresponding to the 'wound marks' applied to the mare at La Pileta have also been discovered on Venus figurines depicting pregnant women. The marks, which are also time-factored notations, occur on the breasts and stomachs of the figurines. It may be that the marks applied to the figurines were duplicated by wounds on real women, for the same reasons and in the same places. Such marks may, in fact, give us a clue about the significance of tattooing and ritual disfigurement.

But, however that may be, the evolutionary and environmental experiences of the Neanderthal-Caucasoid stock suggest that this major group of Mankind may be psychosexually and physically-sexually maladapted compared to other races. Sexual dimorphism on the one hand, and the smothering of sexual-sensual adaptations under glacial ones on the other hand, may have combined to render Caucasoids slightly more frustrated sexually with a slightly higher degree of sexual approach-avoidance and aggression; perhaps more alienated because of the difference in appearance between helpmates; and possessing a greater amount of undisplaced temporal territorial aggression.

It would seem reasonable to speculate that Neanderthal-Caucasoid sexual dimorphism has resulted in somewhat more sensitivity to the physical differences existing between major groups of human beings, *and is therefore the root of both our penchant for sexism and our penchant for racism.*

I do not mean to suggest that the Neanderthal-Caucasoid psychobiological characteristics are absolutely compelling. But I do believe that a reasonable argument can be made for the proposition that these psychobiological characteristics are sufficiently strong that, over the course of many generations, they have made an identifiable impact upon human history. This does not mean that all Caucasoids are always more aggressive and sexually maladapted than people of other major groups, but I think it is reasonable to speculate that, as a group, the Neanderthal-Caucasoids manifest these tendencies strongly and consistently enough that the profile of the contemporary world becomes explicable.

Alone among major groups of men, we Neanderthal-Caucasoids crossed the *sapiens* threshold... and succumbed to the common cronos complex... in a glacial environment. Our necessary glacial adaptations largely cancelled out those common human sexual adaptations intended to relieve the worst symptoms of the cronos complex. We were deprived of much of the power of Nature's talisman against Man's potentially self-destructive behaviour.

A uniquely aggressive creature shivered beside his cave fire during icy Würm, a uniquely alienated creature, a creature uniquely conscious of physical differences among people... and distrustful of those differences. It has always seemed to me that a few lines by Canadian poet Leonard Cohen describe well the crises that this creature's dilemma would become:

Yes, you, who must leave everything
That you cannot control.
It begins with your family, but
Soon it comes 'round to your soul.
Well, I've been where you're hanging and
I think I can see how you're pinned.
When you're not feeling holy
Your loneliness says that you've sinned.

Part Three

*The
Iceman
Inheritance*

7

The Iceman Inheritance:
Love and Expression

We will take a brief respite from the hardness of bones and purely
material evidence of Western man's maladaptations and look inside
the psyche of this uniquely alienated creature who has historically
hung, writhing, pinned somewhere between loneliness and holiness.

We are told that 'love makes the world go round', or that 'what
the world needs now is love, sweet love.' 'Love', as undefinable as it
is, has been enshrined as the goal of both personal satisfaction and
harmony with the eternal. 'Love' is so central to Western culture
that, in spite of the fact that we cannot define it, no one doubts its
existence or importance. The concept is so familiar to us, so
intimately associated with our most important aspirations, that we
may be excused for assuming that the concept of 'love' is universal to
all Mankind.

It may come as something of a shock, therefore, to discover that
most of Mankind is innocent of anything like the Western notion of
'love'. Whatever it is that we mean by 'love', it is simply irrelevant to
most of Mankind. The Chinese do not even have a word
corresponding to 'love'. The Ancient Egyptians' two favourite words
and concepts were 'ankh' (life) and 'djed' (stability). There is a
good deal of uncertainty about whether the Ancient Egyptians even
possessed something similar to our idea of 'love', but, if they did, the
notion did not enjoy the degree of importance it boasts in our

culture. It is difficult to find either words or concepts analogous to 'love' among the languages and peoples of Africa and the New World.

Indeed, it has been the proud claim that in addition to the gospel, Christian missionaries introduced 'love' to previously benighted non-Western peoples.

Perhaps it is time to analyse our notion of 'love' from a psychobiological perspective. As a more or less uniquely Western invention, 'love' must somehow be connected with our evolutionary experience and with our peculiar motivational requirements.

If we will accept tentatively the argument that territorial behaviour in the dimension of time must cause ambivalence toward sex and reproduction, and if we accept the corollary proposition that aggression and frustration result from this ambivalence... then the identity of 'love' begins to take shape. If we further accept the argument that Western man suffers *more* sexual-reproductive aggression and frustration due to glacial adaptations conflicting with sexual ones, then it becomes clear why 'love' is so important in the West.

'Love' is that middle ground between aggression and the ability to reproduce. 'Love' is that place where we can feel unthreatened in sex, and the place where we can have sex without directing aggression toward our partner. The place where 'sex' and 'respect' can co-exist, for both ourselves and our partners. Given the greater degree of reproductive threat for Western man, and given the greater degree of consequent frustration and aggression, that place called 'love' can be very small and exclusive, but of utmost personal importance.

It is not surprising, therefore, that love dominates our prose, our poetry, the lyrics of pop songs and much day-to-day conversation. The necessity of finding that small area of truce where the imperative of reproduction balances our fear and aggression is the primary task of each Western individual and the importance of that search is reflected throughout all levels of our culture.

When the search is successful, a 'pair-bond' is formed. The fact that a pair-bond is, simultaneously, a gravitation toward sexual reproduction and a mutual escape from aggression has been well-known to students of both animal and human behaviour for a long time.

A pair-bond, 'love', is displaced aggression. It is aggression 'shoved aside', literally, so that the partners can reproduce without threat.

Courtship is the subtle process whereby initial and natural aggression is 'turned aside' so that, in the end, the courting partners stand side by side to face the world with their combined and allied aggression directed outward. Courtship can be a lengthy and anxiety-provoking process in the West. 'Falling in love' is a more or less traumatic event filled with uncertainties, 'lovers' quarrels', 'playful fighting', etc.

The courtship antics of Western man differ little from the courtship process common to all pair-bonding species. Konrad Lorenz has studied the courtship ceremonies of creatures as diverse as cichlid fishes and geese and has demonstrated through behavioural analysis that courtship ceremonies are ritualized fighting. The courting partners begin their relationship by aggressive 'sparring' with each other, with fighting motions directed toward each other. But, as courtship progresses, the aggressive movements are directed increasingly 'to the side' of the partner until, eventually, the courting pair find themselves side by side with their combined aggression directed outwards. Their aggression has been displaced, in a very literal sense and by movements which can be measured, until the pair stands together in a small place free of aggression or threat emanating from either toward the other.

The fascinating analysis of this process is fully covered in Konrad Lorenz's *On Aggression* under the chapter entitled 'The Bond' (pages 141 to 188, the Methuen 'University Paperback' edition).

The interesting problem in applying aggressive pair-bonding to human beings as a whole is that human beings are closely related to a group of animals, the great apes, which are not, strictly speaking, always pair-bonded. Among the great apes, only the gibbon appears to be strictly pair-bonded. Chimpanzees, gorillas and orang-utans all show some modest tendency toward polygamy.

Although Man is morphologically related to the great apes, Man's natural habitat and some aspects of his morphology would seemingly place him closer in 'psyche' to some of the ground-living apes like baboons and drills... and these apes are not at all monogamous.

Regarded in their totality before the enforced dominance of Western culture, human beings exhibited a rather modest tendency toward polygamy, like the other anthropoid apes. Occasionally, human beings insisted upon the more exuberant polygamy characteristic of the ground apes.

Only in the West has monogamy been consistently, and at least nominally, enshrined as the 'norm.' We may wonder why this is, and whether it has something to do with 'love.'

If it be granted that Western man suffers from a higher level of sexual-reproductive ambivalence, threat, frustration and aggression... then it becomes obvious that these forces cannot be neutralized easily or with just anyone. The psychosexual 'truce' that we call love will be a relatively rare occurrence between any two partners. Such a truce may be negotiated with only one or two partners in the course of an individual's life. The higher level of threat and aggression may be difficult to neutralize, if it is neutralized at all, and few partners of all the biologically available ones will be inclined, or able, to enter into successful negotiations of the psychosexual 'truce' permitting pair-bonding.

Perhaps we are now willing to grant that our curious Western concept of 'love', and the monogamy 'love' demands, are merely adaptations and behaviour patterns impelled by our evolutionary experience, our iceman's maladaptations.

The delicacy of the reproductive-aggressive balance, and the consequent extreme difficulty in finding a partner who is psycho-biologically compatible and with whom one can negotiate a successful pair-bonding, has forced Westerners to institutionalize behaviour and attitudes which are not typical of the human norm.

Among all peoples there is a degree of courtship between mating individuals, but generally the choice of partner is severely limited by group or family taboos. Sometimes there is no choice at all because the complexity of the taboo structure may narrow the field of available partners down to just one permissible candidate. Or, if the individual's choice isn't restricted by a taboo structure, a marriage between partners may be arranged long before the partners themselves have reached reproductive age. Courtship among most human groups consists of a formalized ritual between partners who have been destined for each other by either social conventions or family decisions.

In the West, too, arranged marriages have been common. But there has always been an enduring tradition that the arrangement dictated by society or family may prove intolerable to the individuals involved. In the West, it has always been recognized that the pair-bond is a delicate and personal matter, and not only a social and family matter. It is understood and agreed that individuals have the 'right' and 'obligation' to rebel against social and familial convention to pair with a partner of their choice. Perhaps it is not too much of an exaggeration to say that most Western literature deals with the 'love conquers all' theme in which two partners strive against great odds and convention to effect a pair-bonding tolerable to them as individuals.

This sort of 'love conquers all' theme is exceedingly rare in the literature and traditions of non-Western peoples.

We have touched upon literature very briefly and we will return to take a closer look at that medium of expression later, but, for now, we will take a short detour to remark upon the association of 'love' and the Western insistence upon 'the freedom and independence of the individual'.

Effecting reproduction is the fundamental business of all creatures. From a purely biological point of view, reproduction *is* the justification for living. Although Man is not a purely biological creature, the business of reproduction is still of crucial, if not total, importance.

We have seen that the higher level of aggression in Western man has forced and institutionalized a higher degree of permitted individualism in searching for a suitable partner. Since finding reproductive partners is of such fundamental importance in the life of any creature, it is not at all surprising that our permitted individualism in pair-bonding has tended to institutionalize a higher degree of individualism in other aspects of living as well. Just as we have been forced to concede a higher level of individual choice and 'input' in the important sphere of basic family and reproductive relationships, so have we automatically extended the notion of individuality in wider social relationships.

Thus we see, by various stages, that our Western ideal of freedom and dignity of the individual proceeds from a higher level of psychosexual alienation due to physical adaptations to a glacial environment, and proceeds from the higher level of undisplaced aggression resulting from an evolutionary experience unique to our 'major group' of Mankind.

To return to 'love'. So far, we have dealt with sexual-reproductive behaviour. We have looked at the kind of 'love' which the Greeks called *eros*.

But our Western concept of 'love' has been applied also to non-sexual and non-reproductive behaviour and orientation. We have 'brotherly love', or 'platonic love', or 'love of God'... what the Greeks called *agapé*.

We do not call both things 'love' by accident, although it is recognized that *eros* and *agapé* are not only dissimilar, but also antithetical.

Why do we in the West recognize the similarity of *eros* and *agapé*, and why do we call both 'love'... even though we realize that the two concepts are, in some ways, opposites?

Perhaps we will get a glimmering of an answer if we return to the cronos complex and the beginning of temporal awareness. As was said earlier, Man's recognition of time forced conflicting realizations upon humanity. Man became aware of a continuum that transcended birth and death and realized that each individual was a part of that eternal continuum. At the same time, and in spite of being a part of 'eternity', Man's thought, energy and behaviour were also mortgaged to the brutal business of surviving, and reproducing, in the biological and material world. The conception of time was, and is, a brutal and soul-tearing reality. There is the desire to become a part of a gentle human continuity consisting of past-present-future relationships and reunions with those who have died and those yet to be born... and at same time there is the biological necessity to survive and to assert our temporal territory so that we may reproduce and preserve that continuity. The paradox and the irony is that to preserve the continuity biologically, our territorial mechanisms force us to do violence to nature, our fellow men and to the integrity of the continuity itself. Territorial law demands that the territory must be defended before we gain the identity and the confidence to reproduce. But, with temporal territory, our territorial adversaries are our own past and future... the dead and the yet-to-be-born whom we love.

The outlines of *agapé* become biologically clear. Just as the 'love' we call *eros* allows us to reproduce in the face of threat and aggression, so the 'love' we call *agapé* allows us to live in the material world while yearning for the relationships awaiting us in eternity. *Agapé* is that place where the needs of material survival are met while the realization of a past-present-future continuity is preserved.

It is worth noting that *agapé* has never been as popular as *eros*. Most people are capable of negotiating some form of 'love' permitting more or less aggression-free reproduction, but fewer people are capable of appreciating *agapé*, the 'love' of life itself. One has to be sensitive enough to be aware of the continuity of past-present-future, and one has to be relatively non-territorial in terms of biological behaviour, in order to appreciate the 'love' we call *agapé*. And those conditions mean, by biological definition, that the individual possessing those characteristics will likely be non-reproductive. We should not be surprised, therefore, to learn that the 'love' called *agapé* is that thing which celibate priests and religious functionaries are always, and more or less vainly, trying to explain to *eros*-dominated Western man.

We have seen that the high level of sexual-reproductive ambivalence among Neanderthal-Caucasoids is such that even successful *eros* is very difficult to attain. We may be excused, I think, for failing to attain an appreciation of *agapé* in significant numbers.

It may be granted now that 'love', including both *agapé* and *eros,* are special adaptations of Western man demanded by his psychobiology. If they have not been invented by other groups of Mankind, and they have not, it is because the rest of Mankind does not require these adaptations. The non-Western majority of Mankind is not so aggressive. The non-Western majority of Mankind does not share the Neanderthal-Caucasoid maladaptations.

Without 'love', non-Western peoples have proved able to reproduce in a relatively untraumatic manner according to socially convenient conventions. They have made do with the notion of 'compassion' and with the reverence for stability. Loveless, the majority of Mankind has succeeded in constructing enduring societies of an environmentally tolerable nature.

With 'love', we have done much worse.

It is at least arguable that what the world needs now is 'love, sweet love.' 'Love' as a symptom of, and compensation for, Western psychobiological maladaptation has done at least as much harm as good. On a purely personal and inter-sexual level, love is, as certain feminists have noted, 'a four-letter word'. Much connected with the Western notion of 'love' has proved inhumane.

We observed many pages ago that the territorial urge in most species works through the male. In human beings, the temporal territorial urge apparently operates mostly through the male and we have noted the frequency of aberrant male psychosexual activity which indicates the strength of sexual-reproductive ambivalence. In Western man this is even more pronounced, as we have seen.

It is not particularly surprising, therefore, that the negotiation of the 'truce' of 'love' permitting more or less aggression-free reproduction has often taken the form of female surrender, rather than an equal truce. Our Western notion of 'love' has traditionally involved immense restrictions upon female behaviour and the development of female social rights and individual personalities.

The forms of this restriction have been too numerous, and are too obvious, to deserve much discussion. But it may be justifiable to note that in the 'loveless' non-Western societies which we criticize for having 'no respect for human life', the status of women has usually been higher than in our own. Women had more personal and property rights in XVIII Dynasty Egypt than in Victorian England. When the 'advanced' Victorian English opened up backward China in the mid-19th Century, one of the peculiar things the English found was that Chinese women could own property in their own names... while in progressive England women were chattel and could own nothing.

Because Western males have been so threatened by sexual-reproductive activity, the 'truce' of 'love' has historically involved the curious notion that women could not, or should not, respond enthusiastically. Female response is frightening to Neanderthal-Caucasoid males and reminds them too clearly of the threat that reproduction represents. In consequence, Western culture has institutionalized the protective adaptation that women must at least *appear* to shrink from sexual encounters, must at least *appear* to be vulnerable and must *appear* to fail to enjoy sex. This is, of course, a mythical restructuring of the 'natural' female personality. Yet, it was a lie told so often that it began to be believed. Until recently, there was apparently serious debate about the female capacity to achieve 'orgasm'. As late as 1972 it was still possible to read in an 'advanced' publication like *Playboy* a discussion among 'experts' as to whether multiple female orgasms were possible, since, by then, the existence of the 'single-orgasm female' had been established.

The problem of female sexual response has never been physiological. It has been cultural. Almost every aspect of female expression, including sexual expression, has been sacrificed to the psychobiological protective adaptations required by Neanderthal-Caucasoid males.

On a much broader social level the Western concept of 'love' has brought inhumane repercussions. We have demanded all the female restrictions involved in 'love' and we have proved intolerant and hideously cruel when the restrictions have been removed... and when common human compassion has been substituted for 'love'.

In order to understand what follows in terms of psychobiological analysis, we have to remember that both *eros* and *agapé* represent places in which ambivalence is balanced and neutralized. Yet, we also have to realize that *eros* is an affront to *agapé*. Those, like non-biological and celibate priests and functionaries, who appreciate *agapé* have a great animosity for the reproductive and crassly 'material' activities of *eros*. Physical love is an affront to those who presume to dwell in eternity and who claim to have an intimate understanding with God. For non-biological priests and religious functionaries, *eros* and reproduction constitute, at best, something tolerable. Sex under the impetus of *eros,* and without at least the justification of reproduction, is intolerable. Along with the affront that material, sexual reproduction represents, there has always been a deep suspicion of women as 'temptresses'. The myth of female non-enjoyment of sex was institutionalized, but, deep down, everyone in the Western male world knew it was a myth.

The solution was to keep female personality and expression restricted, to tolerate sex only when justified by reproduction, to keep women defined only as vehicles for necessary, but somewhat distasteful, reproductive duties... and to institutionalize everything 'powerful' and 'good' as male, including the Godhead itself.

And, since the fall of Rome and the final flickering out of the Ancient World built on Ancient Egyptian lines, that pattern has been the cultural foundation of the West... but there have been rebellions of humanity and compassion.

The Albigensian Crusade involved such a rebellion. It was a struggle between the Western concept of 'love' and a foreign influence of compassion. Compassion lost.

Steven Runciman, in his *History of the Crusades,* states that the Albigensians were 'Western Buddhists', while other scholars believe that they were more or less Christian. While both views are defensible, there are still other experts who believe that the Albigensians were Sufis who had a philosophy of human spiritual development and fulfilment which could be adapted to any formalized religious 'shell', as the Sufis say. It is known for certain that the beliefs of the Albigensians came to southern France from the East.

The philosophy, whatever it was and whatever its origin, lodged in southern France in the province of Languedoc. There, blessed by a temperate climate, a civilization developed based upon a philosophy and way of life completely alien to the West.

In contrast to the totally male domination of the Church in Catholic Europe, the leaders of the Albigensian civilization were *perfecti,* or 'completed ones', and the ranks of the *perfecti* included both men and women. In fact, by the time the Church launched the crusade against the Albigensian heresy, there were rather more women *perfecti* than male *perfecti.*

The *perfecti* preached no formal religious creed. Rather, they were teachers and 'masters' in the Buddhist or 'Eastern' manner. Ascetic and virtuous themselves, they encouraged the development of tolerance and compassion toward all fellow men (and women), and toward non-human species. 'Catharism', as the Albigensian heresy was called, was an appealing philosophy that captivated Europe's nobility and intelligentsia. In spite of the destruction of the civilization built upon 'Catharism', the philosophy itself, and its literature, survived to influence Western thinkers and even some priests. Gentle St. Francis was, by the evidence of contemporary writers, a 'Cathar' as well as a Catholic deacon.

With a gentle climate and a gentle and humanistic philosophy, Catharism in southern France blossomed into a prosperous and enlightened civilization centred in the area of Montségur. Too prosperous. Too enlightened.

Catharism and the Albigensian civilization might have been left alone to flourish in peace in one small, mountainous corner of Europe had the culture not called attention to itself with the creation of a literary form so beautiful that it immediately enraptured barbaric Europe... even if the message of that literature was rarely understood. The literary form that evolved in the French province of Languedoc (i.e., langue d'oc — 'tongue of the West') was a poetry in the vernacular which we have come to call, in gross distortion, poems of 'courtly love'. But the original meaning of the Albigensian *amour courtoise* can be more correctly rendered as 'gentle love', as opposed to that rather ungentle and restrictive 'love' that we have analysed and which is characteristic of the West.

Troubadors from Languedoc, and later from other areas embracing Catharism, spread across Europe as minstrels and sang their ballads about the kind of regard and compassion that *could* be applied to women specifically and to life in general. Often, as a literary device, 'life' and the human 'spirit' were personified in a woman's name and the ballad of compassion and respect sung to 'her'. There is little doubt that, in addition to the message of compassion and respect, many of the ballads also referred allegorically to the old, pre-Christian worship of the Earth Mother.

'Courtly love' as proselytized by the Troubadors turned Europe's eyes toward the Cathar civilization of southern France. There, the Norman barons of the north saw a rich and militarily weak culture ripe for the picking. There, the Church saw heresy.

The male-dominated Catholic Church saw male and female 'completed ones' held in equal respect, saw a way of life so successful and brilliant without the benefit of male-dominated Judeo-Christian dogma that it must be destroyed. More especially, destruction of the *perfecti* was necessary because the corrupted clergy of the Church suffered by comparison with the undoubted virtue, asceticism and integrity of the Albigensian teachers.

A crusade, the *first* crusade of many, was initiated by Pope Alexander II in 1163. It was the first time that Western psychosexual and religious intolerance was institutionalized as *the* proper spiritual orientation of an entire continent. One historian, Maurice Magre, has declared that the holy war against the Albigensians was the greatest single turning point in the religious history of Mankind. Magre may be correct if we consider that this first crusade began a justification for Western expansion that was not discredited until the middle of the 20th Century when 'missionary zeal' lost much of its currency. We should not forget that the nominal justification for *all* European colonialism was, originally, religious. Africa, the New World and the Far East were invaded, and exploited, under the pretext of 'saving the souls' of the 'natives'. The war against the Albigensians was the first step in institutionalizing and justifying expansive Western psychosexual intolerance and aggression.

Norman troops under the command of Simon de Montfort destroyed the Albigensian civilization.

Terrible cruelty was unleashed against the *real* enemy of the Church... the free women *perfecti*. The psychosexual nature of the conflict demanded that the women *perfecti* die at flaming stakes or in agony on the rack.

Western man, that creature pinned, as Leonard Cohen would have it, between loneliness and holiness, extracted a terrible price for his discomfort... and continues to do so throughout the world.

Catharism vanished from the West as a culture, but the literature of the Troubadors survived. Within that literature lay the seeds of 'gentle love', seeds which might germinate at any time to sow another Albigensian heresy. At first, the Church sought to eradicate the literary form itself, but this effort proved impossible. Rude Europe, barely awakened from the ugliness of the Dark Ages, petulantly refused to surrender a literary form which represented some small token of beauty.

The Church then undertook to subvert the message of 'gentle love' and to distort the ballads into 'courtly love'... and that is the form in which we study this literature today. Instead of the Cathar ideal of free women who could attain personal and spiritual 'completion' in equality with men, the Church-approved 'courtly love' substituted adoration of pallidly virtuous and essentially powerless women. The Church transformed the Cathar ideal of compassion into a reverence for an asexual *agapé* which restricted female personality development and sexual expression. From the status of total spiritual and social equality under the Catharism of Languedoc, the women celebrated in the ballads of Church-approved 'courtly love' became transparent and impotent creatures whose only recommendation was the preservation of anatomical virginity. Thus, the Church was able to keep women in the place which Western psychosexual maladjustment intended for them by using and distorting a tradition which had originally offered freedom.

In our own time of permissiveness, many people in the West seem tempted to look back upon 'courtly love' with fond nostalgia, believing it, in error, to have been an epoch of a sort of vague respect for women coupled with enjoyable romanticism. The era of Church-approved 'courtly love', as most contemporary feminists would agree, was in actuality just another mechanism for the restriction of female personality and intellect, and a mechanism for the valuation of women as chattels whose primary worth was virginity... vulnerability and non-threat to men.

I have discussed the Albigensian crusade in some detail, and commented upon the literature at some length, because the war against the Albigensians seems to be an important turning point.

With respect to the history of Western literature and our view of ourselves and 'love' as reflected in writing, the songs of the Troubadors stand at the beginning of Western national literary tradition. The ballads were not sung in the *lingua franca* of Rome. The ballads were sung in the native 'langue d'oc' of southern France and they inspired the creation of national literatures in the native languages of France, Germany, Spain and Italy. With the creation of these national literatures, the West came into its own and ceased to be detritus from the collapse of the Ancient World, communicating in a language 'left over' from that vanished world. For the first time, Western identity was completely free to assert itself along lines molded by Western psychobiology.

I can anticipate that there may be some degree of puzzlement at this point. In the last chapter we were discussing Western, Neanderthal-Caucasoid maladaptations that date from a remote period 40,000 years and more ago... yet, now it is being claimed that the full force of these maladaptations began to be asserted only about a thousand years ago. What happened in the intervening 40,000 years? Was not the force of Neanderthal-Caucasoid maladaptations a factor during these eons?

The answer is yes, of course... and no.

We read in our history texts that Western history began with the Ancient Egyptian civilization. In every such text there is an introductory chapter on the 'Land of the Pharaohs'.

Yet, the civilization of Ancient Egypt was not a Western, 'Caucasoid', achievement. The evidence from the anatomy of mummies, the testimony of fossil skeletal material and the witness of Egyptian art all agree that Ancient Egyptian civilization was a multi-racial achievement. Ancient Egyptian population was composed of a mixture of Caucasoid, Capoid and Negroid elements. We cannot claim the civilization of the Nile as 'ours'. It was not wholly Caucasoid... perhaps not even mostly Caucasoid.

We must remember that the 'end' of the last glacial period may be dated to about 40,000 B.P., but that Europe experienced very bitter and variable weather until the onset of the truly warm climate which set in about 8,000 B.C. It is only at this late date that the Scandinavian glaciers melted away completely.

From the end of Würm I until the final melting of the continental glaciers, Western Eurasia supported Neanderthal-Caucasoid stock, but only a small population. Climatological factors precluded any development of agriculture as an important food source until well into the historical period, and the population subsisted by hunting and gathering. As is well-known, the hunting-gathering way of life can support only a very sparse population.

Eurasian Neanderthal-Caucasoids existed from the end of Würm I, but their population did not reach a level permitting expansion in force until about 1500 B.C. By that time the climate had moderated sufficiently, and the population had increased sufficiently, so that a 'critical mass' of sorts had been reached. The steppes of southern Russia and the Caucasus mountains began to send forth waves of 'Western' people. These people began to invade the area of the Mediterranean basin where the Egyptian civilization had long been established. By about 1500 B.C. the Egyptians began to record the invasions of the 'Sea Peoples', Indo-European speakers who had migrated down the coast of Palestine and who had entered the Greek peninsula and island-hopped through the Cyclades to threaten Egypt.

The Mycenaeans were one wave, the Mittani another wave, the Dorians a third. Perhaps there were earlier waves of 'Western' migrants not recorded and still unknown to archeologists. Long-established empires crumbled under pressure from the newcomers; even Egypt itself was invaded by another wave, the Hyksos, but Egypt recovered to regain its position of cultural dominance.

It is my contention that, at first, from the start of the migrations in 1500 B.C. until the 'final' one about 450 A.D., the migrants from the Caucasus reached the Mediterranean world in insufficient numbers to completely swamp the established Egyptian cultural influence. They trickled into the Mediterranean basin... and were 'Egyptianized' to a greater or lesser degree. This 'Egyptianizing' process of cultural borrowing, I believe, partially nullified the higher level of aggression common to these newcomers. Adopting some of the Egyptian pantheon, adopting variations in Egyptian dress, awed by Egyptian history and culture and borrowing something of Egyptian 'life style' or 'civilization', these barbarians were at least partly tamed. As more migrants entered the Mediterranean world, however, Egyptian influence became increasingly diluted as some of the invaders borrowed second-hand from Western peoples who had arrived earlier.

The 'Ancient World' was, then, a basically Egyptian construct. Mycenaeans, Minoans, Classical Greeks and later Romans all represent varying, diluted degrees and interpretations of 'Egyptianization'.

There came a time, however, when the influx of Western migrants became too vast, and the Egyptian impetus to the Ancient World too attenuated and diluted, to allow the newcomers to be absorbed and civilized. Like a life-preserver of culture afloat for too long and buffeted by too many waves, the Ancient World became saturated and sank beneath the incoming tide of Neanderthal-Caucasoid characteristics.

A fairly rigorous date can be placed on this event. It happened sometime between 378 A.D. and 450 A.D. The handwriting was on the wall at the Battle of Adrianople in 378 A.D. when the Goths defeated the Romans. It was the worst disaster for Roman arms since Cannae more than half a millennium before. The Goths defeated the Romans not only by sheer numbers, but with a new weapon: heavy cavalry. Adrianople was the beginning of the truly Western world because with that battle the supremacy of the horseman was established and with him a new social orientation and order. The feudal order and the social supremacy of the knight was born.

Our modern West still bears vestiges of this ancient transition.

Our words and titles for a man of standing reflect the male-dominated, patriarchal world of the Eurasian horseman, the knight. The French gentleman, or 'cavalier' was, originally, a 'chevalier'... a horseman. The Spanish still retain 'caballero'... horseman... as their word for gentleman. The English 'sir' was originally the feudal and patriarchal 'sire'; the Italian 'messire' was the same.

Along with the Gothic horseman came the Western emphasis on male power as reflected in the 'Godhead'. Where, in the Ancient World, the Earth Goddesses had been at least the equal of their divine male colleagues, with the coming of the horseman in force male sky and war gods reigned supreme. This process of usurping female representation in the pantheon had, in fact, begun long before with the first Neanderthal-Caucasoid invaders, but ancient Mediterranean beliefs remained powerful enough to negotiate a reasonably equal truce. In Greece, for example, where once the Earth Goddess enjoyed absolute primacy, after the coming of the Mycenaeans and Dorians, Hera became the wife of Zeus, Artemis the sister of Apollo. Among the Levantines, once all-powerful Ishtar was made to share her throne with Baal and Marduk. Only among the Jews and Arabs was the female principle almost entirely suppressed while the Ancient World lived. Characteristically, we consider the victory of Jehovah a 'progressive' move... but relics of an older order linger even within Judaism. During the Jewish feast of Purim, an ancient fertility feast commemorating the harvest and the generosity of the Earth Mother, pomegranates, a fruit sacred to the Goddess, are much in evidence. And, during our time of the revival of feminine power and identity, one can see automobile bumper stickers bearing the gentle reminder: 'Mothers and Daughters light shabbos candles'... a remembrance of the time when the holy days were sacred to females and the regenerative principle.

Among the Semites, uniquely in the Ancient World, female submersion occurred earlier and more completely than among other peoples. The anti-feminine taboos and injunctions within Judaism are particularly strong. Witness the frequent prayer of Semitic males: 'Thank God I was not born a woman', or the Talmudic warnings against males being near a menstruating woman, or the ritual baths imposed against women following menstruation.

Much of this anti-feminism was transferred to fledgling Christianity by St. Paul — 'It's better to marry than to burn' — the converted Jew, Saul. Our institutionalized religions still bear witness to the power of male Neanderthal-Caucasoid fear of women and determination to deep them down. As late as 1974 there could be a controversy among *Protestants* as to the suitability of a woman to interpret and to transmit the words of our male God and male saviour. Female Episcopal minister, Rev. Allison Cheeke, had a hard time finding a pulpit.

It is difficult to explain adequately the localized and absolute island of Jewish anti-feminism in the Ancient World. One cannot ascribe the Israelites to any specific migration of purely Neanderthal-Caucasoid stock. It is quite clear that the genetic Jewish stock has probably 'always' been in the area of Palestine. One is very tempted to suppose that the very definitive Neanderthal series from Mount Carmel formed a far-flung and essentially anomalous pool of Neanderthal genes in the Middle East, a true 'pool' surrounded on all sides by other and very mixed racial groups, and that part of this gene pool centred on Mount Carmel contributed to the later existence of Palestinian Semitic tribes.

If this tentative suggestion has any validity, the world is faced with the ultimate irony: the unsupportable racial theories of the Nazis inspired genocide directed against the Jews on the grounds that the Jews were 'non-Caucasoid'; yet the proximity of the Mount Carmel series of Neanderthal remains may suggest that some Semitic tribes are the 'purest' and oldest Neanderthal-Caucasoids. If the psychobiological arguments presented here have any validity, this irony becomes a definite possibility.

Be that as it may, the male dominance imposed by the Jews as early as 1500 B.C. was duplicated across Europe after the fall of Rome and the dissolution of the Ancient World. The Gothic horseman, patriarchal social structures and a male-dominated 'Godhead' were firmly established... but not cohesively established.

Rome was the foundation of the world; at least, the foundation of the Western World. With the collapse of Rome all cohesive power vanished from the West and peoples entered a period of migration, chaos and jostling for power. This is the period we call the 'Dark Ages'. The darkness began to lift as power began to coalesce in several institutions: the Church, and the French rulers of the Merovingian and Carolingian dynasties. Perhaps it is not too surprising that Europe's secular and social power centred around lost Rome's most civilized 'barbarian' province, Gaul.

And this long detour brings us back to roughly 1100 A.D.... the Albigensian crusade. True, the horseman had been dominant throughout the 'Dark Ages', but the psyche of Western man had been confused and dissipated by the social chaos following the fall of Rome and the migrations of peoples. Five hundred years following the sack of Rome were to elapse before social stability, political and military power, and spiritual dogma embodied in the Church were sufficient to allow Western man to begin to assert himself fully in accordance with his own unique psychobiology... not as a pseudo-Egyptian as in the Ancient World, and not as chaotic flotsam in the wake of Rome's submergence... as himself.

The Albigensian crusade was the first indication, the first proof, of this newly won cohesion. It was first evidence of Western psychobiology symbiotically supported on the secular front by the military aggressiveness of the Norman French and on the 'spiritual' front by the motivational supremacy of the male-dominated Church. It was the first crusade, the first alliance of Western psychobiology on both military and religious fronts.

We may not agree with historian Maurice Magre that the Albigensian crusade was the greatest single turning point in the religious history of Mankind. But it was an important turning point for *something*. If North American writers have not been so sensitive to this turning point, European writers have been. In recent years the spate of European-published books on the subject of Catharism or the Albigensian crusade has been nothing short of astonishing. We have *Actualité du catharisme* by Pierre Durban, *La croisade contre les albigeois et l'union du Languedoc à la France* by Pierre Belperron, *Le Sang de Toulouse* and *Le Trésor des albigeois* by Magre, *Albigeois et cathares*... and may others, most published since 1960 and untranslated into English.

The last book mentioned, *Albegeois et cathares* by Fernand Niel, is a most valuable source book for information on Albigensian and Cathar tenets.

European writers seem convinced that something important happened which involved the Albigensian crusade. If the evidence and argument presented in this essay are valid, then we must disagree with Magre, not because he said too much, but because he may have said too little. The war against the Albigensians may have been the single greatest turning point not in the *religious* history but in the *entire* history of Mankind. As we may now be inclined to grant, this first crusade appears to be the evidence and the proof that Western man had achieved a cohesive expression of his own identity. All the following years, up to the present one, have witnessed the steady and purposeful imposition of Western psychobiology upon the rest of the world.

Since establishing his own identity, Western man has striven to explain and justify himself, to himself and to others, through the medium of his literature and art.

As we have seen, the essentially alien and non-Western literary form of *amour courtoise* proved so popular that, after the defeat of Catharism, the victorious Church was forced to invent a superficially similar substitute: the poetry of 'courtly love'. This somewhat bogus and artificial literary form became the foundation for the national literatures of the West, literature expressed not in the 'left-over' language of Rome, but in the 'native' tongues of European geography. The development of national and independent literatures gave Western man the opportunity to explain himself, and express himself... but the results have not been wholly satisfactory.

The evidence of literature and art reveals much about Western man, but not perhaps what Western man would have chosen to communicate...

Just as the invented ballads of Church-approved 'courtly love' offered an unanalysed thing called 'love', so the subsequently invented forms of Western literature have also relied on the theme of 'love'... but without offering much insight into this powerful and mysterious force. Perhaps *the* characteristic Western literary form is the novel. Novels began to appear in the late 17th Century, at about the same time that the colonial emphasis and impetus shifted from southern Europe to northern Europe, as northern Europe was inventing industrialism. Novels were something 'new', as the name implies, and appeared on the cultural scene simultaneously with the equally new forms of expansion represented by industrialism and regimented warfare.

It is almost as if novels appeared for the purpose of explaining and exploring Western man's motivations, motivations that seemed all the more puzzling because of the birth of much more efficient means of expansion, exploitation and aggression. Industrialism, organized national armies and new forms of commercial organization were giving rise to a new social order — the modern social order, in fact — and some way of accounting for this transition in the level of Western aggression seemed necessary.

Novels were and are the answer, though an inadequate one.

In novels we have an artificial construct which is nonetheless presented as reality. Characters drawn as realistically as possible move and struggle within the plot. Novels are, in essence, like the modern 'computer model'. They present 'possible alternative realities', possible 'scenarios', and by analysing the responses of the characters it is hoped and expected that we may gain some greater insight into our own real behaviour in the real world. The novel is a medium of expression which is uniquely Western. No other people has ever troubled to invent such elaborately constructed pseudo-realities. Non-Western people have apparently failed to experience sufficient puzzlement about human motivation to bother writing novels. They have remained content with relatively simple chronologies for recording important historical and social information, while they have relied upon more or less fantastic stories for sheer entertainment. When literary insight into human motivation has been required, brief parables and fables, and even jokes, have sufficed. Nothing comparable to the novel has ever been invented in the pre-Western world.

Only in the West has humanity felt compelled to create detailed and believable pseudo-realities, and only in the West has humanity analysed the actions of completely fictional characters as if those actions in a make-believe world could be significant in yielding a greater understanding of the human condition. What we have come to call 'legitimate' authors of 'serious' fiction presume to think that their novels are, in fact, 'relevant.' 'Legitimate' and 'serious' literary critics and *literati* agree with the authors' basic premises.

Literary creation and literary criticism enjoy such a predominant place in Western intellectualism that few Westerners, it seems, have stopped to consider the validity of the entire exercise.

Some Easterners have, however. Although born to a Greek-speaking family, mystic George Gurdjieff was influenced from earliest youth by a central Asian literary and philosophical orientation. Gurdjieff dismisses the entire body of 'serious' Western fiction as 'wiseacre'. For Gurdjieff, Western fiction is, simply, irrelevant.

Similarly, although he is more polite about it, Sufi Idries Shah also dismisses most Western literature as irrelevant... except for some works by authors who were influenced by non-Western thought.

We may not appreciate these criticisms of our intellectualism, but they deserve some thought.

Maybe the best place to begin is to observe that *all* Western fiction of a 'serious' nature deals with 'love' in one way or another. The novel is a tale of 'love conquers all', a tale of 'love lost', a tale of 'love searched for' or, occasionally, a tale of the conflict between the pull of *eros* and the 'higher' yearning for *agapé*. All Western novels, except children's stories and 'light' reading, deal with these momentous matters.

Yet, as we have seen, Western man has not succeeded in defining 'love' in any agreed-upon way and the conflicts surrounding the 'love' of novels involve similarly undefined concepts like 'consciousness', 'spirit', etc. If we are sincerely searching for meaning, then we have gone about it using meaningless and undefined tools. It is as if we are searching for insight, but not searching too well for fear of what we may discover about ourselves. It is much more flattering to our self-conceptions to write and read novels which manipulate rather grandiose but ill-defined 'concepts' like 'love', 'materialism', 'spirituality', 'consciousness'. It may be flattering, but it doesn't get us very far in terms of our stated goal of 'searching for understanding'.

The practice does employ 'serious' authors and 'experts' in literary analysis, and it does supply material for endless intellectual conversations... and in these senses Western literature is useful socially, but as a vehicle of supposedly serious enquiry it is 'wiseacre'.

Occasionally, Western authors have been truly serious and, rarely, truly informed. The trouble seems to be that these 'great' authors are esteemed by the literary experts for all the wrong reasons. Shakespeare, Dante and a few other Western authors are more or less acceptable to Eastern critics because these authors were transmitting important religious and scientific knowledge through the medium of allegory and 'fiction'. Unfortunately, the last people likely to understand or accept this truth are those entrusted with literary criticism in the West.[8]

Since most Western fiction of a 'serious' and 'legitimate' nature involves the concept and conflicts of 'love', we can judge that little Western fiction has been either sincere or relevant to the human condition. It has been, at best, an exercise in intellectual ego-gratification for both author and 'critical reader'. We can make this judgment because it has been relatively easy for us to see the Western concept of 'love' for what it is, namely, a pair-bonding adaptation demanded by a high level of aggression [*eros*] and an intellectual construct allowing survival in the present while preserving an appreciation of a time-transcending continuity [*agapé*]. Even without the benefit of modern biological and anthropological data, one would think that honest, sincere and fearless observation of human behaviour must have compelled similar conclusions. And, maybe, somewhere and sometime, some author has actually come right out and stated these simple truths in a more or less straightforward manner. But if there has ever been such an author, the *literati* must not have appreciated his (or her) simplicity because such an author has never been highly publicized and remains unknown to the reading public. It is so much more flattering to explore the 'mystery' of Man and the 'complexity' of Man's psyche than to accept the brutal simplicity of the psychobiological truth.

If our literature's obsession with undefined 'love' unintentionally reveals unflattering truths about Western psychobiological maladaptation, Western art strips us further.

Even the most casual glance through art books will serve to illustrate a very basic difference between Western and non-Western expression: the concentration on people in Western art in contrast to the concentration on non-human species in non-Western, especially oriental, art. In Japan, for instance, entire schools were devoted to the depiction of natural life, and 'lowly' natural life at that. The Heian and Kamakura periods, the Muromachi and Momoyama periods, the Edo and even the Modern periods of Japanese art show a preoccupation (to Western minds) with the small forms of life. We find numerous paintings of blossoms, wasps, butterflies. And in all these paintings the artist is obviously attempting an in-depth study of the creature's essence and primary relationships.

Western art, by contrast, exhibits a preoccupation with the study of humans. And, within this distinction, we can make another: there is a preoccupation with the depiction of nudes, especially female nudes. By comparison, nudes of women are very rare in Far Eastern art. But in Western art, 'nudes' constitute a genre by themselves, an acceptable and understandable subject for artistic expression which would, no doubt, have puzzled any Chinese or Japanese artist.

It is significant to me that female nudes in the form of Venus figurines appear frequently at the very foundation of Western artistic expression and have held a major place in it for the past 30,000 years. It is significant because the female nude is just another indication that Neanderthal-Caucasoid males remain bemused by females, sex and reproduction. The depiction of nudes offers an opportunity, time after time, to examine females and to hope that the view will somehow result in a more complete understanding and acceptance. The sexual difference, the sexual dimorphism, obsesses us.

Human sexual dimorphism, or even the existence of human

beings themselves, has never obsessed the oriental artist or people. Sexual difference was real, and was to be refined, enjoyed and accepted as a normal part of natural life. But human sexual difference was never considered something either so mysterious or so compelling that it must intrude into the attempt to illustrate the harmony and condition of life. A butterfly on bamboo served better.

If we wish to find some analogy to our own Western confusion and concern about human sexual differences, then we are forced to compare our art with that of 'primitives'. Among some peoples of Africa, Australian aborigines, some Amerindian cultures and the Polynesians... only within these primitive groups do we find a comparable obsession with the depiction of humans and human nudes. And, as we shall discover later, only among 'primitives' do we find sexual distortions of normal human physiology comparable to the degree of sexual distortion achieved by Western fashions.

Yet, as we have seen, all these 'primitive' people migrated or were forced into areas of marginal physical and cultural survival. They have some excuse for cultural retardation, some excuse for an obsession with sex and reproduction. We have no such excuse... at least we have had none for the past several thousand years. Our only 'excuse' for sexual artistic obsession is that our psyches are constructed along anciently maladapted lines. Indeed, one of the objective wonders of the contemporary Western world must be that our technological development has allowed the artistic expression of very primitive psychosexual confusions in very sophisticated media. In terms of purely psychobiological analysis, there would appear to be little difference between Degas' series of bathing nudes and sub-Saharan fertility figurines or Bushman cave paintings. Only the medium of expression has evolved: the psyche of the creator has not. Degas had canvas and infinitely varied colours at his disposal. The 'primitive' has only wood and his adz, or treasured containers of a few primary shades. The essential motivation, the psychosexual confusion, the attempt to understand the fact of female existence and the threat it poses to male identity... all remain identical.

Although not pretending to the status of an art expert in any way whatsoever, it may be germane to remark here that the return to primitiveness that characterized avant-garde Western art during the pre-World War II years, exemplified, perhaps, by the work of Modigliani and Picasso, was merely the unconscious realization that the motivations and confusions of Western man differ little from the orientation of primitive people even during a time of unparalleled technological development.

Perhaps, in addition to the evidence of bones, it will be granted that we have at least glanced into the psyche of Western man and have seen there non-material indications of psychobiological maladaptations which support the testimony of physical remains.

We will turn now to somewhat 'harder' evidence, manifestations of psychobiological maladaptation more concrete than concepts, words and images.

8

The Iceman Inheritance: Psychobiology in History and Society

At the end of *The Cronos Complex I*, having viewed the white man's pride in his progress and catalogued the crises, produced by progress, that confront us all, I wrote:

> *In Teutonic mythology, Ragnarok was the measure of all things. It was the last deed and glory of the heroes of Valhalla, the ultimate struggle between good and evil. The cause of Ragnarok will be the escape and revenge of the Worm. The Greeks had re-named him Oroubourous because his more ancient names had been forgotten. At the first light of Mesolithic dawn the Worm Oroubourous had been harried deep into the earth by the fire-brands of Niord, the first hunter. There, Oroubourous became encased in ice. But it is said that he will escape and renew the world-consuming struggle with heroes. That is why the Teutons believed that man lived between fire and ice. I choose to believe that this is a true allegory, that Niord is the spirit of heroic man and that the Worm is his temporal vanity.*

It seems evident that none of us has much choice about believing in the truth of this allegory, and more so now than back in 1972 when these lines were written.

Our technological juggernaut, accelerating geometrically, is not only outrunning the world's resources, but is outstripping our feeble human capacity to distribute what resources remain. We're having trouble feeding our creation. Man still lives between fire and ice, on a very practical level, and the ice is gaining the upper hand. Oroubourous is awakening.

During the winter of 1976-1977 the vulnerability of our vanity became appallingly apparent. Oroubourous, issuing forth from the trough of a low pressure area over Hudson's Bay, and disguised as one of the worst winters on record, sallied repeatedly against North America's proud technological culture.

We could not feed all our furnaces. Factories closed down throughout the American midwest, schools closed, government offices closed. Thermostats had to be lowered to conserve fuel. For some, the fires died completely. Oroubourous took his toll. Several people perished in unheated New York tenements.

And this in a society whose schoolbooks say that Man is dominant because he has learned to control nature. The truth is that our attempts to control almost anything have reached a point of exceedingly diminishing returns. Our attempts to control other men are resulting in rebellion. Negroids in Africa and Mongoloids in China have acquired our own weapons and values in self-defense and are capable of turning them against us. Our attempts to control ourselves have resulted in governmental corruption and increasing crime rates. Our technology, which we used to think controlled nature, is so complex that we have difficulty supplying it with fuel during a tough winter. Our attempts to control our own institutionalized aggression, our military, have been mocked by admissions by the U.S. Army that biological warfare research was conducted on civilian populations in major U.S. cities.

All of these failures of control reflect 'progress' getting out of hand. We can see that much of our white man's progress is merely a vulnerable, dangerous vanity.

Yet so deeply necessary to us is 'progress' that President Carter, in his inaugural address, was forced to mouth obligatory phrases of 'moving forward'. To what?

As long as we continue to define 'progress' as increasing materialism, new inventions, improved production and developing technology, we can only move toward eventual disaster.

There are some who see solutions in new reserves of fossil fuels, cast an appreciative eye toward Canada and the North Slope of Alaska, and envision myriads of nuclear generating plants. But these are not solutions. They are postponements of an inevitable reckoning. There is not enough natural gas and oil either in Canada's Alberta fields or under the Slope to supply growth projections for more than 20 years, if that long. Nuclear generating plants may be an answer, but at the appalling cost of producing age-long environmental poisons we do not know how to dispose of.

The U.S. is not the only exponent of Western progress and continued technological folly, as too many of my Canadian colleagues find it convenient to believe. Great Britain is banking its hopes on North Sea oil which will not last forever... and then on nuclear power with even more acute disposal problems than North America faces. Canada, the smug and self-righteous, supplies Candu nuclear reactors to nations in conflict and extracts 'a promise' that these nations won't make bombs. France and China indulge in open-air nuclear tests in the interest of catching up in nuclear technology.

Go forward?

Has anyone seriously considered going backward?

I am inclined to agree with Ashley Montagu to a limited degree. Man does not seem to be absolutely compelled by biological determinates. But I must emphatically disagree with Montagu at the same time. It is extremely dangerous to accept uncritically — and too many of our mass-produced humanitarians have — what I call 'the Montagu pretension'.

> *It is generally agreed that man is born free of* all *those biological determinates which characterize the behaviour of lower forms.* [*emphasis mine*]

To say that we are free of *all* biological determinates is a dangerous vanity. Like Cyrano's, it may get us in the end. If "the Montagu pretension" is taken as an article of faith we have no hope of dealing with some of our self-destructive tendencies. I think that we can deal with these tendencies, but we have to recognize them for what they are first. I think that Man's intelligence can override biological determinates, and we should have no fear of admitting the possibility that 'instinct' may still influence us. It may influence us, but I don't think it need control us. And I don't think it diminishes Man's stature to admit that he may not be completely beyond biology. Facing truth has never diminished anyone's stature, while courting vanity always has. Ironically, instinct will control us if we don't admit the possibility of its influence on us.

I think I've made a reasonable case for the presence of biological determinates in Man's behaviour. I have outlined the cause and the symptoms of the cronos complex. I have shown how Nature attempted to compensate for self-destructive aspects of temporal awareness. Perhaps I have defensibly argued that one group of men, Caucasoids, may have been cheated by some of Nature's protective adaptations.

We have seen that adverse environments have retarded or reversed full cultural development among two whole races of Man, and have had a similar effect on certain groups of all races. We have also seen that, in general, we Caucasoids seem to be suffering from an extreme form of the cronos complex which has resulted in self-destructive behaviour. It is legitimate to wonder what would represent an optimum human culture norm.

What would be the profile of a fully developed, but not rampant, three-tense cultural expression? Has there ever been one?

I think that there have been two such cultures. Both developed by non-Caucasoids. Both destroyed by Caucasoids. Both incorporating 'progress', but neither threatened by it.

One culture was Ancient Egypt. The other was China before the coming of maritime Europeans. It is my feeling that if we Caucasoids are to survive, and the world along with us, we had better begin emulating these civilizations to some degree.

A 'thumbnail sketch' of Egyptian and Chinese history would not only be something of an intellectual obscenity, but would be a personal affront to Egyptologists and Sinologists who've spent lifetimes studying these cultures without approaching complete understanding and empathy.

But since they've been presented as examples of something rare and important, as civilizations which were full and yet remained environmentally supportable, something must be said about them. Perhaps the following generalities will be judged permissible in the anthropological construct offered previously.

The first things that strike the average Western observer when viewing either of these civilizations are their immense longevity and relative stasis in contrast to comparable Western civilizations.

The Egyptian civilization endured and retained its essential character for almost 3,000 years; China presented a similar profile for perhaps 4,000 years. Egypt suffered several invasions over the course of its history, but only the invasion by Alexander and subsequent Ptolemaic rule finally broke the ancient continuity of life and tradition that had probably been established before the time of Menes (ca. 3100-2890 B.C.). Dr. A. Rosalie David says:

The history of Egypt spans many centuries, from its obscure beginnings through the first great upsurge of brilliance during the Old Kingdom, the periods of decay and renewal, the zenith of international power, prestige and wealth during the New Kingdom to the gradual sad decline during the later years... Egypt became easy prey for successive waves of invaders. Some, like the "sea peoples", were unsuccessful, but others - the Ethiopians, Assyrians, Persians, Greeks and Romans - were able to subjugate Egypt for long periods of time. Yet not until the late Ptolemaic era, when a Hellenistic dynasty exploited the country, did these successive conquerers make any determined attempt to interfere with the deep-seated traditions and way of life they found in Egypt. Indeed, the invaders tended to become "Egyptianized", adopting many of the customs and ways of the country they had conquered.

We recognize the same characteristics with regard to China: the early formalization of the civilization, the brief episodes of Chinese expansion, the successive waves of invaders who, however, were mainly absorbed and became Chinese. In the case of China, modern Europeans destroyed the Middle Kingdom.

Both of these civilizations were non-Caucasoid. With China this observation is merely a truism, but we Westerners generally tend to adopt Egypt as one of the cornerstones of our own culture. This is only partially true, at best. Carleton Coon notes:

The theory that the ancestral Capoids migrated southward from North Africa goes back to the discovery, during the last century, of Bushman-like paintings in the Sahara. In 1905 Biasutti first noticed Bushman-like traits in some of the oldest Egyptian skulls...

In 1924 a Bushman-like skull was found at Singa, 200 miles south of Khartoum on the banks of the Blue Nile, by W.R.G. Bond.

Carleton Coon's theory about the origin of the Capoid race, represented today by the Bushmen and the Hottentots, was that these men developed in North Africa and later migrated south into the heart of the continent around 6,000 B.C. There, as we have seen, they were later almost exterminated by the Bantu expanding from the north and the Dutch coming from the south.

Peoples seldom *all* migrate *en masse*: the excess population migrates. The Sahara was not a wasteland of sand until fairly recently, but a well-watered parkland where numerous rock paintings testify that people swam (and apparently developed the Australian crawl at that). More than one historian believes that the Ancient Egypt we know was developed by people who collected along the Nile when the Sahara started to become desert about 6,000-5,000 B.C. If that is so, and it seems very likely, then we have reason to believe that the very first Egyptians were partially or even predominantly Capoid. Some, after reaching the dependable source of water in the desert, the Nile, perhaps hesitated to settle down and relinquish the nomadic way of life they had had in the Sahara grasslands. Perhaps these Capoids migrated on down the Nile, past the great lakes, and on into southern Africa where they could live on the veldt in much the same manner as they had lived far to the north before the Sahara turned to sand. This scenario fits Coon's theory and the evidence.

But whether or not this happened, it is undeniable that there was a definite Capoid strain in the ancient Egyptians. Biasutti's Bushman-like skulls are one bit of evidence, but there are several more. The 'Hottentot apron', that unique elongation of the labia minora that distinguishes Capoid women from all others, is also called the *tablier egyptien* because the same anatomical adaptation has been observed in several female mummies. Then, those famous almond eyes of the Egyptians are nothing more nor less than an accurate representation of the almost-oriental eyes of modern Capoids.

About 6,500 B.C. a Caucasoid people, the Capsians, moved into the Nile area, but perhaps 'moved through' is a better description of the evidence. There is little doubt that the Capsians came from Palestine because their Mesolithic blade and microlith culture had its origin there, but there are no Capsian sites in present-day Egypt itself. Capsian skeletal material and artifacts have been found in Tunisia and Algeria only, as far as I know. The evidence indicates a strong Capoid presence in the Nile through which the Capsian Caucasoid invaders may have forced or negotiated a corridor, but which they were unable to displace. Negative evidence proves nothing in paleontology, and it is possible that many Capsians settled in what was later to be Egypt.

Later Egyptian art and history also testified to a strong Negroid admixture. The XXV Dynasty was entirely Ethiopian, and statues of the great Mentuhotep (ca. 2133-1991 B.C.), who unified Egypt during troubled times, strongly suggest that he was a Negro. A bust of Queen Tiye, mother of famous Akhenaten, reveals marked Negro traits (see Plate III).

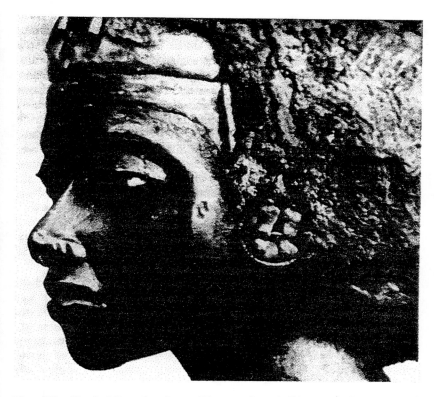

Plate III   *Head of Egyptian Queen Tiye, mother of Akhenaten, showing mixed racial features.*

The evidence forces us to conclude that Ancient Egypt was not a Caucasoid achievement, as we are much too ready to assume automatically, but was a culture built by a composite people exhibiting mixture of Negroid, Caucasoid and Capoid racial traits. I am inclined to believe that the longevity and lifestyle of Ancient Egyptian civilization can be attributed more to the Negroid and Capoid characteristics than to the 'white' ones. Archeologists note a 'sad and gradual decline' of Egyptian culture beginning about 500 B.C., but this period of decline coincides with Persian Dynasties and Caucasian invaders, and includes the XXVII Dynasty (Cambyses, Darius I, Xerxes, Artaxerxes) and the XXXI Dynasty (Artaxerxes III, Arses, Darius III)... closely followed by the Greeks of the Ptolemaic period. What we recognize as the brilliance of Egypt was only partially Caucasoid: the period of decline was increasingly so.

If for no other reason, this somewhat long detour back into Egyptian beginnings is justified by *that* realization. Chinese cultural longevity and refinement were almost totally Mongoloid achievements and need no elaboration.

I have tried to search for one word or phrase which might illustrate the subtle essential difference between these two civilizations and our own when viewed very generally. I have not been very successful in this search, admittedly, but I offer the following inadequate perspective: neither China nor Ancient Egypt showed much interest in the *mechanical multiplication* of power which eventually led, in Europe, to what might be called the 'artificial energy' of the steam engine. This is an oversimplification, and not even totally accurate, but I believe that this notion can be supported by examples, at least to the extent that the *world view* of China and Egypt can be shown, however inadequately, to differ significantly from our own.

Given that all of Pharaonic Egypt and much of Chinese civilization flourished in ancient times when technology and energy sources were limited everywhere, I believe that it can still be shown that Greek, Roman and later European contemporaries strove to mechanically multiply what energy there was, in contrast to the Egyptians and Chinese whose solution was generally to employ more energy units.

Ship design illustrates this: Greeks, Egyptians, Romans, Chinese and Japanese alike employed galleys powered by slave oarsmen. But only among the Westerners do we find any consistent attempt to improve on one bank of oars. The Greeks and Romans tried continually to increase the speed and power of their galleys, for a given length, by placing more than one layer of oarsmen on deck. The mechanical ingenuity devoted to this exercise was immense, and the design of multi-bank galleys became an obsession in classical Europe. The trireme proved to be the most practical limit in the search for increasing power-to-length ratios, given materials available, but even five-banked galleys were used in warfare.

The Chinese and Egyptians, on the other hand, remained satisfied with single-banked galleys, and if greater speed was required the solution was to make the ship longer to accommodate more rowers until materials limitations called a halt to ship length. There was little tendency to attempt an unnatural multiplication of power by mechanical means.

Perhaps the ultimate illustration of this psychological difference occurred during one of the British naval actions against Canton during the opium wars of the 1840's. The British used a steam-paddle gunboat and the Chinese, in desperation, tried to emulate its mechanical efficiency. They constructed a paddle-driven junk in imitation of the British gunboat, but the junk was not powered by a steam engine. It was powered by men working at a capstan.

As another example of the same tendency, we may note that James Watt was not the first to discover the power of steam. There was a Greek-built steam turbine in Alexandria about 300 B.C. and steam power was used to open and close heavy doors in some Greek temples. This was not the expansive exploitation of steam developed during the Industrial Revolution in Europe, but a different principle. These ancient engines worked on the principle of atmospheric pressure working on a piston or diaphragm in a vacuum produced by the condensation of steam. Neither the turbine nor the power-operated temple doors caught on in Egypt.

The Western tendency toward maximizing the power or output through the invention and use of mechanical contrivances is revealed by ancient pottery. Both Greeks and Romans mass-produced their tablewear on multiple, slave-powered lathes, while the Chinese and Egyptians remained satisfied with turning out pottery pieces one at a time on nothing more sophisticated than a one-man potter's wheel. Indeed, at least in the orient, the creation of individual ceramic pieces became something of a ritual, a source of great pleasure and almost religious satisfaction.

Perhaps these few examples are sufficient to hint at a symptomatic Western aggression and frustration. The desire to increase power and output reflects a basic frustration with nature. There is the urge to control it, extract the most out of it and improve on it.

A comparison of contemporary Western cultures with the Chinese and Egyptian civilizations will show that this aggression was also directed against men. Again, for a moment, we will discuss ships. In the ancient world only the Western powers constructed specialized warships. The Egyptians and Chinese, for the most part, simply pressed merchant ships into military service in time of war. This is to say that neither the Chinese nor the Egyptians ever had a specialized *navy* as distinct from a *merchant marine*. This accounts for their singular lack of success against Western adversaries. The aggression of Chinese and Egyptians was apparently not so prominent and therefore not so institutionalized.

And while we're back on the subject of ships, it might be germane to observe here that the entire philosophy of Chinese junks differs from the idea of a European vessel. The junk is designed to go with the sea and the wind and not to strive against them. It is intended to offer little resistance and to ride like a cork in a storm, while the European ship is designed to stand up to the waves and oppose the elements by sheer strength. We will come back to this a bit later.

The Chinese and the Egyptians seem to have had a lower level not only of maritime aggression but also of land-based aggression. In the broad view, neither of these non-Caucasoid powers made a habit of expansion. Rather, the reverse. Both considered themselves uniquely blessed and wished to remain isolated. There were periods of exception in the history of both peoples, but they were rare. On a more personal note, we have this Egyptian view of soldiering:

> *Come, let me tell thee of the woes of the soldier! He is awakened when an hour has passed, and he is driven like an ass. He works till the sun sets. He is hungry, his body is exhausted, he is dead while yet alive.*

And this was not a minority opinion. It was only one of several texts which schoolboys had to copy which illustrated the non-glamour of war. As Barbara Mertz has said, these copy-texts "might be subtitled, 'Why Not to Choose a Military Career' ".

One gets the impression that war was not considered a glorious or even very sensible occuption in Ancient Egypt. True, we have gloomy and bombastic texts carved on steles which recount the incredible exploits of various Pharaohs on the battlefield. The number of enemy soldiers slaughtered is always astronomical and the number of prisoners enslaved is all very impressive... except that some pharaohs simply copied earlier boastings of earlier pharaohs, verbatim. The Egyptian ego did not demand individual recognition for heroic deeds on the battlefield and one cannot help but think that "the Egyptians were never keen on fighting".

There *were* exceptions. Rarely. Thutmose III was an energetic campaigner and a reasonably successful one. So was Ramses II, but more by good fortune than sterling military qualities. In China, the Han Dynasty was exceptionally expansionist. Both countries tended to rely on mercenaries whenever possible. Egypt preferred Aryans (Achaians and Philistines) and Nubians about equally, while the Chinese regarded Manchurians as good war fodder. Both peoples learned to regret their military inadequacy. Both were, at one time or another, conquered by their own mercenaries and both China and Egypt finally succumbed to highly motivated Caucasoid armies which their mercenaries had no intention of opposing seriously.

Perhaps it will be granted that Western cultures have differed from the Chinese and Egyptians in *aggression*, whether directed against Man or nature. These peoples apparently did not share our emphasis on physical opposition and control.

We conceive of these peoples as having been both unrealistic and unprogressive, and thus account for their cultural demise. But, faced as we are by the results of our own practicality and progress, perhaps the Egyptians and the Chinese deserve a closer look.

I believe that the Chinese and the Ancient Egyptians progressed as much as we have, but in a different direction, one offering few material remains. Rather than opposing or controlling nature through the use of mechanical contrivances, I think that these civilizations placed a premium on refining and developing their relationships to nature and to each other. Some of their achievements, when reflected in material objects that have survived the ravages of time, are so subtle that we have difficulty recognizing them for what they are. We are only now coming to appreciate the *efficiency* of these people, but the man in the street is still largely unaware of new discoveries and recognitions.

Ironically, it may be the progress won by this non-aggressive and harmonious world view that can save us from our technological dead end.

I would like to return to the Chinese junk in order to illustrate the *kind* of progress, in terms of psychology and world view, that we will be talking about.

The junk is a unique material and functional creation which crystallizes philosophically the Chinese way of dealing with nature. And, as a solid entity of wood, canvas and iron, the junk is

amenable to Western 'practicality' and offers an easier first glimpse
into an alien world view than a study of poetry, flower arranging or
the symbolism of the oriental tea service.

The junk *is* the refined and harmonious balance of conflicting
forces.

French yachtsman Eric Tabarly electrified the boating world with
his single-handed victory in the 1969 Transpacific sailboat race
from San Francisco to Tokyo. The Frenchman's boat was
thoroughly unorthodox. *Pen Duick V* was 35 feet in length, made of
lightweight aluminum alloy, and displaced only three tons. A
conventional Western sailing yacht of the same size would normally
weigh almost three times as much. The extra weight, perhaps as
much as five tons in an all-out racing boat, would have been
concentrated in a deep ballast keel. *Pen Duick V* did have a keel
and it did have 900 pounds of ballast at the foot of the keel... barely
enough to right the boat in a *calm* with all sails down. But Tabarly
did not sail his boat across the Pacific in a calm, of course. On the
contrary, Tabarly is noted for carrying the maximum amount of sail
in all conditions, even in gales, for that is how ocean races are won.
Tabarly has won more than his share.

What prevented virtually ballast-less *Pen Duick V,* from
capsizing?

A traditionally oriented Western yachtsman, viewing the
underwater configuration of *Pen Duick V*, might be tempted to
jump to the conclusion that Tabarly's boat boasted two rudders.
There was the normal movable rudder blade at the rear of the boat,
but, in addition, *Pen Duick V's* deep but almost ballast-less keel also
had a movable blade attached to the rear edge of the keel-fin. And
this blade, or 'trim tab' as Tabarly calls it, was the secret of the
boat's stability.

The force of water pushing against this tab, depending on the
angle of adjustment, acted to push *Pen Duick V* upright against the
force of the wind, which would otherwise capsize it. The more
forceful the wind, the faster the speed... and the more powerful was
the corrective influence of the rushing water against the keel's trim
tab. *Pen Duick V's* stability was achieved by an automatic *balance*
of opposing forces, not by opposition to just one force, wind, with
sheer weight. Tabarly's creation was viewed as an unorthodox and
impractical design by many. But *Pen Duick V's* revolutionary
method of maintaining stability not only proved its worth in several
long-distance ocean races, but has several inherent advantages. The
lack of ballast means a dramatic saving in weight, which, for

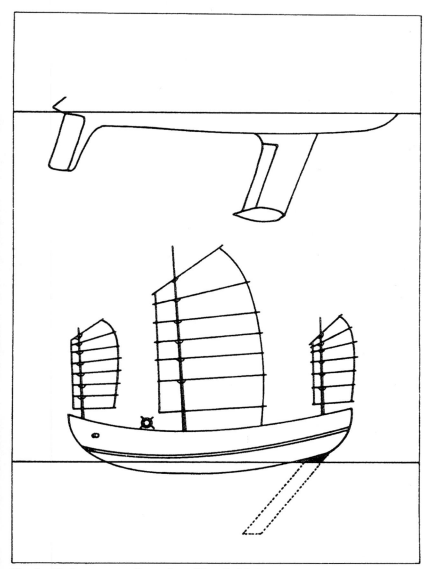

Fig. 9 *Underwater configuration of* Pen Duick V *compared with that of Chinese junk. Keel tab on* Pen Duick V *forces boat up against the pressure of wind in the sails. Long deep rudder of Chinese junk performs the same function.*

Pen Duick V *drawn from* Ocean Racing *by Eric Tabarly, junk drawn from* Jane's Book of Ships.

Tabarly, meant less inertia and more speed in light airs. Weight is cost, not only in speed, but also in cost of construction and in potential payload not carried for any given size of boat.

Tabarly's creation was neither revolutionary nor unorthodox, nor was it original with him. The principle of *Pen Duick V's* stability was the principle of the Chinese junk's stability. The principle is at least 3,000 years old.

The Chinese did not indulge in ocean racing. They sought from their watercraft safety, economy in construction, efficiency, and, above all, carrying capacity. They were traders. The junk has all these qualities in large measure and they derive, at least in part, from the rudder. The Chinese rudder extended very deeply into the water and it angled forward. It was a curious appendage for their typically shallow-draft hulls. This exceptional rudder could be raised and lowered to permit beaching or shoal cruising, but lowered fully it might extend as much as twelve feet below the keel on a 40-50 foot junk.

If you look carefully at the illustration of *Pen Duick V's* keel tab and compare it with the Chinese rudder (Figure 9), you will see that they perform the same function. The junk rudder is not *only* a rudder, it is a lever using the force of the water flowing past to balance the force of the wind in the sails. But the comparison shows that the Chinese have been more economical. The junk's rudder takes the place of both the keel tab *and* the rudder on *Pen Duick V*.

A balance of forces, not brute opposition to them, characterized the ancient junk. Tabarly's *avant-garde* and ultra-sophisticated *Pen Duick V* does not quite show a comparable level of refinement.

While Tabarly the Frenchman was experimenting with the junk's underwater refinements, a British yachtsman, Colonel H.G. 'Blondie' Hasler was studying the Chinese sail rig, the battened lug.

Figure 10 shows the elements of this rig, but the subtleties have to be explained. All sails work on the same principle as an airplane's wing. An airplane's wing 'lifts' because its shape causes a vacuum on the upper surface of the wing. The wing does not 'lift' so much as the wing is 'pulled' into the sky. A boat's sail works in the same way. A boat isn't pushed by the wind, it is pulled along by a vacuum created in front of the sail which results from the wind being 'stopped' or distorted by the sail. The Western notion of the sail does not utilize the aerofoil principle very well because we rely on the force of the wind itself to create a curve in the sail. Often, and especially in light airs, there is not enough wind to push the canvas into the most efficient aerofoil curve.

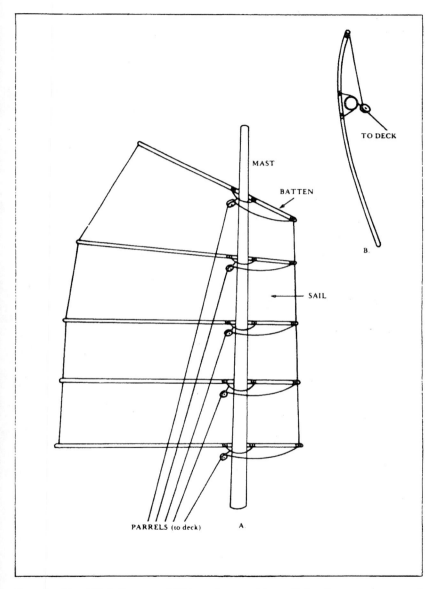

Fig. 10 *Simplified diagram of Chinese battened lug sail showing arrangement of parrels [sheets not shown]. Figure B, a view of sail from above, shows how parrels may be tightened to bend the sail to proper aerofoil shape.*

The Chinese long ago devised a way of preserving an optimum aerofoil shape regardless of wind force. As a result, their sails were efficient even in very light breezes. The parrels can be tightened to bend the sail to the proper shape around the mast.

Colonel Hasler fitted a battened lug to his *Folkboat* and competed in several single-handed races across the Atlantic. He says this of the Chinese rig: "The design of this sail and gear is extraordinarly subtle. The more I learn about it, the more subtle it seems. I suspect I am still missing points known to the Chinese, who started two thousand years ahead of me."

Marine expert Charles A. Borden observes:

> *Having started over two thousand years ago the Chinese sailor added many artful refinements and arrived at a high degree of efficiency hundreds of years before the science of aerodynamics explored and pointed the way for modern Western sailors... the junk master has at his disposal the fastest-reefing rig in the world. With halyards slacked, sails and battens dropped swiftly into buntlines, like a Venetian blind, and even on the largest junk one man can take in a reef three or four battens deep in seconds.*

Joshua Slocum, Canadian-born dean of American sailors and the first man to circumnavigate the world single-handed, has nothing but praise for the battened lug: "the most convenient boat rig in the world." The illustration of the Chinese sail is drawn after the sail plan of *Liberdade*, one of Slocum's vessels.

This discussion of junk design may seem a bit too detailed in view of the fact that our Western scholars and even Western laymen-intellectuals deem it more important to study more profound aspects of Chinese philosophy and delve into things like the *I Ching* and Taoist learning. But I disagree... and so did the Chinese. According to the *shui-jen*, a people representing one of China's most ancient lifestyles, one flourishing before the Chinese could write and still vital, the junk was one of the first gifts of the gods to the Chinese. It *was* a material and concrete crystallization of the wisdom of balance, an immensely practical illustration of yin-yang in balance. On one level the junk was merely a boat, but on another level it was recognized to be a day-to-day reminder or lesson that harmony and balance of forces was the essence of the Middle Kingdom and the secret of civilization itself. For this reason, junks have a peculiar prominence in both Chinese poetry and Chinese law. As late as 1850 the selling of junks to foreigners, especially to

Europeans, was specifically forbidden and the penalty for doing so was death. For, with the coming of the Portuguese to Macao and the opportunity for close observation of Caucasoid behaviour, the Chinese decided that these barbarians, who had no concept of harmony, should not be allowed to desecrate this symbol of harmony, the junk, with ignorant alterations.

As a symbol, the junk often crops up in poetry:

> *When one has good wine,*
> *A graceful junk,*
> *And a maiden's love,*
> *Why envy the immortal gods?*

This sentiment, expressed by Li T'si Po, is a bit more subtle than it might at first seem. It might be translated thus to extract its deeper significance:

> *When a person can taste rich sensation,*
> *Yet be cognizant of living in a balance of forces,*
> *Not only of natural forces as illustrated*
> *by the sailing junk,*
> *But be cognizant of balancing forces of the mind,*
> *permitting love,*
> *Such a person may die content.*

Li T'si Po's poem could perhaps have been sent to King George of England as an instruction, but the Chinese Emperor had no illusions about the message being understood, so he said it without subtlety and in straight prose:

> *The Celestial Court does not rate as precious objects coming from far away;... King, keep peace among your own people... In future it is unnecessary to send further envoys by land or sea. Know only how to open your heart and study benevolence. Then it will be said that without sending envoys annually to my Court you progress in civilization.*

Before leaving the junk, it should be said that it may soon have practical significance for us. It should not be dismissed as a mainly philosophical expression of Chinese life because, as Western sailors have testified, the junk is an immensely efficient water craft. The Chinese, who saw no gulf between 'practicality' and 'philosophy', and who lived their philosophy and reflected it in their works, would not be surprised that even we are being forced to balance yin-yang.

Consider the design study of German engineer Wilhelm Prölss.

The world's economy is dependent on international trade and our comfort and even survival relies upon the importation of goods, like oil for instance. Most of this trade is carried on by ships. Yet, ever-inflating energy economics are having a serious effect on maritime trade. Ships require fuel oil too, an immense amount of it in relation to the tonnage moved by a freighter or tanker. Water transport is only cheap if the motive power of ships is cheap. Otherwise, it becomes inordinately expensive. When ships were powered by sail the motive power was free. Until recently, fuel was so cheap that steamships were not only viable but actually cheaper than sail because of the volume of goods moved according to reliable schedules. Sailing ships died out because they couldn't compete with the economics of steam.

But fuel costs are no longer a minor expense for the ship-owner. Fuel is a major expense. The escalating cost of it is beginning to make the shipment of goods by steamship another exercise in diminishing returns. Not only that, but oil pollution is being recognized as a major environmental hazard. Most of the danger comes from cargoes of oil escaping, but escaping fuel oil from freighters and tankers contributes substantially to shore and open-ocean oil slicks as well.

Ironically, at the apex of our high-energy civilization, computer studies have shown that sailing ships are again becoming competitive... even taking into account the absolute unreliability of wind patterns. Windships could now, statistically, deliver goods cheaper than steam on an over-all, worldwide basis.

It was in response to these computer studies that Wilhelm Prölss again turned to a computer to design a modern windship. The optimum size, number of masts, and sailing rig — according to the computer, at any rate — resulted in Prölss's design study.

At first glance, this ship looks like a Western clipper, but a close look will reveal that the rig is actually a battened lug, the ancient Chinese junk rig. The sails of the Prölss ship are more or less permanent fixtures. They never come down. They are plastic sheets which are curved to the optimum aerodynamic shape by aluminum battens. The sails are trimmed by rotating the entire mast, which is a tripod of aluminum tube. The masts are rotated by servo-motors directed by a computer. In a storm the sails can be trimmed to present almost negligible resistance to high winds.

Computer studies have predicted that the Prölss 'neo-junk' can average 25 days between Hamburg and Hampton Roads "carrying 13,000 tons of cargo with ten less crew than a comparable modern motor ship, at a freight a dollar and a half less per ton than the minimum such a motor ship could accept with hope of payment." But that was back in 1958. The Prölss design is much more competitive now. Fuel costs have tripled, labour has doubled... or more. Perhaps it is enough to say that two keels of Prölss-like 'neo junks' have been laid in Hamburg, West Germany.

I have gone into such length about junks in order to show that *on a very real and practical day-to-day basis the idea of refining natural relationships, rather than 'controlling nature' by main force of technology, is the only true kind of progress.*

What we call progress is not practical because, as we are beginning to discover, it is self-destructive and not environmentally supportable.

With the lesson of the junk in mind then, we are perhaps prepared to see other evidence of progress in Egyptian and Chinese civilization that we have ignored.

And now that the outline of what we will find has been illustrated by the junk, we will not have to spend so much time on other progressive achievements which have more relevance to our crises.

Western medicine is beginning to be aware that some diseases and conditions are apparently caused by 'disharmonies' which can be treated without drugs or surgery. Everyone knows that ancient Chinese acupuncture has earned some popular respect and even a modicum of Western medical acceptance. Less well-known is the fact that colour can have a marked effect on patients' rates of recovery and can even be used to treat some diseases. This was very familiar to the Ancient Egyptians, who pioneered 'colour therapy', and who seem to have designed some of their jewelry in an attempt to treat or correct individual 'disharmonies'. In fact, gemstones were prized by the Ancient Egyptians *because of the pure colours they reflected* which were useful to health.

Equally important to us and our health were advances made in Egypt in the field of agriculture. The appeal of 'health foods' in our society is a measure of our concern over the chemical fertilizers and preservatives our technology has invented in order to increase food production and facilitate distribution. We are beginning to learn that, again, our technology may be killing us.

Consider some 'recent' scientific discoveries.

There are ancient myths, from Egypt, China, India and elsewhere involving the notion of plant growth being stimulated by music. Typically, some hero grows a luscious garden in short order by playing his harp, or else he 'sings' up crops. Until the last decade,

Western science regarded these tales as naive and charming and totally unrealistic.

George Ivanovitch Gurdjieff, a rather mysterious 'mystic' who seems to have had a lot of influence in intellectual circles in pre-World War II Europe, claimed, among many other things, to have discovered secrets of 'pre-sand Egypt' relating to stimulating plant growth with music 'based on the Golden Section'. Needless to say, this claim was regarded as mumbo-jumbo nonsense.

In the mid-1960's two researchers at Canada's University of Ottawa, Drs. Mary Measures and Pearl Weinberger, undertook a series of experiments lasting more than four years and culminating in the discovery that sound at a frequency of 5,000 cycles a second could significantly stimulate the growth of spring Marquis and winder Rideau wheat. The results could not be explained, only presented, and Measures and Weinberger did this in the *Journal of Canadian Botany*. Weinberger is willing to believe that basic farm equipment of the future may include sound-generating equipment and loud-speakers.

Previously, an American, George E. Smith, discovered that corn yields could be increased if the plants were subjected to sound at 1,800 cycles per second. Sound-stimulated plants produced 186 bushels of corn per acre as compared to 171 bushels for unstimulated plants.

It seems that not only is the growth of plants stimulated by the right kind of sound, but music or sound which is good for plants is bad for crop pests. Peter Belton, a researcher for the Canadian Ministry of Agriculture, reported that corn plots subjected to 50,000 cycles per second were found to contain 60 percent fewer corn-borer moth larvae than 'soundless' plots and that the corn was three inches higher.

Dorothy Retallack, a student at Temple Buell College in Colorado, discovered that under laboratory-controlled conditions classical music and Ravi Shankar stimulated the growth of four kinds of plants, but that acid rock withered them. L.H. Royster and B.H. Huang, both of North Carolina State University, achieved similar results with tobacco plants.

The research is increasing and a flood of data indicates fairly conclusively that music can stimulate plant growth and increase crop yields in a manner comparable to the addition of chemical fertilizers and insecticides... but with no known harmful side-effects.

Egyptologists have been hard put to explain how Ancient Egypt, with its assumed primitive agriculture, could have supported the population required for pyramid-building and sundry similar tasks. Perhaps Egyptian harps, which are indeed based on the Golden Section, can explain how the pharaohs raised the necessary manpower. For that matter, recent research into plant stimulation by music and vibration may revise our estimates of primitive population levels in many cultures. In 1963, T.C. Singh, head of the botany department at India's Annamalai University in Madras discovered that ancient fertility chants and dances, like the *Charakusi raga*, produced rice harvests from 25 to 60 percent higher than the regional average in the states of Pondicherry and Madras. Singh used live entertainment, traditional musicians and dancers as well as canned music.

So much for 'harmonious' agricultural production. What about non-technological food preservation?

It is now believed by some that the pyramid shape has strange and unaccountable properties. One of these properties is that the shape retards decomposition of organic substances if one face of the pyramid is oriented toward the north, just as the Great Pyramid at Giza was oriented toward the north by the Ancient Egyptians. Milk can be stored for about a week in a pyramid-shaped container before it goes bad and such containers are, in fact, used for that purpose in Czechoslovakia. Another strange property of the shape is that it seems to produce static electricity. None of this is understood yet, or satisfactorily explained, but it works.

From this brief survey of Chinese and Egyptian civilization we can see that these people were not static at all. They progressed in a different direction and apparently achieved significant breakthroughs in areas of contemporary concern. Judging from the various guises in which Oroubourous is now at our throats, we may very well come to accept the possibility that these non-Caucasoid societies were more advanced than we are in *the* really important ways.

This realization is percolating down to an ever-increasing number of people, and heightened interest in various non-Caucasoid or pre-Caucasoid cultures has been the result. In an attempt to understand and appreciate the world view of these advanced cultures, many Westerners are turning away from their own technological values and taking up Chinese or Indian philosophies, studying pyramids or gravitating toward the 'occult'.

But, typically, most of these Westerners are going about it in a Western fashion. The asceticism of some eastern philosophies seems to be the major attraction because of the natural (to a Westerner) idea that if our technology and materialism represents an excess of sensation, then the cure must be asceticism.

Our psychology is treacherous and self-protective.

The asceticism that we Western intellectuals find it easy to profess when taking up pre-technological philosophies was never characteristic of the societies from which we're borrowing. The civilizations of China, Egypt and pre-Caucasoid India were not stable because of asceticism. They were stable, and perhaps more fulfilling than our own culture, because they were *balanced* and because human temporal vanity and aggression were compensated for by sexual adaptation leading to satisfying sexual behaviour.

Far from being ascetic, the civilizations of China, Egypt and pre-Caucasoid India were highly erotic. They refined *that* too, as we in the West have very seldom done, and I offer the irreverent thought that Chinese, Egyptian and pre-Caucasoid Indian [9] civilizations owed their stability and humanitarian natural progress to sexual-sensual factors *at least* as much as they owed them to ascetic-esoteric-intellectual ones. Since it is undeniable that primate sexual adaptation has been developed and refined in direct relation to the increase in 'intelligence' and the cultural and technological ability to alter the natural world, culminating in Man in both respects, and since we have already discussed Caucasoid sexual-sensual maladaptation and cultural aggression in comparison with other races, it would seem that sexual-sensual factors may be *the* most important.

Sexual-sensual adaptations seem to be a compensation for temporal aggression, in short. We have become more sexy, as a species in direct proportion to the increase in our intelligence and ability to conceive of time as a cultural environment. We Caucasoids have a greater degree of temporal aggression, as reflected in our wars against nature and Man. We Caucasoids are also less well evolved sexually because, as we have suggested, sexual adaptations conflicted with glacial ones.

The conclusion is becoming inescapable that the Chinese, Egyptian and pre-Caucasoid Indian civilizations avoided our rampant temporal aggression because of a greater degree of sexual-sensual activity. This is well documented in the art, fashion and sexual mores of all these peoples.

And it is perfectly consistent with our sexual maladaptation that Western intellectuals and Western technological cop-outs, when viewing these civilizations, would recognize the ascetic and philosophical aspects of them but ignore their sexual-sensual aspects. Any objective analysis, however, demands that these cultures be considered *in toto*. We must look at everything, and no objective observer can deny that sexual-sensual refinements requisitioned much of these peoples' time and energy.

I think it was time and energy which would otherwise have been employed in using their intelligence and temporal aggression to develop 'our' kind of 'progress'.

If we are going to borrow something of the world view from these civilizations in order to combat our own dangerously anti-man and anti-nature psychology, then we have an obligation to borrow something of everything from these cultures. We have this obligation *because we do not know which of their cultural and racial traits prevented them from making our mistakes.*

Western intellectuals and Western cop-outs from our rampant technology *assume* with immense certainty that it must have been Chinese, Egyptian and 'Indian' philosophy which prevented them from taking our naturally disharmonious course of development. Little thought is given to the possibility that the lifestyles of these civilizations contributed much to their relative environmental sanity.

We meditate, yes, or we study Egyptian music and pyramids, or we delve into Zen, or we profess Mahayana Buddhism, we learn mantras... but we do not emulate Egyptian fashions, we do not study Chinese sexual refinements, we have little patience with 'Indian' temple dances, we disregard their concern with cosmetics and body adornments. We are sure that these must be irrelevant.

Yet, the ascetic philosophies of these cultures existed in a balanced symbiosis with the day-to-day lifestyle. Perhaps one could not have existed without the other.

If we know to our regret that something is amiss with Western philosophical values, we may suspect that something may be wrong with Western sexual-sensual values, too.

It is obvious that our world view differs philosophically from the attitude toward the natural world held by non-Caucasoid high civilizations. But it is even more obvious that our sexual-sensual mores also differ from the lifestyles depicted in the art of these peoples' cultures.

The sexual-sensual behaviour of these civilizations will horrify *all* segments of contemporary Western society, however much these segments profess to oppose each other philosophically. The sexual-sensual attitudes of Chinese, Ancient Egyptians and pre-Caucasoid

Indians will be unpalatable to intellectuals, hippie commune members, women's libbers, male chauvinist pigs, businessmen, gay libbers and religious ministers alike. Since all these supposedly divergent factions would be united against the sexual-sensual lifestyles of these civilizations, I believe it is a safe bet that sexual-sensual matters are *the* functionally important difference. But this is merely repeating what was learned about Neanderthal evolution, about our inherited racial traits.

If we are going to climb down from our precarious technological perch, it will not only be necessary to adopt the more ascetic, intellectual and esoteric aspects of advanced non-Caucasoid civilizations. It will also be necessary to emulate them to some degree in the matters of sexual-sensual behaviour, body exposure, cosmetics, fashion, body adornment and 'morality'. For if it was these aspects which displaced temporal aggression in these peoples, it is obvious that only the same mechanics can displace it in ourselves.

There is a difficulty, a subtlety that we must come to grips with. It was the most 'intelligent' and sensitive members of our Western civilization who first drew our attention to the environmental and human dangers posed by our 'progress'. And, to a great extent, it is still only this relative minority which is vocally concerned and which proposes solutions.

We have seen a general human tendency, common to all races, for the most intelligent and temporally sensitive to have a greater degree of sexual approach-avoidance. It is no accident that both Caucasoid and non-Caucasoid exceptional intelligences tend to be somewhat asexual, as reflected in reproduction. Buddhist and Christian priests have, alike, preferred celibacy statistically. Chinese and Western philosophers have, alike, left fewer offspring than their average fellow men.

Therefore, it is very natural that the most aware and sensitive Western people, those who are concerned with the catastrophic direction of Western civilization, should have turned to the most aware and sensitive aspects of successful non-Caucasoid civilizations. Intellectual turned to intellectual, philosopher turned to philosopher, mystic turned to mystic across cultural and racial barriers. And each found the other very nearly similar in the matter of sexual outlook... an asexual world view, a tendency toward statistical genetic oblivion.

It is therefore natural that Western intellectuals and refugees from rampant technology would recognize and emphasize the ascetic, esoteric and asexual aspects of those high civilizations which have avoided our unfortunate direction.

But societies, either Caucasoid or non-Caucasoid, reflect not the philosophies of the minority but the behaviour of the many. Just as our own Western culture has been molded by the passions and violence of average men, and not by the temporal and intellectual benevolence of the few... so have non-Caucasoid civilizations been molded by the behaviour patterns of the many and not by the intellectual positions of a temporally aware elite.

It is my feeling that the sexual-sensual behaviour of the average person in Egypt, China or pre-Caucasoid India displaced aggressions which are more apparent in less adapted and sexually-sensually less evolved average Caucasoids.

It was a lower *average* level of aggression, made possible by a different sexual-sensual outlook and different sexual-sensual behaviour by *average* people, that allowed these non-Caucasoid civilizations to reflect *as a whole* pacific and benevolent values which have been common to philosophers of all races. It was a lower average level of aggression due to sexual-sensual behaviour which permitted the average man in Egypt or China to share more closely the non-aggressive values of his philosophers. In the West this has not been the case. The values of our sensitive and intellectual elite have more often been mocked by the more violent and aggressive behaviour of average men.

And the point is this: those who wish to lower the level of temporal and technological aggression in our entire society must encourage the average person to indulge in aggression-displacement activities of a sexual-sensual nature.

But this has never been the case. Traditional philosophical-religious doctrine in the West has stressed discouragement of satisfying sexual-sensual behaviour.

And our so-called "progressive" contemporary intellectuals have done the same, and are doing it still. The average Western man is being offered the asexual values common to exceptional intelligence, not the sexual-sensual values common to *average* people in environmentally sane non-Caucasoid civilizations.

We have seen that Chinese and Egyptian civilizations were less aggressive than ours. But the art of these cultures shows us that the average people were not ascetics even if their intellectual elite tended to be. These cultures incorporated a high degree of sexual experience and sexual-sensual stimulation. In general, it was a much higher level than has ever been manifested in the West by Caucasoids.

The insight offered seems to be that exceptional intelligence, sensitivity and awareness tend toward non-aggression because of a more complete understanding of time. A feeling of continuity with past and future promotes both benevolence and functional, statistical leanings toward sterility and self-imposed celibacy. But aggression in the average man, the man who defends and asserts his temporal territory, must be displaced by sexual-sensual mechanisms. Caucasoids have confusing sexual behaviour because the sexual adaptations were distorted by glacial ones.

If our aggressive technology is to be curbed the average man must be given sexual displacement mechanisms which Nature partially denied him. If intellectuals are smart and truly wish to curb technology they will stop staring autistically at their statistically asexual navels and begin thinking about encouraging the average man to improve his sexual-sensual satisfaction.

But we find that our progressive intellectuals are not very objective after all. Advanced feminist thinkers maintain that no one should be a sex object. Progressive nature-lovers and anti-technological hippie commune members rage against the fashion and cosmetics industries. Television commentators, newspaper pontificators and psychologists rail against permissiveness. Our religious leaders fight pornography.

And the irony of it.

The high non-Caucasoid civilizations of China, Egypt and pre-Caucasoid India, the philosophies of which our intellectuals are increasingly adopting and the lower aggression of which we recognize to be a valuable example... all were exceptional examples of cultures maintaining that both women *and* men were sex objects, all were obsessed with fashion and cosmetics and jewelry, all incorporated sexual freedom with which our 'permissiveness' is but a pale reflection in comparison, and all of them valued art and decoration which was 'pornographic' in the literal meaning of that word.

The Middle Kingdom achieved relatively uninterrupted survival for 4,000 years and produced Confucius, the *I Ching*, marvels in ceramics and textiles and painting, superb cabinetwork and mathematics, gunpowder, the compass, aluminum and very advanced medicine... and exquisite refinements in what we would call 'perversion' and immorality. The Chinese refined physical pleasures every bit as much as they refined aesthetic ones. Their women were stimulated by vaginal inserts of various sorts and by cunnilingus performed by both human and animal partners.

Fellatio was enjoyed by both men and women, and males indulged extensively in intercourse with animals. Male and female prostitution were regarded as a normal and sensible arrangement and especially adept prostitutes of both sexes were highly respected. Most chemical research conducted by the Chinese had the goal of developing ever more effective aphrodisiacs. It must be recorded that about the only example of Chinese behaviour resulting in the near-extermination of a species involved the search for aphrodisiac ingredients. Traffic in rhinoceros horn, conducted by the African Arabs for Chinese customers, very nearly decimated that species.

We know that similar sexual activities do occur within our own Western culture, but they are regarded as something improper and even criminal. The Chinese, however, regarded such experience as a normal part of life and talked about their enjoyments openly, boasting or offering advice.

Ancient Egyptian art shows that this people devoted a good deal of thought to developing fashions and sheer fabrics which exposed the body while jewelry adorned it. Female fashions of the XVIII Dynasty were not only sheer, but completely open down the front. Ancient Egyptian art aptly testifies to the Egyptian love of cosmetics, and nipples as well as eyes were emphasized with colour. The major purpose of Egyptian international trade was to obtain incense and we are told that it was used mainly for religious purposes. This is true, and the volumes of frankincense and myrrh used by priests were enormous, but much was used in the production of scented cones of fat which perfumed party-goers.

The Egyptians would go far afield in search of cosmetic ingredients. Antimony from a princess's rouge-box was discovered, by chemical analysis, to have come from southern Africa. And, aside from the monumental stonework along the Nile, the most characteristic Egyptian artifacts consist of personal jewelry... necklaces, jewelled collars, fillets, anklets and ornamental belts. As Milada Vilímková says:

> *Ornamental belts for women are common in the scenes of social occasions from the time of Thutmose IV... in the Dier el-Bahari relief is a scene in the tomb of Wah showing two girls playing a lyre and a double pipe, wearing transparent sleeved dresses reaching almost to their ankles, and belts made up of large plaques painted in red. The belts appear to have been worn under the dress next to the skin. At a slightly later date music and dancing girls, servants and very young*

Plate IV *Egyptian relief showing little sexual differentiation between male and female dress. Note dress open completely down the front.*

girls are usually shown naked in social life, wearing only ornamental belts around their hips.

The common image of Egypt seems to be that it was a rather gloomy place, obsessed by thoughts of death. This impression is inaccurate and is fostered by the fact that things made of stone are more likely to survive the ravages of time. Thus we have many examples of temples and tombs, but few examples of harps, lyres and other musical instruments and no very good idea of the non-religious lifestyle. However, an immense amount of personal jewelry has been found, and there are quite a few scenes of gay social occasions depicted in reliefs. The average Westerner's notion that the Egyptians were a people subdued by the knowledge of death is contradicted by the fact that the *ankh* (life) is the most common type of pendant found and the symbol *djed* (stability) the next most common. Social scenes illustrated in relief show that the Egyptians enjoyed life sensually and sexually somewhat more than we do, balancing the present's assertion with the right of both past and future to exist... *djed*... stability. With us, by contrast, present-tense assertion, contemporary industry and technology threaten to prevent the future from happening and threaten the past with oblivion.

Mertz translates:

> *Spend the day merrily; put unguent and fine oil to thy nostrils, and lotus flowers on the body of thy beloved. Set ringing and music before thy face. Cast all evil behind thee and think thee of joy — until that day comes when harbour is reached in the land that loves silence. Spend the day merrily, and weary not therein; lo, none can take his goods with him; lo, none that has departed can come again.*

This sounds suspiciously like an Egyptian version of 'eat, drink and be merry, for tomorrow we may die.' Except that the Egyptians did not try to avoid acceptance of death implied by the 'may' of the Western phrase. The Egyptians knew death, faced it and probably lived more joyfully as a result. The small goods of Egyptian day-to-day life testify to sexual-sensual enjoyment, and humour. Again, Mertz:

> *When I kiss her, and her lips are open,*
> *Then I am happy — even without beer!*

India before the domination by Europeans which began in the 16th Century presents a picture similar to that of China and Ancient Egypt. The subcontinent which produced the Buddha and which now produces a seemingly inexhaustible supply of Masters,

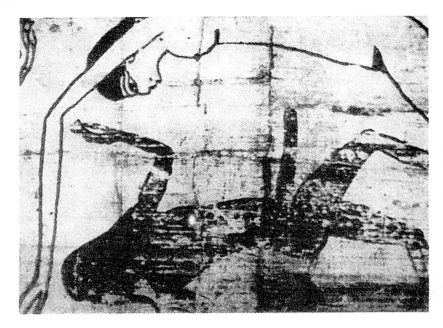

Plate V *Symbolic painting from Egypt showing sexual-religious content. Note also 'Feminist' sexual position. Would an Egyptian understand our concept of 'pornography'?*

Teachers, gurus and bikkhus who captivate alienated Western young once balanced the meditation with a highly erotic 'secular' life. To the sexually maladjusted Western mind some Hindu temples are simply monuments to pornography, and hard core at that, with dominant motifs of well-rounded and smiling girls intertwined with excitedly erect males. The *Kama Sutra* needs no discussion because its sexual advice is too well-known, if shocking, to Western morality.

It would seem that the 'optimum human culture norm', a culture which does not destroy itself because of rampant temporal

Plate VI *Indian woman. Acceptance of natural body form with no attempt to distort sexual parts, fondness for adornment.*

Plate VII   *Cretan bell-skirt of 1,200 B.C. showing early hip-emphasis in Western civilization.*

aggression and one which is yet fully developed in terms of present-past-future communication, incorporates a high level of sexual-sensual stimulation. For reasons outlined previously, I think there is evidence that such a civilization *must* offer a high level of such stimulation.

If we take a very brief historical look at our own sexual-sensual lifestyle in the West, and compare certain gross features with Egyptian, Chinese and pre-Caucasoid Indian civilizations, we will receive some shocks.

The first thing to realize is that our sexual-sensual behaviour is not typical of civilized society but resembles more the sexual-sensual behaviour of 'primitive' cultures retarded by adverse environmental conditions. This should not come as a surprise since we evolved

Plate VIII *Parisian lady of 1777 in* grande toilette *being escorted through door sideways because of exaggerated hips. Compare with Venus of Laussel.*

partially under adverse conditions during Würm. A cursory glance at Western fashion suggests that we seem to be puzzled by reproduction, disturbed and obsessed by sexual difference. Our fashions reveal a historical inability to accept *all* of the natural human body. In addition to a general Western tendency to demand a high degree of sexual differentiation in costume, we note that certain periods have emphasized sexual parts of the body, particularly of the female body, in an almost cultish or fetishistic way.

Compare the costumes illustrated in Plates VII-X with the 'Venus figurines'.

Some periods of Western history have featured women's dresses which so over-emphasized hips that women could only pass through

Plate IX   *Woman's dress of 1870. The 'Venus of Lespugue' clothed.*

Plate X   *Extreme distortion of hips, waist and bust in women's clothing, 1890-1918.*

doors sideways. This development reached its apex about 1780 in Paris with the *grande toilette*, but unnatural emphasis of the hips has been a more or less constant feature in Western fashion from the time of the Minoans until the very recent past. Other periods have so over-emphasized the female buttocks that women could not sit down in their bustles, or so over-emphasized the hip-waist-bust curve that female ribs were actually permanently distorted by corsets.

Males have not been ignored. In several periods of Western history the penis has been emphasized by codpieces. The Minoans did this and it crops up again in Elizabethan England and Philip's Spain (see Plates XI-XII). In Elizabeth's England codpieces grew so large that men began the custom of tying ribbons around them at one-inch intervals in order to advertise their prowess. Some cheated a bit on the interval and Elizabeth was forced to pass laws guaranteeing the one-inch measurement... a progressive bit of consumer protection for the female population. Masculine shoulders have been exaggerated by huge puff sleeves and corseted waists.

Even when our Western clothing has not actually distorted the natural body, we have demanded a high degree of sexual differentiation in dress and grooming. We have ensured that the 'social silhouettes' of the sexes were different and easily identifiable. Western males have generally worn hose or trousers and our women have worn dresses. We have only to recall that a few years ago parents were concerned that long hair on boys made them more 'female' and that long hair might pose some difficulties to normal sexual development. Many parents were upset that 'you can't tell boys from girls' and feared that the younger generation itself might be confused. One psychologist wryly remarked: "*They* can tell the difference and that's all that matters."

Our sexual jealousy has been taken to extremes, too, compared with civilized cultures. We have put a great deal of emphasis on 'sexual fidelity' and have never really accepted 'pre-marital sex'. For us Westerners, *the* sexual behaviour has always been a pair-bond, although we have always cheated on this concept. Sexual fidelity in women has always been emphasized and the 'chastity belt' is an understandable concept to us. This ferocious emphasis on pair-bonding occurs also with very primitive cultures, Australian aborigines, for instance, and the 'chastity belt' idea is reflected in the practice in a couple of very primitive African tribes where the husband will sew up his wife's labia before going off to war.

Andreas Lommel and many other art experts maintain that the 'Venus figurines' of the European Upper Paleolithic were not naturalistic but symbolic of fertility. The words 'symbolic' and 'religious' are over-used in the West to explain things which are otherwise inexplicable. If the 'Venus figurines' are indeed symbolic of reproduction and fertility, then our Western fashions reflect a very primitive culture trait of being confused and awed by reproduction and sexual difference.

It must be granted that some of the Venus figurines are exaggerated and stylized and, therefore, 'symbolic'. But the word

Plate **XI** *Codpiece on Cretan fresco illustrates the Western tendency to em-phasize sexual parts of the body. Circa 1,200 B.C. Compare with Spanish codpiece 2,500 years later.*

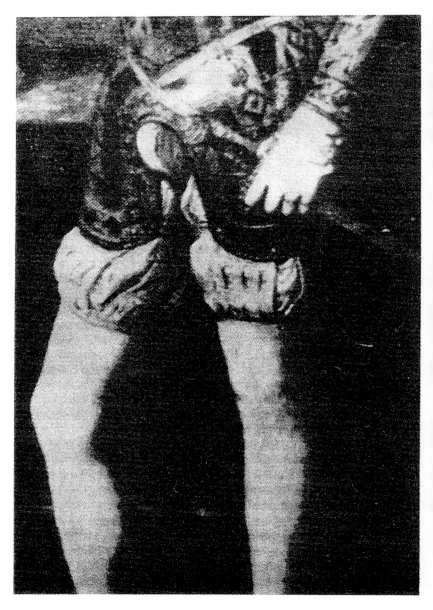

Plate XII   *A.D. 1550-1600. Close-up of portrait of Philip of Spain featuring codpiece. Follows tradition of Western sexual distortion.*

means nothing. Our 'symbol' for fertility must have a template...
and that template was the real appearance, often exaggerated and
stylized, of Upper Paleolithic women. And, from the peculiarities of
Western fashion, it is obvious that we are still fixated on a high
degree of sexual dimorphism. Our psychology seems to demand it
and we recreate in our fashions the dimorphism which has been
diluted in nature.

Our fashions resemble the sexual fertility obsessions of primitive
people now living in the world, and primitive people of our own
past. We might take a closer look at this because it might give us a
better insight into the world view of primitives.

Some peoples were prevented by hostile environments from fully
developing a three-tense understanding of time and full
communication with human past-present-future continua. These
people could be said to be alienated in a present that is not
completely understandable in the human context. Reproduction
leads to a psychological door, the future, which a retarded culture
has not opened sufficiently. They are quite naturally awed by this
unknown, and sex and reproduction become mysterious keys.

Our case is somewhat different. Our geographical environment
was sometimes harsh, but sometimes inordinately rich. We were
able to develop a full three-tense culture, but glacial adaptations
robbed our race of sexual adaptations which would have made it
easier to come to terms with reproduction.

Our sexual-sensual behaviour resembles that of some primitive
people... but for completely opposite reasons. Our racial physical
characteristics have posed a psychological limitation comparable to
environmental limitations experienced by primitives of our own and
other races. We, too, have been prevented from accepting
reproduction and sex in a mature way because of the degree of our
racial dimorphism and lesser-evolved sexual adaptations of
pleasure. We, too, are somewhat trapped and alienated in a present
tense bounded by our approach-avoidance of reproduction and
bringing the future into being. Because we are racially more tied to
this present-tense territory by sexual maladaptations, we war on the
past and future, and our 'progress' and aggression are
manifestations of territorial assertion and defense. Unlike the
Chinese and the Egyptians, we have difficulty in seeing the past and
future as real entities with a right to exist.

If we compare our own fashions with the clothing of Chinese and
Egyptians we will see immediately that these peoples were more able
to accept the natural form of the human body, did not need to

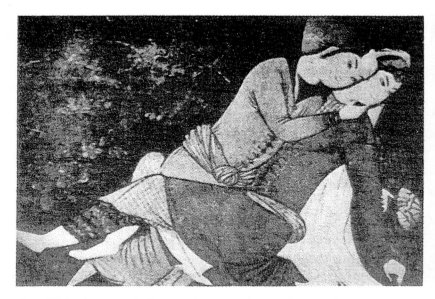

Plate XIII *Seventeenth Century Persian painting of Tartar lovers. Very little sexual dimorphism in dress as compared to Western fashion.*

exaggerate sexual parts, and did not demand a high degree of sexual dimorphism in their dress (see Plate XIII). Wealthy Chinese of both sexes customarily wore robes, while the lower classes of both sexes wore 'pyjamas' familiar to us in China today under elite-less Communism. The Egyptians did have some degree of sexual dimorphism in dress, but not much because they didn't wear much. Men and women went as nearly naked as possible and the natural body form of both sexes was accepted and adorned, not distorted.

Such is our sexual maladaptation that we give clothing characteristic of 'optimum human culture norms' a special name. We call it 'unisex'. Our label would be incomprehensible to a Chinese or an Ancient Egyptian. Our notion that sex should, ideally, be completely restricted to a pair-bond would be equally incomprehensible. A pair-bond was a necessary economic structure for these people: one might say that it was the 'basic minimum' economic and breeding unit... as indeed it is. It was the minimum to which most people were, perforce, restricted. But, among Chinese and Egyptians, sexual-sensual experience could be acquired outside the pair-bond and in mixed social situations if one could afford more than the basic minimum.

But such is our sexual maladaptation and consequent obsession that, for us, the pair-bond has been tied into our religion, tied into our philosophy of past-present-future continua.

Before leaving this discussion of psychobiology reflected historically and socially, a few words must be said about recent developments in Western fashion.

Our clothing is becoming less sexually differentiated. It is now acceptable for women to dress in pants and the 'social silhouettes' of the sexes are converging. One might say that we are evolving, perhaps, in the direction of an 'optimum human culture norm'.

Perhaps we are. On the other hand, perhaps we're not.

'Unisex' and the feminist push toward the wearing of what is basically the traditional Western male costume template does not seem to be motivated by a decreasing need for sexual differentiation in satisfying human sexual relations, but by a determination to share in male-dominated society. Rather than encouraging a greater degree of sexual-sensual stimulation in society, the contemporary feminist and 'liberated' view seems to be a denial of much sexual interaction and stimulation altogether. No one should be a sex object. Sex in society, and purposeful sexual stimulation in books, films and advertising, are reprehensible. Anti-technological young people have taken a viewpoint similar to Feminists who wish to obtain increased entree into the technology. Commune members and members of naturalistic and anti-technological groups allow both sexes to wear the same costume, generally blue jeans, but these groups value 'naturalism' and are opposed to cosmetics, fashions, and sexual stimulation in the society.

In the short view we may conclude that the decreasing sexual differentiation demanded by both Feminists and anti-technological groups is, basically, a 'good thing'. The history of Western fashion shows that extreme sexual differentiation in costume has been characteristic of extreme aggression. The fashions of the colonial period of European expansion show this particularly, but a similar degree of sexual differentiation in costume was manifested during the Mycenaean-Minoan expansion, and during the Teutonic invasions of the Mediterranean world. Just as racially characteristic sexual dimorphism seems correlated with our higher level of aggression generally, so extreme sexual dimorphism in Western fashions can be correlated with periods of exceptional aggression or conflict.

But, in the long view, we may wonder at the value of contemporary 'sexless' trends. Anti-sexist attitudes of Feminists and anti-technological young, symbolized by 'unisex' costumes, is basically motivated by aggression. Feminists are opposing male-dominated technology and industry, while pacifists and anti-technologists are opposing the aggressive values of the same society. Both groups have merely picked the 'opposite' as a costume to illustrate their aggression. Feminists adopt the male costume which has become symbolic of control... 'wearing the pants'. Anti-war and anti-technological young have adopted a dress which reflects opposition to stylized sexual differentiation in the aggressive society they oppose and, with a touch of feminism thrown in, this results in standardized blue jeans. Both oppose sexual adornment and purposeful sexual stimulation.

Our Caucasoid psychology and sexual maladaptation are treacherous.

We may observe that both our aggressive mainstream society and those who oppose it incorporate elements of the 'spiritual-material' dichotomy, the 'sexual-ascetic' dichotomy, dictated long ago by Caucasoid sexual maladaptations which hampered our adjustment to the temporal, spiritual territory of time and human continuity. Both our society and those who oppose it are but two sides of the same racial coin of sexual maladaptation leading to abnormal aggression.

9

Oroubourous Unfettered

The contemporary world is threatened with many crises on many fronts. We recognize the fact that most of our contemporary problems have their sources in the activities of Western man. We presented the world with nuclear threat. Our invention of industrialism and technology brought pollution and resource wastage to the planet. Our aggressiveness has resulted in the expansion of Western culture until the entire world is beginning to reflect what anthropologist Claude Levi-Strauss characterized as an ugly monoculture 'thrown into the face of Mankind.'

The profile of the contemporary world is self-evident. It needs no in-depth depiction. It is all around us. Similarly, it is self-evident that this profile was drawn by Western man. We must explain why Western man has been so strongly motivated to undertake the activities which present our world with multiple threats.

I believe that I have offered some explanation of Caucasoid motivations. As sketchy as it is, the explanation offered here is supported by bones, art, literature, the gross pattern of history... and the evidence from these diverse sources coalesces into a consistent, cohesive whole. It is an explanation with broad circumstantial, if not in-depth, support.

If the argument presented here is judged to be valid or even defensible, we must look at ourselves in a new light. We may remember the statement by Ashley Montagu:

> *It is generally agreed that Man is born free of all those biological determinates that condition the behaviour of lower forms.*

That statement has been the foundation-truth of our self-conceptions and world view for the past three decades. If the argument presented here is judged to be defensible, then the foundation-truth provided by Montagu and two generations of social scientists must be re-evaluated. Our foundation-truth will have been eroded, and the structure of self-conceptions resting upon it will begin to sway.

But perhaps there is more at stake. If there is indeed an iceman inheritance, then it would seem that human disaster is inevitable.

It would seem that biological determinates must triumph over intellectual pretensions, must humble the vanity of free will. Perhaps we could tolerate being left without delusions, but can we tolerate being left without hope?

If the arguments presented here are valid, then, logically, the future holds only one of the following scenarios in store:

1. Western man will succeed in destroying, at least, all viable human life on the planet.

2. Western man will succeed in destroying only his own creations of Western culture and industrialism, and the rest of Mankind will eventually establish something similar to the social constructs of the Ancient Egyptians and Chinese with, perhaps, some vestige of Western technology.

3. There is the bare possibility of extra-terrestrial intervention which might impose some new pattern upon human life.

4. Western man, through valid self-examination, can overcome the motivational hold of biological determinates and modify his own behaviour with the aid of consciously created cultural mechanisms.

5. Western man, and the world along with him, can continue to 'progress' along the lines already established by contemporary culture and technology.

Perhaps each of these possibilities deserves some discussion. I think that the first and last possibilities can be dismissed. Both are vanities of power. Human life is too resilient and adaptable to be completely destroyed by the folly of Western activity. Similarly, the environment is both too limited and too delicate to permit the continuation of our present technology and industrialism. We will not destroy all human life, nor can we continue indefinitely on our present course.

That leaves three more probable future possibilities. Of these three, I think that the pattern of past history and present environmental limitation indicates that Western culture as we know it has reached its peak. In my opinion, the most probable future is one in which we will witness Western civilization collapsing upon itself, crushing its own spiritual and material foundations, and flickering out. This opinion is neither unique nor new. More than half a century ago, in his *Decline of the West*, Spengler offered the same opinion... but the argument of the iceman inheritance adds a new, biological dimension to Spengler's largely spiritual and material construct.

We are left with two other possible future scenarios: the idea of extra-terrestrial intervention; the hope of voluntary cultural adaptation.

Extra-terrestrial intervention has always been the fondly-held hope of a certain segment of society, whether that intervention takes the form of direct influence from the Godhead... or from 'benevolent Venusians'. Recently, however, the possibility of extra-terrestrial intervention has achieved some aura of scientfic credibility. Some exobiologists seriously consider the possibility that alien contact may already have taken place and may occur again. Scottish astronomer Duncan Lunan, author of *Man and the Stars*, advanced the theory that long-delayed radio and television echoes received mysteriously on earth since 1927 are intelligent signals from an alien space probe in a lunar orbit. Lunan's theory is that an alien probe has been returning our own radio and television signals. We receive these signals as 'echoes' with varying periods of delay. Lunan has plotted the variation in delay of echoes received by an experimental radio station operated by the Philips Electronics company in Holland during the late 1920's... and found that the graph depicted the constellation of Boötes.

In a similar vein, Soviet astronomer, Professor Sergei Kaplan of Gorky University, announced in December, 1973, that he had detected apparently intelligent pulsed radio signals coming from inside the solar system. Kaplan speculated that the signals originated from an alien space probe in a lunar orbit.

Data like those collected by Duncan Lunan, Kaplan and many others decided the United States government to attempt the 'official' interception of intelligent radio signals coming from space.

Project Ozma, headed by Dr. Frank Drake of Cornell University, was initiated in the early 1960's at the radiotelescope facility located at Greenbank, West Virginia. Ozma concentrated on listening for emissions coming from the star Tau Ceti, and there is some uncertainty about whether intelligent signals were, or were not, received. The official pronouncement was that Project Ozma failed to intercept intelligent signals from outer space. On the other hand, it is simply a fact that Project Ozma and Dr. Frank Drake were relocated to a specially constructed and much larger radiotelescope located at Arecibo, Puerto Rico. Since the move to Arecibo, official progress reports have been few and far between.

In addition to the attempt to intercept intelligent signals coming from outer space, there has been an effort to comb historical and anthropological material for evidence of extra-terrestrial visitation. This search has turned up some surprising results.

Two Chinese archeologists, Chi Pu Tei and Tsum Um Nui, discovered 716 stone discs in a cave in the Baian Kara Ula mountains. These discs were found in association with dwarf, large-headed skeletal material unclassifiable with known hominids. All of the discs have double spiral grooves inscribed outwards from the centre with accompanying symbols. The discs are 'stone', but of a material with a high metallic content, allegedly cobalt. According to exceedingly scanty reports, some of these discs have been taken to Moscow for analysis where they have been dated to approximately 12,000 B.P. Allegedly, some of the discs have been 'translated' and tell of a space-ship crash. Adequately trustworthy information concerning this find is very hard to obtain.

Another interesting bit of anthropological information concerns the cosmic beliefs of the Dogon people of West Africa. French anthropologists, Marcel Griaule and Germaine Dieterlen, discovered that the most closely-held secret of the Dogon people was a tradition about the nature of the Sirius star system. The Dogon believe that the bright star Sirius has a smaller, dim companion composed of extremely dense material. This is, in fact, true. The star we know as Sirius is accompanied by a white dwarf companion designated as Sirius B and this star is composed of material so condensed that a thimbleful would weigh 10,000 tons on earth.

It is difficult to explain this Dogon knowledge. Sirius B is totally invisible from earth and was only discovered by the use of powerful telescopes. Western astronomers did not know about the incredible density of white dwarfs in general, and Sirius B in particular (Sirius B was the first white dwarf discovered), until the 1920's.

The Dogon themselves say that their knowledge about the Sirius system was given to them by an extra-terrestrial visitor, an aquatic creature they call 'Nommo'. It is known that the Dogon people originally lived in ancient Egypt and migrated to West Africa in the relatively recent past. It is therefore of interest to note that the two ancient civilizations of Egypt and Sumeria both preserve traditions of contact with an extra-terrestrial, aquatic, being. The Sumerians called their visitor 'Oannes'. The Egyptian tradition of visitation is associated with the Goddess Isis.

There is no doubt that the world's space agencies take these data seriously. NASA exobiologist, Dr. Carl Sagan, refers to the importance of 'sub-Saharan' contact myths... and here he must be referring to the secrets of the Dogon and allied peoples as recorded by Griaule and Dieterlen.

The contemporary scientific opinion seems to be that extra-terrestrial contact in the past must be regarded as a probability. Therefore, it follows that extra-terrestrial visitation now and in the future is at least a possibility.

But there is no reason to assume that intervention in human affairs by alien beings would alleviate our problems. There is no reason to assume that alien intervention would be benevolent. There is some reason to assume otherwise.

There seems to be some sort of unexamined assumption that 'progress' must result in increased 'humanity'. Therefore, those who hope for extra-terrestrial intervention seem to assume that aliens must be more advanced than we are on earth, and therefore must be more 'humane'. George Adamski and other 'contactees' claim to have communicated with advanced and humane beings who will come to us from outer space and solve our problems.

Perhaps.

On the other hand, our own Western evolution on earth shows no strong correlation between 'progress' and 'humanity'. Indeed, it is the argument of this essay that our own technology is the result of aggression rather than the result of intelligent and 'humane' evolution. Why should it be otherwise elsewhere? If our world is suffering from undisplaced aggression caused by temporal territorial behaviour, perhaps other planets bearing intelligent life have a similar burden. Oroubourous, the worm of temporal vanity, has been released on earth. He may have been unfettered elsewhere in the cosmos.

In their independent studies of UFO sightings, both French scientist Aime Michel and American zoologist Ivan T. Sanderson have been forced to conclude that a pattern of intelligent and potentially hostile surveillance is indicated by the evidence. NASA, through the Rand Corporation, has commissioned a number of studies concerning the probable psychological profiles of hypothetical space visitors. If General Douglass McArthur's last official statement is any guide — "the next war will be an interplanetary one" — then there is a definite concern in both academic and military quarters that the 'Venusians' may not prove to be 'benevolent'. The argument presented in this book implies that *any* technological and expansive intelligence is aggressive by definition. Oroubourous is probably at large elsewhere in the universe and, doubtless, other worlds have reaped their own version of the iceman's inheritance of temporal vanity and inadequately displaced aggression.

Alien intervention is definitely a possible future scenario, taken from the realm of Buck Rogers into the bosom of contemporary science by qualified experts. Yet, though a possibility, the idea of extra-terrestrial involvement in earthly affairs may be improbable as a scenario for the immediate future. Many space scientists, Lunan, Sagan and Drake among them, accept contact between galactic intelligent communities... but accept it as a relatively rare occurrence. Lunan believes that earth may have been visited only once by alien intelligence during the tenure of morphologically modern man. It is Lunan's view that all of earth's 'contact traditions' can be traced back to just one encounter which happened perhaps 14,000 years ago.

Similarly, a 'think tank' of space scientists including Carl Sagan and Frank Drake, informally called The Order of the Dolphin in honour of Dr. John Lilly's apparent success in communicating with a non-human intelligence on earth, concluded in 1966 that contact between space intelligences was probably a rare event. The distances separating intelligent communities in space must be vast. But, more important, the period of high technology permitting contact might be very limited. The Order of the Dolphin noted that technology on earth was in grave danger of destroying the intelligent community. The scientists concluded that the duration of a technology permitting contact might be very short — if events on earth are any reliable guide, perhaps less than 100 years. If that is indeed the case, then it is obvious that only rarely will any two communities in space be close enough, and at the appropriate technological stage of evolution, to effect contact.

It seems as if our space scientists, while allowing the possibility of alien intervention, consider it an improbable influence for the immediate future. The consensus is that we will be left alone to solve our own problems.

And that judgment brings us to the last of our possible future scenarios. Are we capable of consciously changing our behaviour, utilizing consciously constructed cultural mechanisms? Or, to put it another way, as Dr. Carl Sagan put it in the last chapter of *Intelligent Life in the Universe*, "is there intelligent life on Earth?"

We have Ashley Montagu's dictum asserting Man's freedom from biological determinates. But, if my thesis is defensible, it is clear that we are not free of "all those biological determinates" and it is obvious that the pattern of human history was conditioned by them... to a degree which threatens us with converging catastrophes.

There is no reason, however, why these undoubted biological determinates must be absolutely compelling. We do possess intelligence and a great capacity for independent thought in spite of motivational tendencies forced upon us by our evolutionary experience. There is no reason why we cannot use that intelligent and thoughtful capacity to consciously structure cultural norms and values and to encourage behaviour patterns which will partly compensate for the more destructive biologically-impelled motivational proclivities.

There have been times, after all, when Neanderthal-Caucasoid stock has been able to live in relatively gentle and non-expansive communities. Rare times, and short-lived times, but such times have existed.

Under the impetus of Cathar doctrine coming from the East, the civilization of the Albigensians in southern France was, for a century or so, an island of humanity in an otherwise unrelieved sea of Dark Ages brutality and ugliness. Leaders of this civilization, the Cathar *perfecti*, may have exhibited a very real asceticism — they were sworn to poverty, chastity and vegetarianism — but the larger secular population of Languedoc indulged in a degree of intellectual and sexual permissiveness that has seldom been equalled in the West. Some of the troubador ballads reflected other than purely spiritual love. Indeed, in addition to the female social and spiritual equality practised in Languedoc, the freedom of female sexuality proved to be just as offensive to the Church. One of the oft-cited justifications for the crusade were the 'courts of love', alleged orgies of sensuality, which also took place within the castles of Languedoc. One of the most famous, or infamous, 'courts of love' was presided over by the Viscountess of Carcassone in the castle of Puivert.

One can also point to some of the cultures of central India which, though largely Caucasoid genetically, had an Eastern philosophical orientation due to the influx of Mongoloid peoples. A 'golden period' of artistic expression coupled with non-expansion occurred from about 850 A.D. to about 1100 A.D., before the area was overrun by aggressive Islam. The only monuments of this civilization consist of ruined temples whose 'pornographic' sculpture titillates Western visitors today.

In a sense, it is possible to say that the Ancient World until the fall of Rome represented a non-Western orientation in spite of the fact that the peoples living around the Mediterranean became increasingly, and more purely, 'Western' and 'Neanderthal-Caucasoid' as successive migrating waves of Indo-European speakers arrived in the area. We recognize that the 'ambiance' of the Ancient World differs in some way from the character of the Western World... even though both 'worlds' occupied an identical geographical space. The difference between the modern Western world and the lost Ancient one is cultural.

It has been my argument that this subtle difference is a result of primary Egyptian influence in the Ancient World. This influence became exceedingly diluted and attenuated in the later Classical and Hellenistic periods, but it was there and potent until the final fall of Rome. It was an influence with a profile which included a greater degree of sexual-sensual freedom, a reverence for the female principle in the 'Godhead', the pantheon, a tendency toward intellectual and not technological expression. Human life was not so alienated, the gods and goddesses, and nature, were kept very close and very interrelated.

Though the Egyptian influence stretched very thin toward the end of this Ancient World, I think that we can discern its influence even in expansive and Imperial Rome. Much that we characterize as 'decadence' in Roman society was actually 'civilization' acquired gradually as the Italic barbarians became exposed to Egyptian culture through contact with other Mediterranean peoples and the Egyptians themselves. The 'decadence' of Rome included, at least, a degree of religious, racial and sexual tolerance that we could well emulate. And, though expansive, the Romans attempted on several occasions to 'fix' and stabilize their frontiers and the extent of the Empire. Successful in stabilizing much else, the Romans failed at this. Barbarians from across the frontiers continually invaded Roman territory. In the North and East, where pulses from the Caucasus beat, Rome was forced to expand continually or be overrun. In a very real sense, barbarian pressure never allowed Rome to fix the geographical extent of the Empire. In some places, such as Scotland, the Romans built viable walls to keep themselves in and the barbarians out. But no walls could be built between Rome and the steppes of Russia.

Perhaps we can also grant that around the fringes of Europe there is, or was until recently, a certain 'non-Western' ambiance. The 'Celts' seem to preserve some Egyptian-like traits, including the insistence on preserving female expression in divinity. The 'Celts' are on the fringes of Europe for two reasons: they seem to have migrated largely by sea and therefore tended to locate around the shores of Europe; later invasions pushed them into fringe areas and mountainous areas whenever they expanded outwards from their beach-heads. The Celtic reverence for the female principle and their penchent for artistic and literary expression rather than industrialism may be due, in part, to the cultural influence of Ancient Egypt. It is now known that the ancient religion and at least the Ogam alphabet of the Celts came from Libya across North Africa and hopped to the British Isles and Brittany coasts via the Iberian peninsula. All along this route we find Ogam scripts, dolmens and characteristic bronze weapons and tools. It is possible that even the Celtic languages, as distinguished from the Ogam alphabet, were heavily influenced by ancient North African tongues.

We may speculate that one of the reasons why Catharism took such firm root in the Pyranees was that the area was one of those Celtic 'fringes' and refuges. The Cathar sanctuary of Montségur was, in fact, built upon an older Druidic structure.

Neanderthal-Caucasoids *can* achieve cultural norms and values much more characteristic of the norms and values shared by the world's majority of non-Western people. But, with only one exception, the Celtic-Cathar civilization of the Albigensians, the Neanderthal-Caucasoid adoption of more typical human behaviour has always been due to force of circumstance. It has not been voluntary. As we have conjectured, the Neanderthal-Caucasoid migrants into the Ancient World trickled in to become naturally dominated by the established Egyptian culture. In India, the lascivious and civilized cultures of the central plateau were strongly influenced by Mongoloid migration into the sub-continent.

Only once have Neanderthal-Caucasoids voluntarily adopted something approaching the world's norm of psychobiological outlook and behaviour. Catharism and the civilization of

Languedoc show, at least, that it *can* be done. But the utter and savage rejection of that civilization indicates that a wholesale acceptance of any similar outlook by the majority of Westerners is not very likely. It is our need for a feeling of superiority that is the problem. Our vanity.

It is not the mere existence of biological determinates which threatens us: it is our shame about admitting their existence that does.

I am reminded of my favourite literary character. Rostand did not 'say it straight' about the condition of Western man, but, in his creation of Cyrano de Bergerac, 'wiseacred' with an allegory that comes very close to the mark. Cyrano is, in my opinion, a character through which Western man can very nearly discover himself. Aggressive, brilliant, protective, romantically shy towards women. Cowardly. Endowed with more than adequate courage for facing any external threat, Cyrano dared not look himself in a mirror. Unafraid of facing a hundred swordsmen in an alley, Cyrano could not face himself.

Cyrano's problem was a minor physical deformity... his nose. It was overly long and he was sensitive about it. Hating it, he also took an inverse pride in it. Because of his deformed nose, Cyrano was certain that no woman could ever come to love him.

Thinking himself unloved, Cyrano flung himself into one danger and adventure after another. In the vacuity of modern psychiatric parlance, our Cyrano was supremely 'alienated' and 'acted out' a 'death wish'. In spite of all his achievements and adventures, Cyrano led an empty life. He had always loved the beautiful Roxanne, but, shamed by his nose and believing that Roxanne was revulsed by the sight of him, Cyrano never courted her.

Only at the end of his life did Cyrano realize that his beloved Roxanne had always loved him. It transpired that she had never really noticed his nose. In spite of its objectively large dimensions, it was yet dwarfed in Roxanne's mind by much more important considerations: Cyrano's intellectual brilliance, his undoubted courage, his capacity and determination to protect the powerless, his thwarted capacity to love.

At the end of Rostand's play, Cyrano laments the waste of years and the emptiness of both their lives. At the end Cyrano recognizes his life-long enemy. He says:

> *"Ah, you too, Vanity! I knew you would overthrow me in the end —"*

A quirk of nature, a small deformity, keeps us from looking in the mirror. Like Cyrano's nose, it is not the mere existence of biological determinates which threatens us: it is our shame and denial of them which may overthrow us.

Our Neanderthal psychobiological maladaptions... our nose. Like Cyrano's physical defect, our psychobiological one is real, but its importance is magnified out of all proportion by our vanity. And, like Cyrano, Western man has escaped his shame by filling his life with grandiose adventure and arrogant behaviour.

Perhaps the key lies in Cyrano's last speech. He knew the identity of his ultimate and final adversary. We know, too. It is our vanity.

Instead of denying the existence of biological determinates in our behaviour, we must somehow find the courage to look them straight in the mirror. If we can only find the courage that Cyrano lacked, we may yet live. And if we do not find love, we may at least discover compassion for ourselves and others.

Appendix:
Objections, Counter-arguments...
and Retorts

Since 1965, when I first began to develop the biological notions of human temporal territoriality in general and the higher level of Caucasoid aggression resulting from this type of territoriality combined with glacial maladaptation, I have taken every available opportunity to discuss these ideas with experts in whose fields I've trampled. Particularly after the publication of *The Cronos Complex I* in 1973, I found myself involved in a lively correspondence with scholars and interested laymen on three continents. Then, too, following lectures and interviews on radio and television, listeners and viewers have sometimes felt compelled to respond to the ideas I'd put forward.

Most respondents and correspondents offered objections and counter-arguments to the ideas I was advancing. Some of these I had considered myself, others I had not thought of. Some of these objections and counter-arguments have been incorporated into the text of *The Iceman Inheritance* by coverage of historical and intellectual points which I would not have thought necessary had it not been for this sort of contribution. The outline of Caucasoid invasion into the Mediterranean basin and the stages in the development of 'Western Civilization' is an example of an explanation offered because of the observations and objections of manuscript readers and correspondents. The attention given to the

Western concept of 'love' is another example of material included because of criticism and discussion, while the comments regarding the possible 'aggressive' psychological profile of hypothetical alien beings stands as yet another. The contributions of critical readers and correspondents have been acknowledged in the opening pages of this book and some criticisms have been incorporated in the Introductions.

There is another category of objection and counter-argument, however, which I did not feel sufficiently relevant to be included in the presentation of this thesis directly... mostly because, although they immediately spring to mind, refutations of them would also spring to mind almost as quickly among readers who have special knowledge. Unfortunately, however, this particular category covers a wide range of topics and no reader, however informed, is likely to be aware of the facts which argue against some of these apparent objections. In fact, following the presentation of some of these objections and counter-arguments by experts and laymen, I found myself scrabbling around researching topics as diverse as the archeological digs in Alaska and specific tactics of war in the Middle Ages.

Therefore, I offer the following 'refutations' and 'retorts' in answer to some of the most common objections which have been raised against this thesis. It is convenient to group this material in two major divisions: some comments upon 'comparative aggression'; and the discussion of 'biology vs. culture.' The outlines in both cases will be as brief as possible because a so-called 'popular' book is no place for extremely detailed discussion of very specialized matters.

Comparative aggression

It has been asserted that exceptional aggression has been manifested by non-Western and non-'Caucasoid' peoples, and some examples have been offered. I have not intended to suggest that Neanderthal-Caucasoids have *always* proved more aggressive than anyone else... but merely that this major group of Mankind has a *tendency* toward higher aggression and that this has, in the aggregate, affected the pattern of history in obvious ways.

On the other hand, some examples given for exceptional non-Caucasoid aggression do seem to evaporate under closer scrutiny, especially with respect to the *quality* of the aggression manifested.

The Religions of Mexican Indians.

Many people have pointed out to me that the Amerindians of the Valley of Mexico and other places in Middle America indulged in ferocious religious wars, just as the West did when Europeans indulged in Crusades and the Arabs indulged in their Jihad. What, therefore, is the difference in aggression and religious intolerance?

A study of these wars in the Valley of Mexico reveals, in my opinion, that the religious wars of these Amerindians were of a different quality than the religious conflicts of the West. They were not motivated by intolerance as was the case in the West. The religious wars of the Middle Amerindians were apparently purely 'economic' in nature.

Religions in the Valley of Mexico had a bloodthirsty character and involved frequent human sacrifice. The Amerindians of Mexico engaged in 'religious wars', not to impose one set of religious beliefs on another, not to proselytize their beliefs, but simply to acquire prisoners-of-war who would serve as suitable human sacrifices. In fact, faced with this religious necessity, the Middle American communities took care *not* to annihilate each other so that the supply of sacrificial victims would never cease. Eventually, the 'warfare' evolved into a stylized and carefully arranged conflict. In the interests of obtaining sacrificial victims who were unmaimed by combat and therefore presumably more acceptable to the gods, some of these Amerindians gave up the use of weapons altogether in their warfare. 'Paintbrushes' (or the Middle American equivalent) were employed by the warriors. Each side had an agreed-upon colour. The object of combat became the attempt to smear opposing warriors with paint. A warrior so marked became 'wounded' and a 'prisoner' and, eventually, a sacrifice.

One may legitimately ask, however, if the bloodthirsty character of these religions was itself a manifestation of aggression comparable to anything witnessed in the West. Of course it was. On the other hand, we do not know the origins of Middle American religions... and some authorities believe that these religions were heavily influenced by Old World ideas and behaviour.

When the Spaniards first invaded the New World of Middle America they found many religious parallels between Europe and Mexico. The Spanish, and almost all scholars up until about 1850, accepted the 'naive' notion that the Amerindians either *were*, or had been culturally influenced by, wandering Canaanites, Phoenicians, Carthaginians and Early Christians and that much Amerindian culture and religion consisted of a mixture of these disparate elements. With the rise of modern archeology and so-called critical scholarship, these 'naive' notions — and the evidence that supported them — were rejected.

But modern archeology is in the process of undertaking a painful and embarrassing re-think, although the most pedantic and 'establishment' scholars still have their minds suitably and tightly shut.

Professor Barry Fell of Harvard University, Professor George Carter of Texas A. and M., and a few other courageous scholars have been recently re-introducing these 'naive' notions and rejected evidence into the academic community. Fell's book, *America B.C.*, documents monumental linguistic evidence that the New World was indeed visited often, and in force, by Canaanites, Phoenicians, Libyans, Egyptians, Celtiberians and others for many thousands of years before either Lief Erickson or Columbus waded ashore. Further, Fell demonstrates that these visits influenced the culture and religions of Amerindians to a great extent. In the light of Fell's work, it may very well be that the bloodthirsty aspect of Middle American religion simply aped the religious ceremonies required by the Phoenician Baal. There is now solid evidence to support this conclusion, or at least to argue for it. The final verdict is not yet in. However, we must now accept at least the possibility that the ferociously inhumane religions of Middle America were yet another iceman inheritance imposed upon non-Western peoples. Until there are more data, and data are analysed and a final judgment effected, the religious wars of Middle America's population cannot be used as an argument against this thesis.

The Mongol Expansions.
Several critics have pointed to the expansionism of Genghis Khan as an example of non-Western aggression. He is not alone... Timur-i-lang ('Tamerlane'), Babur, Jahangir could have been mentioned in company with Genghis Khan as examples of 'Mongol' or at least Central Asian conquerors who, for a brief period, terrorized the world of Eurasia. The word Mongol is in quotes in the last sentence simply because Timur, Babur and Jahangir were partly, if not mostly, 'Caucasoid' in this area of racial boundary, but operated within a mostly Mongol culture.

There is no doubt, of course, that the Mongol horsemen were fierce warriors, and cruel ones, who very nearly conquered Europe. We tend to forget that Timur's armies came within sight of Vienna. Europe was saved only because Timur turned back to deal with the rebellion of a vassal, Bayazit... but this 'vassal', Bayazit, had almost overwhelmed Europe, and Europeans of the time found it difficult, and horrifying, to conceive of the fact that Bayazit himself had an even more powerful overlord. Kings of Europe wrote to Timur pleading for mercy.

Yet, even considering the sheer magnitude of the Mongol expansions, involving numbers which panicked the population of the European peninsula, I submit that there was a difference in quality about this Mongol aggression. It was aggression, but it was 'normal' aggression. It was motivated by overpopulation in the Central Asian steppes and was expansion and migration of a people based on environmental necessity, not on psychological motivations. Mongol peoples have periodically pulsed outward in response to population and environmental pressures... but the waves have just as periodically subsided, usually within one or two generations. Only in one instance did a Mongol conquest last permanently and that was in China when, at the time of European contact, the rulers of China were (in theory) Manchurians. But, as is well-known, these invaders became absorbed by the Chinese culture and were only nominally 'barbarians' after two generations.

But, in the West, Mongol expansion never resulted in any permanent imposition of Mongol culture and language. After the pulse was over, the Mongol and Timurid polities disintegrated with the passing of the population peak which had brought them into being. Neither Genghis Khan nor Timur (or Babur or Jahangir) ever brought any proselytizing of culture, religion, politics or philosophy when they invaded. They merely temporarily required more room to live as they always had. When the population pressures eased, the Mongol incursions evaporated back into the steppes.

I do not think that these Mongol expansions can be compared to the expansion of Western peoples. The West has expanded, even when unnecessary because of 'normal' population and environmental factors, in order to impose Western culture and religion on others. Or, from the motivation of sheer greed, or from all these motivations combined in a mutually supportive justification structure. It is this expansion and aggression based upon the notion of cultural-religious-moral-racial *rightness* and intolerance that makes Western behaviour unique. I submit that no other people has shared this justification for aggression and expansion... certainly not the Mongols.

The Case of Japan.

Many people have mentioned the aggression of Japan, not only military, but also commercial and technological. It certainly seems obvious that the Japanese are the most aggressive of the Mongoloid major group of Mankind... they have been sufficiently aggressive to remain uncolonized by Europeans (uniquely among Eastern peoples) and to adopt our Western forms of militarism and technology and commercialism in successful self-defense. Some people have pointed to the development of martial arts in Japan as evidence of aggression.

The argument presented in *The Iceman Inheritance* is offered as a factor in the pattern of human history, but not as the *only* factor. There are, of course, *other* factors. In explaining why the Japanese should appear to be the most aggressive of Mongoloid peoples, I thing that Toynbee's environmental 'stimulus-response' construct is most relevant.

Japan and Great Britain have often been compared. The two island groups are roughly the same size, in roughly the same latitude, and share a roughly similar geographical relationship with their respective neighbouring continental land-masses. As Toynbee points out, there seems to be something special about the environmental conditions and cultural possibilities afforded by these two island groups. According to Toynbee, the latitude and climate promote vigor. Also, there is enough room for the development of a sizeable population... but enough geographical restriction to promote a high and constant level of friction between islanders. There is enough isolation from continental land-masses to prevent absolute submergence in the continental culture, but sufficient proximity to prevent insular stagnation.

We see that all of this appears to be relevant to the case of Japan and Great Britain. Both peoples, in their respective geographical and 'racial' spheres, proved to become particularly dominant once the insular population had reached a certain critical mass. Both peoples exhibit in their histories a high degree of internal friction. Both peoples exhibited a relatively high degree of externalized aggression in comparison with neighbours. The British became the premier colonial power of Europe, and the premier technological power.. and their American descendants have further spread their culture, technology, language and political institutions throughout the world.

In the East, the Japanese have been the most facile adopters of Western militarism, technology and industrialism... and the

Japanese expanded to impose their culture and language upon other East Asian peoples, until defeated by an even more aggressive and expansive Anglo-American alliance.

I think that Toynbee's 'stimulus-response' construct, and the comparison of Japan with Great Britain, explains adequately why the Japanese emerged as the most aggressive people of the Mongoloid domain. But, while granting this, we must yet concede that the Japanese were not as expansive or as aggressive as the West. *We* came to *them*. We *developed* the military and technological forms of aggression which the aggression of the Japanese allowed them to *adopt* successfully in self-defense.

With respect to the development and status of martial arts in Japan, it must be conceded that this culture trait is evidence of a high level of aggression. However, a biologist, viewing the stylized and ritualized forms of martial art, might very well conclude that such behaviour constitutes an aggression-displacement mechanism. That is, the aggression level is high enough to promote interest in fighting but low enough to be substantially absorbed by stylized and ritualized forms of fighting which have almost taken the forms of abstract studies and *games*.

The aggression level has seldom been low enough in the West to promote stylized fighting. Our aggression was historically of such proportions that it could be satisfied only by un-stylized real mayhem indulged in by many people... instead of highly ritualized mayhem practiced by only a few experts, as in Japan under the code of Bushido. Perhaps the 'jousting' of medieval European knights comes close to the institutionalization of martial arts in a manner somewhat comparable to the Japanese construct.

But, in my opinion, the only European stylization of conflict which truly approaches the Japanese achievement must be the ritualization of swordmanship in France from about 1650 until about 1780 with the development of 'fencing' and the weapon known as the rapier. Conflicts between French swordsmen assumed a great similarity to conflicts between Japanese samurai Zen-trained sword masters, with style and form being prized above the mere lethal results of the art. In France, the stylization was so extreme that a weapon was developed which could kill only with the point, a weapon which was delicate in the extreme. But it is worth noting that other Western nations did not so completely adopt French refinement in 'fencing'. The Italians insisted upon fencing with a dagger in the other hand, while the Spanish, Germans and English retained a cutting edge to their elongated swords.

In any case, Europeans have rarely allowed their conflicts to be settled by a small corps of professional warriors well-versed in the *arts* of stylized aggression. European conflicts, even during the heyday of 'chivalry' were decided by massed weapons wielded by non-expert common men... in spite of the knightly literature. The decisive battles of Europe were won by the commoner's longbow, the commoner's pike... not by the stylized knighthood.

The Eskimos.
The Eskimos presently live in the arctic and are therefore assumed to be 'cold-adapted'... and yet live in a remarkably peaceful society. Does this not refute much of the argument presented here?

No. I do not believe that it does. We must go back again to the last 'Ice Age' for the explanation.

Few laymen suspect that the 'Ice Age' was not a universal phenomenon. Although western Eurasia and eastern North America grew colder and developed ice sheets many thousands of feet thick, it is a fact that eastern Siberia and western Alaska were warmer than presently. While much of eastern North America and western Europe was under ice, the treeline in eastern Siberia and western Alaska was some 750 miles to the north of where the treeline is today. The dissection of mammoth stomachs reveal that flowers grew in Siberia during the 'Ice Age' where there are only tundra or icefields today. The mammoth itself is evidence of a warmer climate in Siberia and Alaska. Contrary to popular belief, the mammoth was not an *arctic* animal, but an animal of the temperate forests. The fact that mammoths ranged so far north in Siberia shows that the temperate forests extended far to the north during the last glacial period.

During the last 'Ice Age' the only entrance into the arctic was through this warmer corridor in Siberia. Mongoloid man lived in this area and was able to follow the warmer weather into the north and inhabit the geographical area of the arctic. Conditions were so bitter in Europe, however, that many thousands of miles of ice separated Europe from the arctic and prevented Man, *no matter how cold-adapted,* from crossing the sterile ice barrier.

Ironically, then, our present-day arctic happens to be inhabited by Mongoloid man, Eskimos, because entrance into the arctic area was permitted during the last 'Ice Age' by *warmth,* and a kind of Man not particularly cold-adapted was able to migrate to the north.

Whereas in Europe Man adapted to the glacial conditions for some 60,000 years during the height of Würm I, conditions only warmed sufficiently in eastern Siberia to permit a non-cold-adapted man to enter the geographical arctic about 15,000 years ago. The Eskimos, per se, are relatively recent arrivals, *coming during a warmer phase,* and staying on after the climate changed to the present conditions.

But are the Eskimos not cold-adapted? Yes, they are... in some ways. Certainly they have developed cultural adaptations to arctic conditions: clothing, weapons and hunting implements, shelter, etc. They also show biological adaptation in terms of being 'round' in accordance with Allen's Rule. They also exhibit some metabolic adaptations.

However, it may be doubted that contemporary Eskimos have the level of adaptation achieved by the European Neanderthals... or are even genetically capable of that level. The roundness of Eskimos is not so pronounced as the roundness of Neanderthals. The Eskimos lack the nasal development and pelt of the Neanderthals. Doubtless, the Neanderthals possessed metabolic adaptations which cannot be analysed because soft tissue does not fossilize. We have only the testimony of Neanderthal skeletal material... but even this hints at metabolic adaptation (i.e. the mental foramena allowing increased blood flow to surface tissue).

Archeological excavations in Alaska indicate that there was once a much larger population in the arctic than is the case today. As the cold increased to the 'normal' level associated with the 'arctic' today, the population of Mongoloid man in the arctic began to decline... *perhaps, because not being particularly cold-adapted genetically, he could not adapt to increasingly cold conditions.* The site at Onion Portage, in Alaska, indicates the decreased population as the modern period advanced and colder weather took hold of the arctic.

Certainly, the Eskimo population in the arctic was never great, and appears to have been steadily declining from the time of first European contact, and probably before. Ever since European man came to learn of the existence of the Eskimo and began to study this people, the population of Eskimos has appeared to decline... but only recently because of factors which can be correlated with the imposition of Western culture, disease, etc. The Norse settlers in Greenland reported very numerous 'skraelings' (i.e. Eskimos) about the year 1000 A.D., but the same coast was uninhabited by Eskimos when the 'modern' Danes returned to the area in the late 1700's.

It is possible, therefore, that the large outline is this: a non-cold-adapted man came into the arctic during a period of warmer weather in the Bering Sea area; he stayed on and attempted to adapt culturally as the climate changed to the present arctic conditions; but his fund of genetic cold-adaptive traits is limited and he has consequently steadily declined in numbers.

The Eskimos belong to the Mongoloid major group of Mankind which is characterized by being the most 'glabrous' (i.e., without body hair) of major groups. It is possible, therefore, that the Eskimo simply lacks the genetic material to grow a pelt to achieve a higher level of arctic adaptation. If the Eskimo cultural achievements (much greater than the Neanderthal) cannot compensate, or if the weather becomes colder, the Eskimo may perish entirely in a 'natural' evolutionary manner. Certainly, the steadily declining numbers of Eskimos during the entire historical period would seem to indicate this trend.

The Capoid and Australoid Extinction at the hands of non-Caucasoid People.

The extinction of the Capoids mainly by Negroid Bantu peoples is often cited as an example of non-Western exceptional aggression. I have dealt with this matter in the text... and also with the extinction, or virtual extinction, of the Australoid group at the hands of the prehistorically expanding Mongoloids.

I do not think that we have to postulate a greater level of innate aggression among Mongoloids and Negroids in order to explain these extinctions. We can rely upon the 'non-racial' doctrines of population and geography. Both the Australoids and the Capoids had the misfortune to centre themselves at the southern extremities of major land-masses. Their neighbours to the north in each case had much more room in which to develop, and much greater continental areas in which to achieve a greater rate of population growth. By the time these groups came into contact and inevitable migratory conflict of the 'normal' variety, the Capoids in Africa and Australoids in East Asia must have been badly outnumbered. Worse, being situated in the southern apexes of triangular continental land-masses, neither the Capoids nor the Australoids could effectively retreat. Their retreat was either wholly or partially blocked by water barriers. Consequently, both groups were virtually annihilated with merely a few survivors lingering in desert areas of South Africa and Australia.

Instead of viewing the virtual extinction of these peoples by non-Caucasoids as arguments against this thesis... we may turn it around. The Caucasoids themselves were mainly restricted to a relatively small peninsula, Eurasia. They had the same neighbours and the same water barriers against retreat. Why were the Caucasoids not overrun by Mongoloids leaving overcrowded Asiatic heartland? or by Negroids coming up from continental Africa across the then-fertile Sahara? The Mediterranean Sea presented a formidable, if not total, barrier to any hypothetical Negroid advancement north into Europe... but there is no natural barrier against Mongoloid invasion.

In fact, we have seen that Europe was *almost* inundated several times by Mongoloid expansion: by the Huns, by Genghis Khan, by the Timurids. Almost.

But not in fact. I believe that the reason why Europe was able to escape this almost-natural inundation (given the realities of geography) was because of the higher level of aggression postulated by this book. The Europeans, though badly ounumbered, fought with special fierceness not previously experienced by Asiatic invaders.

Biology 'vs.' culture

In several conversations with me, Dr. Jagdish Hattingadi of York University in Toronto has based his fundamental disagreement with my construct upon his assertion that, in effect, I am stating that 'culture is dictated by race'. If I am actually stating that, then Dr. Hattingadi's criticism and disagreement are well-founded, since it is obvious that culture may be transmitted easily irrespective of race.

I have thought carefully about this and have concluded that I *am* saying that culture is dictated by race... but I am also stating that this is relevant in only one respect.

It seems to me defensible to maintain that if biology and genetic inheritance compel distinctive psychological and mental traits in a group, then that group's culture must reflect those traits. However, a century of comparative anthropology, sociology and psychometrics has shown pretty conclusively that there appear to be *no significant mental and psychological* differences between 'races', and certainly none in the general area of intelligence (or 'moral stature', 'moral fibre', etc.). I accept this. However, *I do not think that we have troubled to measure 'aggression' as a trait that might differ in equality of distribution.*

My position is that, *except in one characteristic affecting mainly one population,* it is irrelevant and useless to maintain that 'race dictates culture' simply because there are no significant psychological and mental biologically compelled characteristics which *can* dictate culture.

Therefore, as a general rule applying to the total human population, I think that it is justifiable to maintain that 'race' cannot dictate culture.

But it is the position of this essay that there is an exception, a very small exception in the context of the world's population, but a very important one in the context of the world's history. And that exception is that among the Neanderthal-Caucasoids biological determinates resulted in a higher level of aggression as a psychological trait, and that that trait has been reflected in Western culture and behaviour... to the world's sorrow.

In spite of Dr. Hattingadi's stature, I submit that it is not sufficient for him, or any other expert, to argue against the construct presented here by simply asserting that 'race cannot dictate culture'. That statement remains an assumption, one supported by many data, but still an assumption which cannot be enshrined as a foundation-truth until we are assured that *not one* biological determinate in *not one* genetic group has ever influenced culture. It is the contention of this book that an unmeasured psychological trait has, in fact, influenced Caucasoid culture... and the world. Our researches into aggression, and its causes and sources, are still very much in their infancy.

Dr. Hattingadi says that *"culture transcends race and makes race insignificant"* (italics his). I could not agree more with Dr. Hattingadi, nor could I agree more with the many other humanists who have maintained this truth over the course of the last three decades.

The problem may be, however, that this truth may have unpleasant implications unsuspected by the humanists who assert it so proudly.

When a humanist says that *"culture transcends race and makes race insignificant"* he or she means that culture is a progressive mechanism which allows human beings to 'rise above' the 'stasis' of biological and genetic determinates.

There is the underlying assumption in such humanist statements that biology is somehow unresponsive and immutable while culture is adaptive and progressive.

It is a curious notion, an unfounded and dangerous assumption.

If there is one thing that is absolutely characteristic of biology, indeed, if there is one thing that is almost the *definition* of biological life, it is adaptability. Biology is immediately and brutally responsive to reality. In the biological world, an organism adapts or perishes in response to real conditions.

One cannot say the same for culture.

As is maintained by humanists like, perhaps, Ashley Montagu, culture is an intellectual achievement which 'transcends' biological influences. This is another way of saying that culture is not responsible to reality. Culture does not have to adapt to anything other than our own self-conceptions. As such an unresponsive thing, human culture often preserves attitudes and behaviours for which the justifiable reality has long since disappeared.

Until recently, and even in Victorian England, little girls used to dance around the May pole on the first day of the month and adorn it with ribbons. A charming custom... until Sir James Frazer traced the origins of the custom back to the phallus adoration of fertility religion. When *The Golden Bough* was published, the Victorians hastily gave up dancing around May poles.

On the Christian holiday of Easter, it is the custom of adults to hide brightly-painted eggs, and the custom of children to look for them. These eggs are supposedly deposited by rabbits, of all things. Again, this curious behaviour is a cultural anachronism dating from yet other ways of appreciating fertility (which the eggs symbolize and the rabbits personify).

These are relatively harmless examples of culture's ability to 'fix' and preserve human behaviour and attitudes which are inappropriate to existing intellectual and biological reality.

Let's take a more dangerous example. If the premise of this argument is granted, that there *once* was a high level of sexual dimorphism among Neanderthal-Caucasoids which contributed to a high level of undisplaced aggression which, among other things, provoked anti-female behaviour... then we should look at the contemporary reality.

Biology has proved adaptable. Culture has not.

Sexual dimorphism has been much diluted in most Caucasoid individuals. It exists now only in vestigial form after 50,000 years of biological adaptation. But the behaviour it once 'justifiably' provoked in purely biological terms has been unnecessarily perpetuated *by culture*.

Among the oldest and most cohesive Caucasoid cultures, those of the Jews and Arabs of the Middle East, we find anti-feminism as a major characteristic. 'Once — justifiable' biological response has been 'fixed' and perpetuated by culture while the biological maladaptations themselves have become greatly diluted. We see that culture may be reactionary when compared with biology.

This anti-feminist trait has been transmitted *by culture,* and via Christianity, to plague the humanist orientation of the Western World.

Culture does indeed transcend biology... and that is not altogether fortunate.

As I said at the conclusion of the previous chapter, I think that we can modify our behaviour by the application of consciously constructed culture. But our opponent is not the mere existence of biological determinates. Our real enemy is our culture which has 'fixed' and perpetuated behaviours and attitudes long after biology itself has adapted.

Our task of consciously modifying our culturally-dictated behaviour and attitudes, and those few vestigial biologically dictated behaviours and attitudes, will be made much easier if we know and delineate the original biological determinates which may have been institutionalized by culture and which compromise our social goals.

I think it is evident that we are not faced with a question of 'biology *versus* culture'. That is an oversimplification that amounts to a dangerous and self-deceptive distortion of the truth. Rather, we have a matrix of culture *and* biology when it comes to the important factor of aggression. And, in altering this matrix for our own conscious purposes, we are hampered much more by culture than by biology. Our intellectual vanity, the Western notion of separating biological life and intellectual freedom, prevents us from looking in the mirror and seeing the complex of biology and culture that is humanity.

Notes

1. The major references for CBW and other Western-wrought catastrophes outlined in this chapter are: *The Ultimate Folly: War by Pestilence, Asphyxiation and Defoliation, The Weather Conspiracy, The Jupiter Effect*, 'Army Used Bacteria on U.S. Cities' (Newsday Service), 'Death in the Diner' (*Elite* Magazine), 'The Mutilation Mystery' (*Oui* Magazine), field researches by the Society for the Investigation of the Unexplained, and other sources. (See bibliography.)

2. Dates obtained from radiocarbon analysis may be extremely relevant to this thesis in one particular respect. Unfortunately, some background is in order. Radiocarbon dating is based upon the fact that all living organisms assimilate the radioactive isotope of Carbon, C14, at a fixed rate during their lifetimes. The assimilation of the isotope ceases at death. This isotope has a half-life of 5,538 years, give or take 30 years. Therefore, by measuring the amount of C14 remaining in a sample of organic substance, a determination may be made as to the number of years which have elapsed since the death of the organism from which the samples originated. The technique is useful for measuring the ages of bone samples, wood fragments, cereal grains, etc., from archeological sites. However, the accuracy of dates obtained from C14 analysis is dependent upon one major assumption: *that the amount of C14 in the atmosphere has been constant and unchanged during the past 60,000 years.* The first expert to challenge this assumption was the Yugoslav anthropologist Vladimir Milojcic, and later researches by Dr. H.E. Suess con-

firmed a basic inaccuracy in C14 dates. It is now known with certainty that the amount of C14 in the atmosphere has been constant from about 2,000 B.C. until the 'present'(i.e., 1950 by convention). However, before 2,000 B.C. and extending back to some as yet unknown time, there was a higher concentration of C14 in the atmosphere and in all organisms living during this period. Radiocarbon dates before 2,000 B.C. are now known to be too 'young' or recent by a matter of up to 1,000 years. By 1955 a method had been developed to cross-check the accuracy of radiocarbon dates. This method is based upon *dendrochronology* — the counting of annular growth rings of trees. By the use of the bristlecone pines of the White Mountains of California, the oldest known living organisms on earth, it has been possible to establish a *dendrochronology* extending back in time to about 8,000 B.C. and this chronology agrees well with dating methods relying upon Scandinavian varve counts. In short, it is now possible to correct radiocarbon dates for the period 2,000 B.C. to about 8,000 B.C. This correction is called 'calibration'. Therefore, there are now 'uncalibrated radiocarbon dates' and 'calibrated radiocarbon dates'. Only the latter are considered accurate for the period before 2,000 B.C., but, unfortunately, many radiocarbon dates obtained from 1946 to 1960 remain uncalibrated.

A useful convention has sprung up almost spontaneously among archeologists: uncalibrated dates are referred to by lower-case 'b.p.'s' or 'b.c.'s', while calibrated radiocarbon dates are referred to in upper case 'B.P.'s' or 'B.C.'s'. I have spared the reader such dates in the text by sometimes 'splitting the difference between uncalibrated and calibrated dates'... a procedure justified by the fact that this thesis is concerned with very general trends and a long period of time. However, calibration has had a revolutionary effect. It is now known that the megalithic cultures of Western Europe *preceded* the civilizations of the Middle East. This fact has completely upset the established structure of the development of civilization. Only a few short years ago, it was confidently assumed that the megalithic cultures of barbarian Europe had been inspired by the light of civilization coming from Sumer and the Nile. Now, it appears that it may well be the other way around: the stone-building knowledge, the mathematical knowledge making such architecture possible and the astronomical knowledge upon which most megalithic structures are based all travelled from 'barbarian' Europe to the Middle East. This new and revolutionary view of the spread of civilization was forced by the calibration of C14 dates. Megaliths in Brittany are now known to be much older than the pyramids of Egypt.

This new view accords well with the research of Alexander Marshack, which established that the earliest time-factored notation occurred in Europe among the Neanderthals. It is possible, therefore, that there was a continuity of mathematical and astronomical knowledge from about 40,000 B.P. until 5,000 B.C. when the megaliths began to be raised in Western Europe and that *this knowledge* was the foundation of civilization and gradually diffused toward the East.

If this is true, then Western man made a much earlier and more dramatic impact upon history than is reckoned by the 'established structure' of contemporary archeology. It is too early to say yet whether the 'established structure' or the 'New Archeology' based upon calibration will prevail. There may be some other factor affecting dating which will be soon discovered... upsetting everybody's structures! In *The Iceman Inheritance* I have adhered to the 'establishment' chronology and historical structure because of the desire to remain absolutely 'fair' and 'conservative' in the presentation of a provocative thesis. However, the reader should realize that the argument of *The Iceman Inheritance* will be strengthened considerably by C14 calibration and the 'New Archeology', for, under these new data, Western man emerges early as a decisive factor in the pattern of world history and the development of civilization.

The reader is referred to *Before Civilization* for an interesting discussion of C14 calibration and its implications for the changing view of history (see bibliography).

3. The major sources for this discussion are: *Man's Most Dangerous Myth: The Fallacy of Race, The Concept of Race* (see bibliography).

4. I have, for the purposes of my thesis, accepted Konrad Lorenz's definition of aggression: *violence directed against members of one's own species.*

5. The major sources for this section are: *The Origin of Race, The Peking Mystery, Shanidar: The First Flower People, Abominable Snowmen: The story of sub-humans on five continents from the early ice age until today,* and other books (see bibliography).

6. There may be another explanation for the origin of the Neanderthals, although it is an explanation at odds with the 'establish-

ment' view. There is a possibility that the Neanderthals developed in the New World and subsequently migrated into Eurasia, going 'backwards' across the Bering Land Bridge. Neanderthal-like artifacts and skeletal material have been discovered in the Americas, but all such evidence has been ignored by the 'establishment'. However, in 1974 something happened which was difficult to ignore. Three very reputable scholars — Dr. Harold E. Malde and Dr. Virginia Steen-McIntyre of the U.S. Geological Survey, and Dr. Roald Fryxwell of Washington State University — jointly announced the discovery of Neanderthal material (Mousterian artifacts) dating to 250,000 B.P. at the site of Hueyatlaco, Mexico. The artifacts were dated by three techniques. Similarly, Dr. Bruce Raemsch of Onteonta College in New York State has been investigating very ancient Neanderthal material in the New World. The discovery, and verification, of very ancient Neanderthal remains in the New World would, of course, compel a very basic re-evaluation of Man's evolution. Although in the text I have adhered to the 'establishment view' of human evolution, I think that some basic surprises are in store for anthropology. As Dr. Raemsch wrote to me in a private letter: "I think, myself, that knowledge about him (Man) is so scarce compared to what we will know even in the next fifty years that it is almost impossible to say what will be the most productive direction to follow. It behooves us, therefore, to remain very open-minded....."

7. It is now definitely known, if not accepted by all anthropologists, that the Micmac Indians of Nova Scotia and Maine did possess a writing system before the coming of the white man. The reader is referred to *America B.C.* (see bibliography) by Professor Barry Fell of Harvard. If radiocarbon calibration has resulted in a revolution in thinking about the development of human civilization, then Fell's book constitutes another revolution concerning the nature of civilization in the New World.

8. As an example, one of the most enjoyable pastimes of literary experts over the past couple of centuries has been endless discussion and 'dialogue' about the psychological motivations of the Prince of Denmark in Shakespeare's *Hamlet*. Hapless English students of many, many generations have been forced to write papers on this theme... yet, the supposed psychological motivations of Hamlet are both irrelevant and wiseacre. Hamlet's motivations make no sense, nor do many of Shakespeare's

allusions, simply because the true framework of Hamlet has been forgotten by moderns and buried under pretentious intellectualism. This framework has nothing whatever to do with psychology, but a great deal to do with astronomy.

In their co-authored book, *Hamlet's Mill*, Dr. Georgio de Santillana of M.I.T. and Dr. Hertha von Detchend of Heidelberg University rather elegantly demonstrate that the *Hamlet* story merely personifies the cosmic events surrounding the first notice of the precession of the equinoxes, and the various planetary and zodiacal displacements caused by the initiation of the precession. If Hamlet's psychology makes no sense, it is simply because the events which occurred in the distant past made no sense to those who witnessed them. These witnesses saw effects in the sky, but had no real understanding of what was happening or why it was happening since no one on earth at that time had adequate knowledge of astrophysics (a lack still shared by the literati). The *Hamlet* motif simply recorded the events that occurred, with Hamlet (Saturn) being the central character in the cosmic drama. Since the astronomical phenomena connected with the precession made no sense to the ancient audience, the character of Hamlet can make no sense either. This is why all attempts at 'psychoanalysis' of Hamlet have been more or less unsatisfactory. Similarly, Ophelia (i.e., 'snake') begins to make some sense only within astronomical context when it is realized that she is the personification of the zodiacal band and that this band was 'drowned', *sunk beneath the horizon and 'into' the sea*, when the earth's axis inclined at 23½ degrees to the plane of the ecliptic.

Students of Dante's *Divine Comedy* might consider that there may be very simple astronomical reasons — not complicated metaphysical and religious ones — for the 'seven levels' of heaven and hell. Dante's seven levels are the same as the 'seven-lined cup of Jamshayd' in the poetry of the Sufi Kayyam.

My editor tells me that any discussion of this subject, short of a whole book, will be incomprehensible to Western laymen. It should, however, be emphasized that, as Alexander Marshack has shown, the foundation of our civilization is astronomical time-factored notation carried out among cave-dwelling Europeans. This notation has the most intimate relationship to the 'precession of the equinoxes' and the 'inclination to the plane of the ecliptic'. We cannot understand or appreciate *Hamlet* properly without understanding these terms. The true wonder of *Hamlet* is not the subtle motivations supposedly created by

Shakespeare, but the simple fact that the *Hamlet* motif may very well be the most ancient 'literary intellectual' creation of the West. The reader is referred to Marshack's *The Roots of Civilization* and to *Hamlet's Mill* (see bibliography) .

Western writers like Shakespeare and Dante are acceptable to some Eastern critics because internal evidence in works by Shakespeare and Dante shows conclusively that both these authors knew the real, astronomical truth and its relevance to the development of human history and civilization. The skill of these writers was such that this truth was hidden within a meaningless but entertaining literary theme which fulfilled its intended function of disguising the real message from those who could not accept and appreciate the knowledge in any case. The 'psychological' theme in *Hamlet* is such a device and theme... and it has mesmerized those who get more out of 'wiseacring' than out of knowlege, as intended. Dante's *Divine Comedy* was constructed in a similar way. For those who can read the messages, some of the work by Shakespeare and Dante has much more in common with *The Thousand and One Nights* than with other Western work of the wiseacre genre.

9. The term 'pre-Caucasoid' is not, strictly speaking, an accurate one because no one is in a position to say with certainty when the population of the Indian subcontinent was 'pre-Caucasoid'... if it ever was. This term is intended to convey the idea that whereas much of the Indian population is, and has been, racially 'Caucasoid', the culture of this subcontinent has always been heavily influenced by the Far East and Central Asia. Again, in India, we have the 'southward pointing triangle' phenomenon. Earlier peoples were pushed toward the southern tip of the subcontinent with each new invasion. These people either found havens or were exterminated... or, as a third alternative, accommodated culturally to the influences imposed upon them. Although 'Caucasoid' in some measure, the peoples of India have shown a tendency toward a non-Western orientation in religion and in sensuality due to external cultural influences. It may be stated here, however, in support of my major thesis, that one of the most southerly people are the Vedas, a very primitive Caucasoid group pushed south by subsequent invasions. The Vedas are highly sexually dimorphized, both physically and culturally, and, notwithstanding their primitive cultural level, they were a highly warlike tribe until pacified by modern government.

Bibliography

Borden, Charles, *Sea Quest* (MacRea, Philadelphia, 1966)

Bradley, Micheal, *The Cronos Complex I* (Nelson, Foster & Scott Ltd., Toronto, 1973).

Bradley, Michael, "Death in the Diner", *Elite* Magazine, May, 1977.

Brown, J.S., *The Motivation of Behaviour* (McGraw-Hill, New York, 1961.)

Broby-Johansen, A., *Body and Clothes*, (Reinhold Book Corporation, New York, 1968.)

Carpenter, C.R., "A Field Study of the Behaviour and Social Relations of Howling Monkeys", *Comparative Psychological Monogram*, 1934, pages 1-168.

Carson, Rachel, *The Silent Spring*, (Crest Books, New York, 1962.)

Chant, Donald A., ed., *Pollution Probe*, (New Press, Toronto, 1970.)

Cleator, P.E., *Lost Languages*, (Robert Hale, London, 1973.)

Coon, C.S., *The Origin of Races*, (Alfred A. Knopf, New York, 1968)

Creasy, E.S., *Fifteen Decisive Battles of the World*, (Dutton, New York, 1952.)

Cummings, John and Fetherston, Drew, "Army Used Bacteria on U.S. Cities", *Newsday*, December 22, 1976.

David, A. Rosalie, *The Egyptian Kingdoms* (Elsevier-Phaidon, Lausanne, 1975.)

Davidson, Basil, *Old Africa Rediscovered* (Victor Gollancz Ltd., London, 1970.)

de Beauvoir, Simone, *The Second Sex*, (Bantam, New York, 1961.)

de Santillana, Georgio and von Detchend, Hertha, *Hamlet's Mill* (Gambit Inc., Boston, 1969.)

Fell, Barry, *America B.C.: Ancient Settlers in the New World* (Simon & Schuster, New York, 1976.)

Freud, Sigmund, *Totem and Taboo*, (Kegan Paul, London, 1960.)

Fuller, John G., *We Almost Lost Detroit*, (Ballantine Books, New York, 1975.)

Garvin, Richard M., *The Crystall Skull* (Doubleday & Company, Garden City, New York, 1973)

Graves, Robert, *The White Goddess* (Faber and Faber, London, 1961.)

Gurdjieff, G.I., *All and Everthing: Beelzlebub's Tales to his Children*, (Harcourt, Brace, New York, 1950).

Herrmann, Paul, *Conquest by Man*, (Hamish-Hamilton, London, 1954.)

Heuvelmans, Bernard, *On the Track of Unknown Animals* (Rupert Hart-Davies, London, 1958.)

Hitching, Francis, *Earthmagic* (Pan Books Ltd., London, 1977.)

Impact Team Report, *The Weather Conspiracy* (Ballantine Books, New York, 1977.)

Ivimy, John, *The Sphinx & The Megaliths* (Turnstone, London, 1974)

Jung, Carl G., ed., *Man and His Symbols* (Dell Publishing Co., New York, 1968.)

Levi-Strauss, Claude, *Tristes Tropiques* (Atheneum, New York, 1974.)

Lorenz, Konrad Z., *King Solomon's Ring* (New American Library, New York, 1972.)

Lorenz, Konrad Z., *On Aggression* (Methuen & Co., London, 1967.)

Lunan, Duncan, *Man and the Stars* (Souvenir Press, London, 1974.)

Lunan, Duncan, private correspondence, May 10, 1978.

Malde, Harold E., U.S. Geological Survey, Denver, private correspondence. August 28, 1974.

Marshack, Alexander, *The Roots of Civilization* (McCraw-Hill, New York, 1971).

McCarthy, Richard D., *The Ultimate Folly, War by Pestilence, Asphyxiation and Defoliation* (Random House, New York, 1969).

Mertz, Barbara, *Red Land, Black Land* (Dell Publishing Co., New York, 1966.)

Montagu, Ashley, ed., *The Concept of Race*, (The Free Press of Glencoe, New York, 1968.)

Montagu, Ashley, *Man's Most Dangerous Myth: The Fallacy of Race* (Oxford University Press, New York, 1974) (5th edition).

Movius, H.L., Jr., "Radiocarbon Dates and Upper Paleolithic Archeology", *Current Anthropology*, Chicago, Vol. 1, Nos. 5-6, pages 355-391.

Muller, Herbert Joseph, *The Loom History*, (Mentor Books, New York, 1961.)

Murdock, G.P., *Our Primitive Contemporaries* (Collier-MacMillan, New York, 1934.)

Neugebauer, O., *The Exact Sciences in Antiquity* (Harper & Brothers, New York, 1962.)

Oman. C.W.C., *The Art of War in the Middle Ages* (Cornell University Press. Ithaca, New York, 1953.)

Pauwels. Louis, *Gurdjieff* (Samuel Weiser, Inc., New York, 1975.)

Renfrew. Colin, *Before Civilization* (Jonathan Cape, London, 1973.)

Runciman. Steven, *A History of the Crusades,* (Cambridge University Press. 1951.)

Sagan. Carl and Schlovskii, Iosif S., *Intelligent Life in the Universe,* (Holden-Day, San Francisco, 1966.)

Sanders, Ed. "The Mutilation Mystery", *Oui* Magazine, September, 1976.

Sanderson, I.T., *Abominable Snowmen: legend come to life, the story of sub-humans on five continents from the early iceage until today.* (Chilton Book Company, Radnor, 1961).

Shah, Idries, *The Sufis* (Anchor Books, New York, 1971).

Shapiro. Harry L., *The Peking Man,* (Simon and Schuster, New York, 1975).

Smith, G.E., "The Influence of Racial Admixture in Ancient Egypt", *Eugenics Review,* London, Vol. 7, No. 3, pages 163-183.

Solecki. Ralph, *Shanidar: The First Flower People* (Knopf, New York, 1971).

Solecki. Ralph, "Three Adult Neanderthal Skeletons from Shanidar Cave in Northern Iraq", *Smithsonian Report, Publication,* No. 4414, pages 603-635.

"Solid geological evidence indicates New World Man older than believed", *UPI,* August 14, 1974.

Stewart, T.D., "Form of the Pubic Bone in Neanderthal Man", *Science,* Vol. 131, No. 3411 (1960), page 1437.

Temple. Robert K.G., *The Sirius Mystery* (Sidgwick & Jackson, London, 1976.)

Tompkins. Peter and Bird, Christopher, *The Secret Life of Plants* (Avon Books, New York, 1974.)

Vilimkova, Milada, *Egyptian Jewellery,* (Paul Hamlyn, London, 1969.)

Wendt, Herbert, *From Ape to Adam* (Thames and Hudson, London, 1971)

Zuckerman, Sir Solly, *The Social Life of Monkeys and Apes,* (Kegan Paul, London, 1932.)

140618-500-40-60W